THE DOOR BETWEEN WORLDS

BOOK 5 OF THE *GEMINI GATE* SERIES

STEVEN E. WILDE

The Door Between Worlds (The Gemini Gate series, Book 5)
Steven E. Wilde
Hardcover edition 978-1-77342-106-3
Paperback edition 978-1-77342-105-6
Ebook edition 978-1-77342-104-9

Produced by IndieBookLauncher.com
www.IndieBookLauncher.com
Cover Design: Saul Bottcher
Interior Design and Typesetting: Saul Bottcher

The body text of this book is set in Adobe Caslon.

Dedicated to my readers. Without you, my efforts to tell this story would be meaningless. Thanks for your support.

And he said unto them … ye are of this world; I am not of this world.
—*John 8:23, King James Bible*

Prologue

Twin World—Lobby of the Crowne Plaza Hotel, Columbus, Ohio
Newly elected Senator Gregory McCormick walked briskly over to the smart-looking couple that had just passed through security, threw his arms around the elegant woman and gave her a hug.

"Lillie, it's good to see you again. You too, Amos," he added unemotionally, then smiled widely and gave Amos a hug as well. "Come on. We've been waiting for you."

The senator hooked an arm with each of them and walked casually into the ballroom, smiling and waving to guests—friends, fellow politicians, and supporters—as they wound their way between round tables filled with people, eight to a table, to the front-center of the room. The senator's wife, Elizabeth, and two other middle-aged couples, sat at the table. Amos and Lillie bent to give Liz a hug, then Amos shook hands with the other two men, who stood to greet him.

"Dr. Blund," the first man said, "it's a pleasure to meet you. Nick James. I've heard a lot about you."

"A pleasure," Amos said. "If it was Greg who told you about me, you can believe half of it, maybe."

They all laughed politely, but Amos felt uncomfortable, as he always did when he had to make polite small-talk.

"Dr. James is one of the foremost nuclear scientists in the country," Greg said, grinning. "I stole him from MIT. And this is his better half, Sharon, or should I say Representative James from the Michigan House of Representatives." Amos and Lillie nodded to Sharon, who nodded in return.

"Brian Chalmers, nuclear medicine," the second man said as

Amos shook hands with him.

"As Dr. Chalmers's said, his background is nuclear medicine," Greg said. "I stole him from Mount Sinai Beth Israel hospital in New York City. He's one of the top ten doctors in his profession. His wife, Toni, is a surgeon at Montefiore military hospital."

"Military?" Amos asked politely.

"Cancer care," Toni said. "I received my training in the Navy and at the Huntsman Cancer Center in Salt Lake City. And yes, I know you're from Utah. It's a beautiful state. We enjoyed camping and hiking in your national and state parks while we were there."

Four professionals, scientists, doctors and a politician. When Greg had pressed Amos into attending this fundraising banquet *free of charge,* he had suspected that Greg had an ulterior motive. A few years earlier, Greg had tried to recruit him to serve on a House committee, but his family, medical, and scientific pursuits were a higher priority. Tonight's meeting might be an attempt to draft him again, this time for a Senate committee. They'd known each other for many years and Greg had never done anything this bold and blatant before.

Lillie and Amos took their seats and everyone started in on their salads, which had already been served. The talk at the table started out with the usual chit-chat about family and careers, quickly focusing on medicine and medical research, the topics that the three couples had in common and were obviously passionate about.

The salad plates were soon cleared away and dinner was served, then dessert, and the discussion continued. At some point, Amos realized that the McCormicks were not part of the conversation and glanced their way. Greg's smug expression convinced him that this was exactly what the senator had wanted to happen.

The dinner dishes were cleared and coffee served to those

who wanted it. They were all distracted when the senior standing senator from Ohio stepped to the podium and introduced his new colleague, former state Representative, and Ohio State Buckeyes hall-of-famer, Senator Gregory 'Buck' McCormick. Greg stood, amid applause and cheers, bobbed his head a couple of times in acknowledgement of the gracious reception, and strode confidently to the podium.

Greg thanked everyone for coming, naming a few key supporters by name and waving to each of them, then started in on the usual political rhetoric that everyone expected. Amos listened with half of his attention, while the other half reminisced about experiences he and Greg had shared over the years, starting as teenagers at a National Science Foundation summer science course in Arizona, and including being best man at each other's weddings and god-father to each other's children.

Amos's attention was drawn back to Greg's speech when Greg announced that he had been appointed chairman of the Senate Committee on Commerce, Science, and Transportation, and had already started to select key committee members, some of whom were in the audience. Amos's heart pounded when Greg started naming names and having people stand. He expected Greg to announce that Amos had agreed to serve on the committee when he definitely had not. The look he gave Greg said, *Don't go there.*

"Dr. Nicholas James, one of the foremost nuclear scientists in the country, formerly associated with MIT, please stand," Greg said, grinning widely. Nick stood. "Dr. Brian Chalmers, nuclear medicine, formerly of Mount Sinai Beth Israel hospital." Brian stood.

They both looked pointedly at Amos, perhaps expecting his name to be mentioned next; but when Greg continued, he mentioned two women and two other men, prominent in commerce and transportation, sitting at an adjacent table. Having introduced his new committee members, Greg thanked everyone again and wished them a good evening, then he returned to his seat.

There was an awkward silence at the table as everyone looked around at each other, as if waiting for some kind of announcement or confession. Around the room, people stood and began leaving, amid the noise of scraping chair legs and friendly greetings. Greg thanked everyone at the table for coming, stood and shook hands with Drs. James and Chalmers, and promised to be in touch. Amos shook hands with them as well, then with Greg.

"Stay for a minute, will you, Amos?" Greg asked.

Amos sat and told Lillie what Greg had said. They waited patiently as people made their way over to shake hands with the newly elected senator. Amos was introduced to many of the guests and stood each time, overwhelmed by the number of people who already knew who he was or knew of him.

When the stream of well-wishers ended and most people were headed for the exits, Greg sat and looked Amos in the eyes.

"Amos," Greg said, "I know you're not comfortable in the limelight, but did you notice how many people know who you are?"

"Your doing, I'm sure," Amos said, politely.

"I may have had some influence on that," Greg replied, "but you are well known and well respected in this country. With your brilliant scientific mind and medical background, you would be an immense asset to me and to the country we both love."

"Your flattery, Greg—"

"Amos," Greg cut him off before he could finish his sentence, "I want you to chair my subcommittee on science. James and Chalmers will work for you. And the other subcommittee chairmen, for transportation and commerce, will also report to you. You will, in effect, run my committee. Say you'll do it."

"Greg," Amos demurred, "I'm not a manager—"

"I'm not looking for a manager, Amos. I'm looking for a leader, and you're one of the best I've known. People will stand in line to be associated with you and do what you want."

"But what about my research and medical practice?" Amos asked, looking at Lillie for support, but she gave him an *it's your call* expression that was no help at all. "And, I suppose you'll want us to move to Washington D.C.?" Amos sputtered.

"I'll take you around the area so you can decide where you want to live," Greg said, smiling.

Amos turned to Lillie. "What do you think?" he asked, expecting her to object to a cross-country move, which would uproot their three children.

"I'll support you in whatever decision you make, but if you do take the job, I'll have to start calling you *Doc* again, to remind you of your roots." They'd met when he was in his residency and she was a volunteer in the hospital, before becoming a nurse. 'Doc' had been her nickname for him back then.

"What do you say, Doc?" Greg asked, grinning at the use of Lillie's nickname for him. His look said he was certain he had Amos hooked now.

"If you're going to call me Doc, I'm going to call you Buck," Amos said.

"How long do you think you'll need me?"

"I'm planning on becoming president of the United States after this, so at least ten years, maybe sixteen if I run for another Senate term."

Amos groaned.

1

Family Chaos

Old World—The Preserve, 5 June

"Do you know where Mike is?" Emily asked Terry as he was leaving the dining room after breakfast. She breathed heavily, held one arm under her large belly and leaned against the table with her other hand.

Terry knew that Mike had been avoiding everyone since his father, Amos, had died from a gunshot wound to the head, two weeks earlier, during the battle for Aspen Valley. At twenty-four years of age, he'd been elected chairman of the board to replace his father. But he had no interest in the board or the running of the Preserve. It had been their underground home in Logan Canyon, ever since Al Qaeda had threatened, then succeeded in destroying Washington, D.C. with a nuclear bomb. Emily wasn't the first to ask about Mike, and Terry was tired of making excuses for him. At the same time, he was concerned about Emily.

"How's the baby, Emily?" Terry asked.

"He, or she, is very active. Usually kicking my rib cage or bladder."

"You know, we can tell if he's a he, or a she, any time. We don't have to wait another month until he, or she, is born."

"I'm fine with not knowing, Terry. I just need Mike to help out a little. Where did you say he was?"

Terry smiled. She knew he hadn't said and was being polite, as she usually was.

"I'm sure he's in the lab, Emily. That seems to be the only place he goes anymore. Is there something I can do for you?"

"He's chairman of the board, right? I thought that meant he was supposed to help us manage problems with the running of the house." That's how most thought of the Preserve, which had been their home for almost a year now. It was either 'the house' or 'home'.

Terry pursed his lips in thought and choked back tears. He had been Amos's partner, probably his best friend, next to Lillie, for over sixteen years. Amos's death had hurt him almost as much as it had hurt his family, maybe more. "You know," he said, "Mike accepted the role of chairman reluctantly, because your mother turned it down. Have you spoken to her lately?"

"You know she's been a wreck since Dad's death," Emily said, tears coming to her eyes. "She hasn't left her room, except for meals, and has barely spoken since the board meeting last week."

Almost everyone had been sullen and moody, but Lillie had been especially impacted, as one would expect after the unexpected and violent death of her twenty-plus year best friend and mate. She had nominated Mike to be the new chairman and the other board members had immediately approved it. Then Lillie had resigned from the board and turned the house over to twenty-two-year-old Emily. Those had been big changes, and the family was still adjusting to them.

"That's what I heard," Terry said. "I don't think Mike's heart is in it yet. He's more interested in what's going on in the twin world."

"Well," Emily said, "I'm not getting around so well these days. So, when you see him, will you tell him I need his help?"

"I'm going to the lab now, Emily. I'll tell him, if he's there."

"Hi Mike," Terry said. "What are you up to?"

Mike was reading a newspaper that he'd brought—stolen, according to his mother—from the twin world through the Gemini Gate. He still had trouble believing that they had built a machine that cut a hole in the fabric of space, between their world and a parallel world—a twin world—where they might all exist. He had seen references in the newspapers from the twin world that convinced him that his dad, at least, was there and had accepted a role as an advisor to the president of the United States, Gregory 'Buck' McCormick, as everyone referred to the president. Now, he was looking for proof.

He looked up when Terry entered the lab and spoke to him.

"Huh? I'm still trying to find a way to contact Amos Two," Mike said with a sigh. Amos Two was what they had agreed to call the Amos in the twin world, to differentiate him from Mike's dad, Amos, in their world. "I may have to go through the gate to continue my research."

"Emily's looking for you," Terry said, missing or ignoring what Mike had said about going through the gate; he leaned against the table and folded his arms across his chest.

"What does she need?" Mike asked indifferently, returning to his review of the paper.

"We all need you to act like the chairman of the board," Terry said.

Mike bristled. He wanted to research the twin world. He wanted everyone else to do their jobs and leave him alone.

"You know I was railroaded into accepting when Mom turned it down," Mike said. "I don't want to be chairman. You do it."

"No Mike," Terry said sternly, drawing Mike's attention back to him. "We need a doctor and that's my role. Your role is to run the Preserve."

Mike studied Terry while Terry stared back at him. There was no way he was going to get out of this. Why did his dad have to die? The thought brought him close to tears, again. He needed his dad back.

"Okay," he said, sighing again, "I'll go find Em and see what she needs."

"You should also talk to Katie. She's having trouble managing the gardens." Katie and Mike had been married for several months and Katie had been helping Mike in the gardens for longer than that. Mike had been responsible for the gardens for the past year, but had handed it off to Katie when he had taken an interest in the twin world.

"She hasn't said anything to me," Mike said in frustration.

"She wants you to think she can handle it without you, but she's struggling. Be kind. She's trying. It could hurt her feelings if she thinks you don't approve."

"And she told you instead of me . . ." Mike started to say.

"Because I'm her father and problem solver." Terry interrupted Mike. "Give her time to get used to you being her 'go-to' guy."

"Great! What else?" Mike asked, wondering when Katie would start confiding in him before her father. His agitation increased the more he thought about it.

"Mike, calm down. Your dad's death was less than two weeks ago. Everyone's trying to adjust. Emotions are on the surface. Confusion is normal. Be patient."

"His death affected me, too," Mike said defensively. "Don't think I don't have feelings."

"Mike," Terry said, probably more calmly than he felt, "I know how much you loved and admired your dad. He felt the same way about you. He was proud of your accomplishments and how much you contributed to the building of the Preserve." Mike had degrees in engineering and geology and had been a major contributor to the construction of the Preserve.

Mike thought about the time his dad had scolded him for going through the gate without permission. According to his Mom, who'd told him much later, he had almost died, and his dad had blamed himself for not preventing it. Mike felt guilty, all over again, because he knew he had intentionally been secretive so no one would discover what he was doing.

His breath caught and a tear ran down his cheek. He wiped it away angrily. He felt so inadequate. How could he ever fill his dad's shoes? What did everyone expect of him?

Terry could see Mike's anguish—could feel it—since he had been affected the same way by Amos's death. He and Amos had been partners since Mike was in grade school and had pulled Katie's pigtail, which was how he and Amos had met and become good friends, then later partners. Almost everywhere he went in the Preserve, and everything he did, brought a memory of Amos. He owed it to his good friend to be patient and help Mike become the man he was meant to be. Suddenly, a thought struck him; something he and Amos had done whenever they became frustrated with a problem in their research.

"Hey Mike, let's go get a burger and shake," he said, and started to laugh.

"What?" Mike asked, obviously confused.

"That's what your dad and I used to do whenever we became stumped. Come on, I'll ask Becca to break out the homemade ice cream and cook us a veggie-burger." They didn't have meat in their underground retreat, because it wasn't renewable; like the vegetable gardens; so they'd have to make do with a vegetable substitute. He stood and waved to Mike to get up and go with him. When Mike stood reluctantly, Terry put an arm around his shoulders, squeezed, and led him out of the lab.

"There you are," Emily said when she saw Terry and Mike walking into the dining room.

"Hi Emily," Terry said good-naturedly. "I found Mike and we're going for a burger and shake. Want to join us?" They kept walking and Emily followed them toward the kitchen where the dinner crew was beginning to prepare their next meal.

"You're what?" Emily asked, as confused as Mike had been.

"If it's not too late, I'm going to ask Becca if we can have a good, old-fashioned ice cream and veggie-burger lunch. There's nothing like a burger slathered with mustard, relish and onions. Umm. And after I talk to Becca, we can sit at the table and you can explain to Mike what help you need." When Emily looked at Mike for confirmation, he returned her gaze, obviously clueless.

"That would be fine," Rebecca, Terry's wife of twenty years and the board member responsible for meal preparation in the Preserve, said. We're not so far along that we can't change the menu.

Having spoken to Becca Terry went back to the dining room to sit with Mike and Emily, who were already talking quietly. Emily's concerns turned out to be all the things Terry had already discussed with Mike, plus more. Terry sat quietly and listened as Emily broke it down for Mike.

Katie, Mike's wife and Terry's twenty-two-year-old daughter, lacked the confidence to manage others in the garden and needed reassurance that she was doing things correctly.

Rachel, Mike's nineteen-year-old sister, had only a vague idea of how to manage Rylee's and Sydney's education and needed help or some training herself—Katie had a teaching certificate, but Rachel didn't.

Lillie and Brittany were still in mourning—grieving their losses. Lillie had lost her husband, Amos, but Brittany had lost her husband, Jason, in the same gunfight, plus her second son, Nathan, to a knife wound a few weeks earlier. With the death of her first son, Aaron, in the auto accident the year before, all that was left of her family was Sydney, her fifteen-year-old daughter.

Matt, Emily's husband, punished himself emotionally for his lack of experience in the operating room and blamed himself for Amos's death. He had told Emily several times that they would have been better off if he'd stayed in medical school instead of coming to the Preserve. Emily cried every time he talked that way, asking how anything would be better, since that would mean he wouldn't be there for her, she wouldn't have a new life inside her, getting ready to join the world, and there wouldn't have been anyone else to take Matt's place in the operating room. Speaking that way to Matt only made him feel guilty in addition to being inadequate.

Chris, Terry's twenty-year-old son, thought he should have more responsibility, but no one was talking to him about what he could do. Being a political Science student before coming to the Preserve, he didn't know what he could do either, since there was no need for the skills he'd been learning; but he'd been studying operating manuals on all of the life support systems in the Preserve and had told Terry that he thought he might be able to help run things.

Becca appeared to be the only one who was handling the stress, since she was already doing what she did best, which was preparing food; but Terry knew she cried herself to sleep every night in sympathy for Lillie.

"I have no idea what to do," Mike said, after hearing all of Emily's concerns, shaking his head and looking at Terry for help.

"Think about it, Mike," Terry said. "Let's start with Chris, the only one who wants more to do. Where could you use him?"

"Maybe he could help Katie," Emily said. "He's helped out in the gardens a lot and knows them well. He's intelligent, with a good memory for things"

"Good idea. But, what if you give him responsibility for the gardens?" Terry asked.

"You mean, give Katie something else? Wouldn't she be offended?" Mike asked.

"Emily, what do you think?" Terry asked.

"You'd need to ask her," Emily said, "but I think she'd feel better teaching or helping Sydney and Rylee with their gymnastics. That's what she's best at." As a former college gymnast and trained teacher, Katie had originally been responsible for education and physical exercise for the whole group.

"I'll ask her," Mike said enthusiastically. "What about Mom and Brittany?"

"I think Mom needs more time to work through her emotions," Emily said. "Let's leave her for now. But I could sure use some help."

"Would Brittany be willing to help?" Mike asked.

"You can ask her," Emily said. "But if not her, I don't know who. Maybe everyone will settle down if you make those changes."

"And I'll work on Matt," Terry said. "I've told him that I appreciated his help in surgery and that he did everything I asked of him, but he needs positive reinforcement."

"I wasn't in the hospital with you," Mike said, "but if you think it would help, I'll tell him what you said."

"That might really make a difference, Mike," Terry said. "He really respects and looks up to you. Do you have what you need now?"

"Wow, that wasn't so hard," Mike replied. "Maybe I'll schedule a board meeting once a week for a while and let everyone say what's on their mind."

"Hmm," Terry said, "sounds like something your dad would do."

"And did," Emily added.

☢

"Hello? Mike, are you there?" Dr. Beth Byron's voice came over the radio sitting in its holster in the lab. Beth was the leader of the Outcasts, the victims of the mutated Smallpox virus, who had travelled all the way from the Johns Creek shelter near Atlanta, Georgia to Utah to avoid being found and killed by the military. Of the original twelve, only seven had made it to Bear Lake Valley, had met Jason Carlsen, and had been duped into following Jason to Aspen Valley in his attempt to take over Amos's Preserve.

Mike had forgotten all about the Outcasts. His focus had been entirely on the twin world and finding Amos Two. He realized that Beth still had the radio his dad had given her before the battle in the valley. It had to be just about out of power.

"Hi Beth," Mike replied self-consciously. "What can I do for you?"

"I'm sorry to bother you, Mike. You're probably still in mourning, but we still have five invaders locked up out here. We're feeding them and we've just about run out of food. What would you like us to do with them?"

"Oh, Beth, I'm the one who's sorry. We've been so preoccupied with our own problems that I'd totally forgotten about the surviving invaders." And you, he thought. But maybe he could handle this. Since his meeting with Terry and Em, his confidence in his ability to resolve problems had increased. "What do you want to do with them?" he asked, and realized immediately how stupid that sounded. It wasn't her decision, it was his dad's . . . well, his, now. Maybe he still had a lot to learn.

Beth hesitated, likely coming to the same conclusion.

"Uh, they want to stay and they want to bring what's left of their families from Garden City. But I told them it wasn't my decision." Jason had been captured once, then escaped and returned to Garden City to raise an army. He'd returned to Aspen Valley with an army of nineteen men, women and teenagers, with guns and dynamite. Jason had been killed in the battle for Aspen Valley along with. all but six of the invaders. The only casualty in the Preserve had been Amos, who had been hit by a nearly impossible shot that had gone through a small hole in the gate and hit him in the face.

"Wait, did you say five invaders? I thought there were six."

"The one that was injured didn't make it. He was the father of one of the boys, by the way. He'd lost his wife and daughter to the virus in Garden City. His son, Zach, his brother-in-law, Justin, and his nephew, Isaac, are three of the others. Justin has a wife and two other children still in Garden City. The other two men have no family left. That's part of the reason they followed Jason. I count a total of six people, in addition to the seven of us—eight now, counting Sheryl's baby."

"I need to talk to the board about this," Mike said. His dad's original goal was to keep the location of the Preserve a secret. Jason had brought the Outcasts, so they knew about it now. Then Jason had returned, leading the invaders that they had killed or captured. If they let Justin bring his family, that could be a lot of extra people to feed and take care of. He didn't know if they could handle that large a group long-term.

"Okay. Let me know. How is Lillie holding up?"

"It's a struggle for all of us, but especially for her. Thanks for asking. We'll get you more food, fresh batteries for the radio, and I'll get back to you as soon as we can make a decision."

"Thanks, Mike."

Mike went to find Emily, so she could collect the food and put it outside, then realized that, in her condition, she would just have to find someone else to do it. So, instead, he went to the gardens, found Katie, and together they collected some fruits and vegetables into a box. Then Mike carried the box to the secondary door, wearing a hazmat suit for protection against the nuclear radiation, and left it outside the secondary door. He called Beth on the radio to let her know.

☢

"Hi Mom," Mike said, "mind if I join you?" He had just filled his lunch plate with home-made ice cream, two veggie-burgers and assorted fresh fruits from the kitchen and held it with both hands to keep it from tipping.

Lillie motioned to the chair on her right without looking up or speaking. Everyone else was already seated, eating quietly at the end of the table closest to the kitchen, while Lillie sat by herself, farthest away, pushing food around her plate, and eating little. Everyone knew by now, that to avoid triggering another emotional response, they needed to give her some space.

Mike sat and started eating while he tried to decide how to say what he needed to discuss with her. Quiet conversations from the other end of the room hummed in the air.

"I'm experiencing some problems managing the board," he

finally said.

Silence.

"I wondered if I could ask you a couple of questions?" he continued.

Lillie stopped and looked at him. There were dark rings around deep-set eyes, her skin was pale, her clothes wrinkled, and her hair needed a brush. He felt so bad for her, he wanted to cry.

"I thought I'd adjust work assignments," he said, when he could speak, "to fix a couple of problems that we've encountered, and wondered what you thought about the changes." He had her attention, so he explained the changes that Terry had suggested to him and Emily.

"That sounds like a good idea," Lillie said in a hoarse, unsmiling whisper, as though she had a cold, or more likely, was hoarse from crying.

"Great," Mike said enthusiastically, trying to get his mom to smile. "One problem just came to my attention and it's got me perplexed."

Lillie nodded encouragingly, but didn't speak.

He told her what Beth had said about the invaders wanting to stay in the valley and bring their families, which was contrary to what his dad had wanted. At the mention of his dad, Lillie started to cry, breathing heavily and hoarsely.

"I'm sorry Mom," Mike said and started to rise, picking up his plate. "It can wait, or I'll discuss it with the board."

"Sit," Lillie said through her tears, putting a hand on Mike's arm. Mike returned his plate to the table and sat nervously.

"Really Mom, we can deal with it," he said apologetically, as she shook her head emphatically. He sat quietly, upset at himself for making her cry.

"Mike," she finally said, when she had herself under control "tell me about the captured people." He told her all that he knew, which was what Beth had told him.

"Three of the five are from one family, a father, son and nephew. All three of them say they just wanted to get out of Garden City. Jason gave them someplace to go even though they only believed half of what he told them about the Preserve.

"The nephew's father was killed in the gunfight. They said the father was angry because his wife and daughter had died from smallpox and he wanted revenge on the Outcasts for bringing it to Garden City. The other two survivors tell stories similar to the first three and both lost their families in Garden City. Beth said that would make between five and seven more people, in addition to the seven Outcasts."

"Eight with the baby?" Lillie asked quietly, then waited for Mike to agree before continuing, trying to decide whether or not to tell him about Amos's video message to her. "Mike, I haven't told anyone, and I would appreciate you not sharing this, but your father left a message for me."

"Can I . . ." Mike started to ask his mother if he could see it, but she interrupted him.

"No, you can't see it, but I'll tell you the part you need to know." She had watched Amos's message so many times in the last week, that she could recite most of it from memory. "He said, 'Keep the family looking toward the future. Mike will want to continue looking for us in the twin world. Maybe I should have let him. Maybe some of what we've experienced would help the twin world.'" She skipped over some personal content, then continued.

"He said, 'Beth and her people will make a contribution to the community if you encourage them. Knowing that Sheryl's baby was born immune to smallpox, there's no reason not to allow Rylee and Sydney to find partners on the outside, if that's their choice.

We don't know how long the radiation level will be too high to allow free movement in and out of the Preserve, but Terry can figure that out. Maybe the world will heal itself in your lifetime.'"

She thought about his comment that she should find joy in loving their grandchildren and his expressions of love for her, and choked up. She placed her fingers to her lips, shook her head, then got up and left the room without explaining to Mike.

Mike felt a tear run down his cheek. He wanted to console his mom, but no words came to mind. Then she was gone.

2

Through the Gate Again

Old World—The Preserve, 5 June

"Terry," Mike called as he entered the hospital in a hurry, "are you in here?"

"We're in the operating room," Terry said.

Mike found Terry and Matt looking at Emily's arm. She had broken it when the nuclear explosion at Hill Air Force Base had shaken loose the Wasatch Fault in a 7.4 magnitude earthquake. The quake shook the Preserve hard enough to knock everyone down. As Mike approached, he realized that Terry had the gate open in front of him, large enough for both he and Matt to see what they were talking about. That meant that the other side of the gate was inside Em's arm and that they were looking at the healed bone. The gate acted like a magnifying glass, and Terry could control the level of detail by changing the size of the opening. Terry had worried about blood or bone coming through the gate early on, but had discovered that unless a blood vessel were broken, the blood stayed where it belonged.

Amos's original goal had been to develop a medical device that he could use to diagnose medical problems and study the healing process, by going inside the body non-intrusively. It was ironic that the first use of the device had been when Terry had used it to perform surgery on Amos's head. Amos had lost a lot of blood, but Mike and Matt had gone through the gate and robbed the blood bank at the McKay-Dee hospital in Ogden, Utah. They weren't caught, but had the gate ready for a quick escape if necessary. Amos had died, but the gate had performed flawlessly.

Mike had asked Terry why Amos's blood or tissue didn't come through the gate that was inside his body during the surgery. Terry reminded Mike that they couldn't force anything through the gate by passing through it. The animals that had come through the gate had moved on their own power.

"Wouldn't pumping blood be acting on its own power and pass through the opening?" Mike had asked.

"Apparently not," Terry said, "since it isn't doing that. Don't ask me to explain it. It just works."

Terry had said, afterward, that it had been a little awkward, having Mike in the lab to operate the controls, while Terry was in the hospital, giving him directions by speaker phone. Mike was not surprised to see that Terry had rigged up a portable control panel, so that he no longer needed someone in the lab to maneuver the gate. He was able to tweak the gate remotely now, as needed.

"Hi Michael," Terry said, breaking off his explanation to Matt and looking at Mike. "What can I do for you? Has everyone adjusted to their new assignments?"

"It looks like everyone's pleased with the changes," Mike said, feeling a little guilty for interrupting. "No complaints from Em, that I've heard so far, or from anyone else. Chris is especially happy about being in charge of the gardens, and Katie is relieved to be back in the classroom with the girls."

Emily, lying on the table, looking like a beached whale, didn't comment, although she did turn her head and look at Mike. She had one hand on her pregnant belly, moving it around as though checking on the baby's position.

"Thanks for your suggestions," Mike continued. "It looks like the gate is working as intended."

"It is. You see I built a portable control panel," Terry said, smiling and pointing at the control panel he had set on the table next to him.

"Yeah. That was clever. Good idea. Uh . . . when will you have a few minutes to talk about the gate."

"Now would be as good a time as any. I can tell Emily's tired and her baby is restless." Terry turned a dial on the control panel and the gate closed. Matt helped Em from the table and they left together.

☢

"Okay, Mike. What's up?" Terry asked when they were alone.

"I'm not getting the information I need from the newspapers, so I'm going to go through the gate to research Amos Two online in the twin world. I'll take my laptop and connect to the internet by Wi-Fi, if I can find a way to log in to the internet."

"No Mike," Terry said seriously.

"What do you mean, no?"

"I mean, you can't use the Observer or the gate without my permission, in advance."

"What? I'm chairman of the board, remember? I make the decisions around here, don't I?"

"Actually, Mike, I control all of the technology in the Preserve. Your dad and I have a partnership agreement that states that, should one of us die, our spouse inherits our share of the partnership, but control of all of the technology belongs to the surviving partner. That makes me the senior partner and sole decision-maker, when it comes to the technology."

"Impossible," Mike stammered. "I helped build the Preserve and everything in it. Now, I'm the chairman. I should have some say in its use."

"No one questions your role in building the Preserve, or your contribution to the development of the technology. Unfortunately, that doesn't grant you any rights to the technology."

Mike shifted from foot to foot, nervously. Terry could tell he was struggling to think of an argument that would sway Terry in his favor. Terry wasn't trying to be mean or belittling, but he and Mike needed to have this conversation, sooner rather than later, before Mike, who tended to be head-strong and goal oriented—consequences be damned—got himself, and maybe the rest of them, in trouble.

"Mike, your dad and I spoke often about your role in the Preserve, just as we spoke often about the rest of the family. I wish your dad had had this discussion with you, instead of leaving it to me by default. I know he intended to; he just didn't get the chance."

"What have I done to deserve this lecture?" Mike asked sarcastically.

"I can see I've insulted you, Mike. That's not my intent. I want you to understand what your dad had in mind for you, why you were elected, unanimously, as chairman." Terry could see his words were having the desired effect. Mike wanted to be insulted and angry; but his curiosity silenced him. That was a good sign. He might be quiet long enough to hear Terry out.

"I'm listening," Mike said. His anger appearing to give way a little.

"Your dad told me he was just like you when he was your age. When he met your mom, he mellowed quite a bit, but he was head-strong, just like you."

Mike opened his mouth, probably to object, but Terry raised a hand to stop him.

"Hear me out, Mike," Terry said. "You have the capacity and

ability to be anything you want to be in life. Your dad and mom made sure that you gained self-confidence by letting you make your own decisions, even if they sometimes back-fired on you. He wants me to give you control of the technology," —he held his hand up again to stop Mike from interrupting— "but you need to learn to control yourself first."

"What does that mean?" Mike asked, obvious confusion distorting his features.

"It means, did you even once consider that you might get stuck in the twin world and get beat up, and that it would take the actions of five people who love you, to keep you from dying?"

Mike looked at the floor and his shoulders sagged. Terry knew that Mike hadn't been told the full truth about what happened until he'd recovered from the beating. His body had been busted apart at the hands of three angry men. His rash decision to go alone to the twin world through the Gemini Gate had caused serious problems for his dad and mom.

"Mike, look at me."

Mike looked up slowly, but clearly had trouble looking Terry in the eye.

"Mike, I love you. I see your dad in you. I want you to be as competent and aggressive as he was. He accomplished a lot in his life, but he didn't do it carelessly. He thought through every action, every possible consequence, he talked at length about possibilities and options. Nothing was left to chance. I know you saw that in him, and it sometimes frustrated you. You want to rush off and do something, even if it's the wrong thing."

Mike was looking at the floor again, likely because he knew it was all true. Terry knew enough about Mike to know that Mike understood his own limitations. Mike knew that he was impatient and impulsive, and he knew that most of the family knew it too.

Terry decided he'd beat up on Mike enough. Now he had to hold out a carrot.

"Mike," Terry said, "here's what we'll do. You can go to the twin world."

Mike looked up, excitement dancing in his eyes.

"But we're going to do this together. We'll make a plan, consider consequences, plan for contingencies. And I'll be there with you, controlling the gate and ready to pull you out if all of our planning fails."

Mike was paying attention now. Terry could see the wheels spinning as Mike thought about what he wanted to do.

"Have you talked to my mom about this?" Mike asked.

"Yes, and she's in agreement. If you'll let me coach you, together we can do whatever we want. If you violate that agreement, I have her permission to lock you out of the Observer."

Mike looked deflated. Terry knew Mike would do whatever it took to have continued access to the technology. But he moved around like he didn't know where to go. Terry wondered if he was considering going to his room to have a good cry. He waited patiently to see if Mike would come to some kind of personal decision. Finally, Mike stood up straight and looked Terry in the eye—a good sign.

"Terry," Mike said contritely, "I came to tell you that I think I've found Amos Two and I want to try to meet him."

"I thought you said you weren't having any luck finding him in the papers," Terry said. "I thought that's why you wanted to go through the gate to use the internet."

"That was yesterday," Mike said. "Today I found information that convinces me that I've found him."

"Okay, Mike. Let's go to the office where we won't be disturbed, and talk about it."

They talked for hours, interrupted only by the alarm that Amos had set, to remind them to go to dinner, something that Lillie had made him do after they'd missed too many meals. When they stopped for the night, Terry was convinced that they had a good plan, but wanted to sleep on it, a practice that had served him and Amos well during their years of research. Mike was more excited than Terry had seen him since they'd discovered that the gate was more than just an image on the wall, almost a year earlier.

6 June

Mike stood quickly from the couch in the common area of Terry's bedroom wing as Terry opened the door and stepped out of his bedroom.

"Terry," Mike said.

"How long have you been sitting here?" Terry asked with a laugh.

"About twenty minutes," Mike said. "I didn't want to miss you. Can we talk?"

"Let's get some breakfast, then we can go to the office."

Mike ate so quickly that Terry suspected he wouldn't be able to tell anyone, later, what he had eaten. Terry considered taking his plate with him to the office, then decided that Mike would just have to be patient. He figured he was almost as excited at the prospect of talking to Amos Two as Mike was, but he wasn't willing to skip breakfast.

Mike showed Terry the newspaper story that said President Gregory 'Buck' McCormick would be in Salt Lake City, at the Grand America Hotel, for a fund-raising dinner the next day and that he would be accompanied by some of his key advisors.

"Do you think everyone calls the president, 'Buck' McCormick?" Mike asked.

"It would appear that they do, since the reporter is calling him that," Terry said.

Mike was obviously convinced that Amos Two would be at the fundraising event. He told Terry that he had even worked out how to confirm the details and how to get past security, which they knew would be tight, as it always was when the president was travelling. He showed Terry the notes he'd made on his tablet, including options and contingencies, in case any part of the plan didn't work out as anticipated. Terry had a few questions and suggestions, which Mike added to his notes. Terry liked the plan and its chance of success.

"I'm impressed, Mike," Terry said. "That's exactly what I was talking about yesterday."

"I know, and don't remind me about yesterday. I'm still embarrassed."

"Well, it appears that you took it to heart. Okay, I approve the plan. Do you want to start now or after lunch?"

Mike's eyes lit up. "Now!" he said.

Twin World—Salt Lake City, 6 June

Mike had been to the Grand America hotel in his world and thought he knew the layout of the main floor, but he wanted to check it out, to make sure, before attempting to meet Amos Two the next day. He and Terry went to the lab and set the observer to open a gate in the lobby of the hotel, near a cloak room. After setting the gate opening to about an inch in diameter, Mike peered through the opening and moved it around to confirm that he could step through unobserved.

When he was ready, he had Terry open the gate to just over six feet and stepped through into a doorway, in a hallway off the lobby of the hotel. Then, he turned around to see that Terry had shrunk the gate behind him, back to the one-inch size. He spoke to Terry quietly to test the microphone on his lapel and Terry answered through his earbud. Having confirmed the function of the microphone and earbud, Mike walked through the main floor of the hotel, with Terry looking over his shoulder through the gate, still at the one-inch diameter setting. They quietly discussed the most likely places for security to control the guests and located several inconspicuous spots to pass through the gate the next day.

When they'd finished the initial walk-through, the only serious questions they had left were whether Mike could get into the venue without an invitation, and whether Amos Two would be there. And they couldn't answer either of those until the next day, when they saw how security operated and when they asked to meet with Amos.

Old World—The Preserve, 7 June

"You spoke with Mom, didn't you?" Em asked, while the other board members were finding their seats in the office.

"Yeah, I did," Mike said, thinking about what Lillie had said to him and how much of it the board needed to hear.

"Did you upset her? Is that why she left the dining room in tears?"

"What upset her was remembering the last things Dad said to her."

"What did he say to her?"

"Just a minute. Let's wait for everyone to get seated."

"Are you two talking about Mom?" Rachel asked as she sat next to Emily. Emily nodded.

"Okay," Mike said, "let's start this meeting. We have two agenda items from the chair, but tell me what you want to talk about, so we can add it to the agenda, if needed."

"I want to know what upset Mom at breakfast yesterday morning," Rachel said. "She hasn't come out of her room since then, and the only thing she said to me was 'ask Michael'. What did you say to her?"

"That's on the agenda," Mike said. "Anything else?"

"What are we going to do about the Outcasts and their captives?" Matt asked.

"On the agenda," Mike said. "Anything else?"

"What's going on with the Observer?" Emily asked.

"On the agenda," Mike said.

"That's three things," Matt said. "You said there were two things on the agenda."

"They're related, Matt. Anything else? No? Okay. First item: Dad left Mom a recorded message before he died."

"When? Did he think he was going to die?" Emily asked.

"I don't think so," Mike said, "He recorded it before the battle started, apparently. You know how Dad was, always considering possibilities. I guess that was one of them. Anyway, in the message, he said we should keep looking to the future, not dwell on the past. He also said to let the Outcasts contribute to our community. He thought that the world would heal itself and that Terry could determine when the radiation level would be low enough to allow for free movement between the Preserve and the valley. There's more, but that's the pertinent part."

"Tell us the rest," Emily demanded.

"Mom didn't even share all of it with me."

"Well, tell us what she did share."

Mike thought about it for a few moments, remembering that his mom had said to keep it to himself. Well, he was making an executive decision on what to share with the board.

"She said Terry should keep working on the gate as a medical tool. Terry, I think we need to come up with another name besides 'gate'. It works when we're looking at the twin world, but not so much when we're looking inside someone's body."

"Observer works for me," Terry said, laughing. "That's why your dad named it the Observer in the first place."

"Okay," Mike said, his face and neck turning pink with embarrassment. "Mom also said I should continue looking for Amos Two in the twin world, and see if anything we've experienced or learned would help his world."

"Why is that important?" Matt asked.

"Terry and I discussed it and think that since it's a parallel world, they may be having the same problems we are."

"You mean, like terrorist threats?"

"Exactly."

"So, are you going to . . . ?"

"Actually, Yes." Mike said, interrupting Matt. "Terry and I were working on that this morning."

"And . . . ?" Matt asked.

Mike looked at Terry for agreement before answering. Terry nodded.

"And, I'm going through the gate tomorrow to try to meet Amos Two."

Everyone started talking at once. Mike couldn't pick out any specific question to answer.

"Whoa," Mike said. "We have a plan, with contingencies. Terry will be with me the whole time, to rescue me if I get into trouble." He made eye contact with his wife, Katie. They'd talked about this already and he had reassured her that there wouldn't be a repeat of his last escapade, as she'd called it, through the gate. She had stood by him for months while he'd recovered from the beating he'd taken from three men in the Smiths parking lot. She wasn't anxious for a repeat of that experience.

"Amos Two will be in Salt Lake tomorrow, we think, and we have a pretty good plan for getting in to see him. We can't predict how Amos Two will react to us, but we both know him pretty well, so we should be able to get a dialogue going." There was a little murmuring, but nobody had anything else to share with the group.

"The other thing Mom said was that we should let Rylee and Sydney find partners on the outside, if they want to."

"That makes so much sense," Emily said, "but that won't be until Terry determines that it's safe, right?"

"I don't know how to answer that," Mike said. "That's a topic for another day. Maybe it's best we don't bring that up with them until we know what we want to do."

"What about Mom?" Emily asked. "We can't let her continue on her current course. She's wasting away."

"Yeah," Mike said, remembering how worn out his mom looked the previous day. "Well, if anyone comes up with a solution to that one, let me know. She's too strong-willed for me to tell her what to do."

"She's not eating right or getting enough rest," Emily said. "She's making herself sick."

Mike just shrugged.

"And she's not getting any exercise, as far as I can tell," Katie said. "I've checked the log in the exercise rooms and she hasn't signed-in for over two weeks."

"So, what about the Outcasts?" Matt asked again.

Mike quickly updated the group on the status of the Outcasts and their prisoners from the Bear Lake Valley. He shared the details provided by Beth. Several questions and answers were shared.

Finally, several minutes later, Mike said, "I think the only outstanding issue there is Justin's wife and two daughters. I suggest we let Beth escort Justin back to his home in Garden City to determine the status of his family before we make a final decision. We've agreed to let them stay in the valley, but we should discuss details once we have a final head count."

"We also need to decide how they can contribute," Matt said.

"You're right," Mike said. "They've offered some suggestions."

"What kind of suggestions?" Matt asked.

Things like planting a garden and tending the fruit trees, so they're not such a burden on our gardens. Some of them have home building skills, and want to build a bigger house, so we're thinking about that as well.

"We have supplies and tools they can use if we agree," Terry said. "What do you think?"

"As long as they don't destroy the valley by cutting down all the trees," Emily said, "I think it's a wonderful idea."

"Okay," Terry said, "let's all be thinking about other ideas."

"I'll set up a meeting with all the Outcasts to discuss their ideas," Mike said.

Everyone was in agreement and there was no other business, so Mike ended the board meeting.

After the meeting, Mike asked Beth to gather the Outcasts in the clearing in front of the cliff so he could talk to them through the sensors on the cliff.

"Taylor," Mike said. Taylor was one of the captured invaders who had building skills. "I tweaked a couple of things on your house sketches. Let me know what you think. You'll need someone to do some rock work for the fireplace. You'll also need plumbing and electrical work. I can help with those. I'll also make blueprints and teach anyone who's interested, how to read the prints and do the work. I want to encourage this type of creative thinking, so don't hesitate to share your ideas. We still don't want you to cut down too many valley trees; but I have no problem bringing trees from the hillside.

"We'll get you the home-building tools you need. Pick out a spot for the cabin and start clearing the ground."

Old World—Aspen Valley, 7 June

Mike explained their decision about Justin's family to Beth.

"I better take Bryce and Ben with me in case people become difficult," Beth said. "How do you want us to get there?" Bryce was Sheryl's husband and Ben was Beth's boyfriend. They had proven, over time, to be trustworthy and intelligent, and they would protect her, if needed.

"If I send you the gate, do you think you'll be able to resolve everything today?" Mike asked.

"We can try, but I don't know what I'll find. Last time we were there, the virus was still spreading and killing about thirty percent of those who caught it. The survivors were pretty angry; but we really only need to check on Justin's family."

"Take the radio and let me know if you run into trouble."

Mike sent the gate to the valley for Beth to use to get to Garden City, but he kept the controls and helped Beth check the area she planned to travel to, then the three of them, along with a very surprised Justin, stepped through the Gate into Garden City. Justin was hesitant at first, but after Beth showed him that they were indeed going to Garden City—he recognized the destination—he followed Beth and Ben through, and Bryce brought up the rear.

They went while it was still light outside in order to see what was happening in town. They'd agreed on a cover story in case they ran into anyone, then tried to avoid everyone. Beth checked the area immediately around their entry point, to make sure they hadn't been observed passing through the gate.

The town was nearly deserted, as it had been the last time Beth had been there, although she could tell there were people around. They got almost to Justin's house when they had their first encounter.

"Justin," a man said. "I thought you'd left, gone up into the mountains with that crazy guy, Jason."

"I did, but it didn't work out. Everyone died except us. It was tragic." Justin appeared to be trying to force tears to his eyes.

"Even your boy?"

"Yes," Justin said, wiping a lone tear from his cheek with the back of his hand. "Even Isaac. I couldn't save any of them. I'm lucky to have survived, or unlucky really."

"What happened?" the man asked.

"I'm sorry, but I can't talk about it. You understand."

"Sorry for your loss, Justin."

"Thanks," Justin said as he led the others away, his head bowed until the man was out of sight.

A few minutes later, at the house Justin had been using in the valley, he had to force the door open. Bryce and Ben both stepped in to help him because it had been blocked with heavy furniture. When they got the door open far enough for Justin to squeeze through, he called to his wife. "Hailey, are you here?"

Beth heard running footsteps and a woman cried. "Justin, I thought I'd lost you." When she entered the room, she came to a sudden halt. "Where's Isaac, and who are these people?" she asked cautiously.

"Isaac's fine, and so is Zach, and these are friends. Where are the girls?"

Hailey started to cry and hid her face in her hands. Justin went to her and took her in his arms. He waited for her to get control of herself, then asked again.

"After you left," Hailey said, "some men—I've seen them around, but don't know who they are—forced the lock and took the girls. Two of them held me so I couldn't stop them." By the time she had finished her story, she was in tears again and Justin was fired up. His face had contorted with rage, and Beth became fearful about what he might do. She couldn't let him blow their cover.

"I'll get a gun and go find them," Justin hissed.

"We'll go with you," Bryce said.

"Just a minute," Beth said. "Let's focus on finding the girls. If we find the men at the same time, we can deal with them."

"Can you describe the men?" Justin asked, a little more calmly.

Justin was unable to determine who the men were from Hailey's description, but Beth was confident they could find the girls anyway. It wasn't a large town and the population had been decimated by the virus earlier. There just weren't that many people around anymore.

"Don't leave me again," Hailey begged as Justin pulled away from her.

"Mike," Beth said into her radio, "are you there and did you hear?"

"I am," Mike said, "but I don't know how long it would take to find them. Does she have any idea which way they went or where they would have gone?"

Hailey had gone silent during Beth's exchange with Mike.

"Who is she talking to?" Hailey asked, looking at Justin.

"It's another friend," Beth said, "who has resources that we don't. Don't get your hopes up, but he might be able to look for them faster than we can. Can you answer his questions, tell him what the girls look like and what they were wearing when they left here?"

After Hailey gave Mike a description of her daughters, he told Beth he was going to take the gate, so she would need to call if she needed anything. While they were waiting, Beth told Hailey that she should pack a bag and be ready to leave as soon as Mike got back to them. She should also pack a bag for the girls, trusting that they would be found safe. She didn't want to give Hailey too much information before they knew she was coming with them, so she asked Justin to reassure his wife that she would be fine, regardless of what they found or didn't find.

It took Mike almost two hours to locate the girls, and he was sorry he'd found them. They'd been beaten and left in a field north of town, where they'd frozen to death, if they hadn't died from their injuries. He decided not to give the mother the details. He needed Justin to keep his wife calm until he got them all back to the valley.

"I found them," he told Beth through the radio. "I'm sorry, but they're both dead, and there's no sign of their kidnapers. I've returned the gate to you."

"Isn't there something we can . . . ?" Beth started to ask, but Mike cut her off.

"No, Beth. They're dead."

Hailey collapsed into Justin's arms. He helped her to sit on a couch and wrapped his arms around her tightly. Beth knew, from personal experience, that nothing Justin said in this moment would help his wife find peace. Justin, wisely, didn't try. Later, he would be able to console her.

"Justin," Beth finally said, "we don't have much time. Bring her bag and let's go."

"Why do we have to go," Ben asked. "Why don't we bring the gate here."

"Mike," Beth said, "can you tell where we are and send the gate to us?"

"Give me some coordinates," Mike said, "then one of you go out to the street so I can find you."

"I'll go," Bryce said.

A few minutes later, Bryce returned and led Beth, Ben, Justin and Hailey outside. Following Bryce, they all went through the gate to the valley. Hailey was confused, then shocked, when they told her what she needed to do, but trusted Justin enough, or was in shock, so she followed his directions and went through ahead of him.

Old World—Salt Lake City, 8 June

Mike placed his eye up to the small opening in the Gemini Gate. It made him think of a submarine periscope, except that, instead of merely seeing what was around him, the gate rotated on a vertical axis that allowed him to see what was in the space he occupied as well. He was looking through the gate at the security checkpoint in the lobby of the Grand America hotel in Salt Lake City, Utah, in the twin world.

"The guests have invitations," he told Terry, who stood at his side holding the portable Observer control, "but the staff is collecting them before they pass through the metal detectors, and giving them a program on the other side. It looks like hotel security is monitoring the check-in process and the Secret Service is monitoring everything. So, I just need to get a program and step through on the inside of the security perimeter where no one can see me, and mingle with the other guests."

Mike and Terry had discussed the possibility that he would need an invitation, and fancy clothes. They'd also discussed the chances of Mike getting into the lobby without being seen and what to do if he was discovered. Now, it looked like all he needed to do was get his hands on a program. All of their planning, hours of it, might pay off. Mike was now even more excited about trying to meet Amos Two—not his dad, but the man his dad would have become if he'd made different life choices.

"Sounds too easy," Terry said. "Where can you get a program?"

"I think I saw an open box of them on a counter, to the left. Let's look over there."

As Mike had guessed, Terry was able to move the gate into the box holding the programs. He opened the gate about six inches, then Mike reached through, picked up the topmost program and slipped it through the gate. The gate was open for only a few seconds, so anyone who happened to glance that way, might have thought they saw something, maybe a disturbance in the air; but by the time they looked again, the gate would have been gone. At most, they would have only seen the program move, and then, only if they were looking inside the box at the exact moment when Mike took it.

"One hurdle overcome," Mike said. "How do I look?" he asked Terry. In his dad's black suit, black bowtie, white shirt with cufflinks and polished black shoes, he knew he looked good; but he was nervous, and wanted Terry to confirm it.

Terry looked him over and gave him two thumbs up.

"Do it," Terry said and smiled.

Mike made another 360-degree scan of the area through the gate, nodded to Terry to open it, and took one step forward, through the gate. He looked quickly to his right, where a coat check girl was taking coats, scarves and hats, then took a second step into the cloak room. He turned around to look out of the cloak room and noticed that the Secret Service agent he had targeted was looking in his direction; he had possibly seen a disturbance in the air as Mike had stepped through. Mike took a deep breath, let it out, stepped out of the cloak room, and walked deliberately toward the agent.

☢

"Are you there, Terry?" Mike asked quietly, with his hand to his mouth to hide the movement of his lips.

"Present and accounted for," Terry replied through the small earbud in Mike's ear.

Mike had a fleeting image of himself in one of those secret agent movies and had a sudden urge to laugh. He looked down at his shoes and kept his hand over his mouth until he could control himself, then looked around the lobby, checking the position of the security guards. Holding his program in front of him with both hands, Mike walked up to the Secret Service agent that he'd identified from the dark glasses and wire coming from his ear When Mike saw how badly his hands were shaking, holding the program, he realized how nervous he was and dropped his hands to his sides.

The agent had already spotted him approaching and turned toward him before he arrived.

"Excuse me," Mike said, nervously. The agent didn't respond. "Will you please tell Amos Blund that his son, Michael, is here and would like to speak to him?"

The agent continued to stare at Mike for a few moments, then did a double take as Mike's comment seemed to register. He looked Mike up and down, studied his face hard, then spoke into his collar microphone.

"JP, this is Digs. There's a young man in the lobby who says he's Doc's son, Michael. I know," Digs replied to something JP said in response, "but he's the right age and looks just like him. He wants to talk to his dad."

"Wait over by that column," Digs told Mike, then went back to watching the crowd, periodically glancing in Mike's direction. So, the second hurdle was passed; Amos Two was present, but the agent had called him 'Doc'.

Mike figured that JP, who must be someone on Amos Two's security detail, must be delivering the message and waiting for a response. Mike expected to be arrested at any moment and hauled away for being part of a conspiracy or scam. Mike Two was probably already in the building.

"Are you there, Terry?" Mike asked quietly, hoping Terry could get him out if it looked like he was about to be arrested.

"I heard what happened," Terry said. "Hang in there. I'm ready if you need me."

Digs straightened up as another agent opened a door and stepped into the lobby from the grand ballroom. Digs nodded toward Mike and the agent approached.

"Michael Blund?" the second agent asked. When Mike nodded, the agent continued. "Come with me," he said, and started to move away.

"Are you JP?" Mike asked, then wondered where he'd found the nerve to ask.

Without answering, the agent looked at Mike for a moment, then led the way around a corner and down the hall to a small room. He stepped aside to allow Mike to enter, then followed and closed the door behind them.

"Do you have photo ID?" the agent asked.

Mike pulled out his wallet and removed his Utah driver's license, just about the only thing in the wallet, which he hadn't carried with him since they'd moved to the Preserve. Terry had thought of it and had suggested he might need identification. He handed it to the agent.

After studying the license and comparing it to Mike's face, JP returned it.

"I'm Agent Ty Morgan," the agent said. "JP's my nickname. I don't know how you got here, but you appear to be who you say you are. If you'll wait here, Doc will be here shortly."

"Doc?" Mike asked, with raised eyebrows. Then he immediately regretted it. He'd heard the first agent—Digs—use that name. He suddenly felt foolish, and wondered if he had just blown his cover.

"That's what Mr. Blund goes by. I would have thought you'd have known that, being his son." He studied Mike again, perhaps wondering if he was other than what he appeared to be. For all the agent knew, Mike had always called his dad Amos instead of Doc. After a few moments, JP turned and stepped to the door. "Wait here," he said and stepped into the hallway, closing the door behind him.

"This looks bad, Terry." Mike said. "I might have just blown it there." He looked around the room and realized this was set up as a meeting room for side conversations. There were three chairs around a small table, with place settings, coffee cups and a carafe of coffee, in the center of the table.

"Be still. I'm watching," Terry said. "Sit down and relax. It will look more normal."

"But I'm nervous."

"Then don't sit. Act nervous. That works, too."

3

Terrorist Attack

The phone on the situation room conference table rang, interrupting President Gregory 'Buck' McCormick in the middle of a sentence.

"Not now," Buck thought out loud, then answered it anyway. He knew it was his secretary, Jen, and she wouldn't bother him unless it was important. "What is it, Jen?" he asked politely.

"You better get Doc and come to the Oval Office," Jen said. "You need to see this before the phones starts ringing."

"It's that important?" Buck asked, making eye contact with Doc, sitting in the chair on his left.

"It is," Jen said.

"We'll be right there." He hung up. "Doc, come with me. Jim," he said to his SecDef, James Seymour, sitting opposite Doc, "continue the meeting." All of Buck's advisors and key members of the National Security Council were seated down both sides of the table, discussing the latest Al-Qaeda threat of a major attack against the "evil" western empire It was almost midnight, and Buck had been about to explain what the administration was prepared to do if the attack was directed at the United States.

"We received a video from London that you need to see," Jen said as Buck and Doc passed her desk on the way to the Oval Office. "Let me know when you're ready."

Buck nodded and continued into the office without missing a step. He pushed a button on his desk and a wall panel slid back to reveal a video monitor.

"Ready," he said into his intercom as he sat down behind his desk. Doc took a chair to one side, where he could see the monitor.

Within moments, the video screen lit up and they were watching footage from a news camera, of the New Year's Eve celebration on the Victoria Embankment in London. The camera angle was above street level, likely mounted on top of a TV van, looking at a crowd of happy people talking and dancing in the street. Big Ben, the famous clock tower, could be seen in the background as the camera panned the crowd. A reporter's voice talked about the celebration and the dignitaries that were expected to attend from around the world.

As they watched, a black stretch-limousine passed and pulled up to the curb fifty feet in front of the camera. The front passenger door opened and what looked like a Secret Service agent stepped out, looked around, studying the crowd, then opened the back door. Two more agents stepped from the back of the limo, followed by a man and three women in elegant formal wear.

Suddenly, a skirmish broke out in front of the limo and the camera zoomed in to see what was happening. Two of the three security agents moved quickly to the front of the limo to intercept and restrain a bearded man wearing a dark, bulky coat. The man seemed to be very upset, screaming and fighting to get free. A crowd gathered around the group as they struggled; some appeared to be trying to help, while others were probably curious bystanders.

"Arab?" Buck asked Doc, who nodded without speaking; he was watching the four civilians in formal wear who'd exited the limo.

Amos watched the third agent attempt to usher the four in formal wear away, back into the limo. One of them, the man, broke free and ran toward the struggling agents. Amos lost sight of him in the crowd, but not before he recognized his son, Michael. That meant that the other three were his wife, Lillie, and their two daughters, Emily and Rachel.

"No," Amos said as realization hit him. He'd been sent by Buck to represent the United States at a dinner that night at Buckingham Palace. He had taken his family, and they had enjoyed playing tourist for two days, then Amos had been called back to Washington, D.C. to discuss the terrorist threat with the NSC.

Lillie had been excited to meet the Queen, and had suggested that she represent Amos at the dinner. The girls had begged to stay so that they could attend the formal dinner and dance. Michael had suggested that he also stay so that he could keep an eye on his sisters. Amos knew Michael was as excited about attending the events as the girls were. He also knew that the family had planned to attend the festivities at the Embankment, and he had only agreed on the condition that they would stay close to their Secret Service detail.

Amos stood, expecting the worst, not knowing what else to do, but needing to do something. He knew instinctively that this was the terrorist attack that they had been trying to uncover and prevent. It was too much of a coincidence to be anything else. Fear for his family mixed with hope that he was wrong. His gut clenched, as did his fists.

"Doc," Buck said, "I don't think—" but he didn't get the rest of his comment out before the crowd began to scatter, frantically, starting at the point of the incident and flowing outward like ripples in a pool. Before anyone could move more than a couple of steps, due to the press of bodies, a brilliant flash of light exploded at the center of the skirmish. The people closest to the explosion were blown away, catching fire as they crashed to the ground and lay still. Others, caught by the shock wave, were propelled away from the explosion and rolled on the ground or beat at flames, trying to put them out.

Amos stared at the screen, dumbstruck.

"I'm sorry Doc," Buck said.

Amos turned to look at his boss and long-time friend, and saw the pain in Buck's face, which mirrored his own internal agony. He could not believe what fate had just done to him.

"What have I done?" Amos cried. "I should have foreseen this and prevented it. Maybe, if I'd been there, I could have protected them."

"Maybe they were protected by the limo," Buck said hopefully

"Buck, I need to go to London, now."

Buck played back the video and confirmed that the camera had moved away from the limo by the time the bomb had exploded; but Buck suspected that Doc's family had been wiped out by the explosion. The limo was hardened, but they were outside its protective barrier when the bomb went off. This is what the terrorists had meant when they said this attack would hit at the heart of the United States. Doc was a rallying point for the anti-terrorist movement and a thorn in Al-Qaeda's side. He was the heart of the United States, as far as Buck was concerned.

Maybe Buck had placed Doc too much in the public eye. Maybe it was his fault that Doc and his family had been targeted, and there was no doubt Doc had been the target of this attack.

The terrorists would have had no idea that Doc would be called back hours before the attack.

He knew that the best thing for Doc was action, and going to London would give him a goal and something to focus on. Maybe his family had survived the attack.

"That's a good idea, Doc. I'll get Jen to set it up. You can take Air Force One and be there tonight."

Twin World—London, 1 January

Lillie, Emily and Rachel were dead. Amos's whole body shook— convulsed—when he identified their remains. His family, gone in an instant; and he hadn't been there to protect them. Although the women were some distance from the explosion, their bodies were riddled with shrapnel from the bomb, which must have been filled with scraps of metal, possibly nails. It appeared that an agent had attempted to get them back into the limo, but not quickly enough. Amos would bring their bodies back with him, to the United States, along with one of the Secret Service agents, on Air Force One. The investigators had so far been unable to identify Michael's or the other agents' bodies in the carnage that was left after the explosion. It was assumed, since they were last seen closest to the terrorist, that they had also died, their bodies broken beyond recognition. Further investigation might reveal more.

"Thank you for your efforts," Amos said, exhausted and defeated, as he shook hands with the British Prime Minister, Teresa May. She had requested that Amos, and the U.S. ambassador to the UK, Daniel Porter, visit her before they left the country.

"I am sorry it turned out this way," Minister May said, in her lilting British accent, "and I'm sorry you had to face the insensitive media on your arrival. They just don't seem to know when to leave well enough alone."

Amos had been unable to avoid a media barrage upon his arrival at London's Gatwick airport, on the president's personal plane, and had taken a few minutes to express the president's hope that the people of the world would see the senselessness of the terrorist attacks and join in the effort to stop them. In particular, he hoped that the Muslim population would help ferret out those few racist fringe radicals who were causing all the problems and giving the rest of them a bad name on the world stage.

He had tried to cut off the questions, avoiding sharing his own personal grief as much as possible, but the reporters had seen the video and knew Amos's family had been the target of the attack. They had bombarded him with questions about his personal feelings, implying that he probably hated Muslims because of the attack.

"Let's be very clear about where I stand," Amos had said, "in case you haven't been paying attention. I am, and will continue to be, a strong advocate for peace. I respect all peace-loving peoples of the world, which includes most Muslims. I will continue to do everything within my limited power to stop the terrorist attacks, and the misguided people behind them. I hope you of the media can get it right this time, so I don't have to keep repeating myself."

As he had walked away from the microphone, surrounded by his security detail, who scanned the crowd non-stop, the questions from the reporters had continued, variations on the same theme.

"It will always be that way, I suppose," Amos said to Prime Minister May.

"Well, we agree with you, that you were probably the target of the bomb, because of your tremendous efforts to stop global terrorism," Minister May continued, "but Al-Qaeda will consider this attack a success because it has struck you harder than if they had killed you instead. You have my deepest sympathy. Please don't give up the fight, and tell me if there is anything that I, or my people can do for you personally, or for your country."

"Thank you, again," Amos said. "We will be in touch."

As Doc and the ambassador got into the ambassador's car, with its hardened chassis and bullet-proof glass, the Ambassador tried to engage Doc in small talk.

"The president has called me back," Ambassador Porter said, to fill the silence.

"He's not firing you, I hope," Doc said. "You're doing a great job here."

"No. He wants me to be the ambassador to the UN. My wife will see it as a positive change. She's from upstate New York, so this will be like going home."

"Are your kids there?"

"Well, no. The three of them are living in different parts of the country. But we'll still be closer than we are now."

"Sounds like a win-win. Thanks for your help, Dan. It was hard enough seeing Lillie and the girls that way, *with* your help. I don't know how I could have done it without you."

"I'm just sorry we didn't have a better outcome."

Twin World—Air Force One (over the Atlantic Ocean), 1 January

"Hi Doc," the president said, speaking to Amos over an encrypted phone. "I'm truly sorry. I can't imagine what I would feel if I lost Liz that way. Would you like to take some time to be by yourself before coming back to Washington?"

"No Buck," Amos sighed. "I would be lousy company for myself in my present frame of mind. Tell me what you're doing, so I can get my mind off my problems."

"You know, you don't have to pretend to be the man-of-steel. You can let it all hang out. You can curse me and tell me I'm a jerk for taking you away from your family and leaving them unprotected."

"Cut it out, Buck. We both know it wasn't your fault, and there was nothing we could have done to prevent it. Our intelligence wasn't good enough. We need to correct that before the next attack, and we both know there will be another attack, probably sooner rather than later, and probably bolder and more devastating." Amos was sure the president could see through his charade. He was tired, and lonely, and the loss of his family was nearly enough to make him stop trying. But he put on a brave face, and tried to keep his voice neutral.

"I agree, and that's the reason I called, instead of letting you take a long nap. I'm putting the finishing touches on my message to the nation and wanted to run a couple of things past you, if you're up to it."

"Go ahead. I can put off my nap for a few more minutes," Amos joked drily.

"I heard your impromptu press conference at the airport and want to build on your themes of 'peace-loving people' and 'ferret out the racist fringe radicals'. I want to offer financial support and military protection to any group or individuals who will work with us on those objectives. What do you think?"

"As president, you have a lot of latitude in those areas, but you might want to get Congress behind you on that."

"Agreed, and that's what I want you to do, as soon as you're back. I've got my other advisors talking to friendly Senators and Representatives to find sponsors for legislation, and I want you to be our spokesperson before key committees in both houses, to make it happen. We'll have to work on the wording, to give us some wiggle room for sanctions against anyone harboring terrorists, asylum for those who help us, and so on. We'll definitely have better success if we do it now, while the country's sympathy is with you."

"Okay, Buck, I'll think about it on the way home, and show you my notes when you're ready to talk."

"Excellent, Doc. See you in a few hours."

Twin World—Damascus, Syria, 6 January

As Saleh entered the airport luggage area, he spotted his good friend and mentor, Ahmed, across the room. With a subtle nod, Ahmed left the terminal, walking at a moderate pace, along with other debarking passengers, so as not to attract attention. A few minutes later, bag in hand, Saleh followed. He found Ahmed in a drab, tan 1980s sedan at the curb, its engine running and gray exhaust belching from the back. He dropped his bag into the back and climbed into the passenger seat.

Ahmed set a London Times newspaper in Saleh's lap, with the front page showing.

"Good to see you," he said in Arabic, as he pulled the car into traffic. "Another successful mission, my friend."

Saleh looked at the headline: TERRORIST BOMB IN CROWDED NEW YEAR'S EVE CELEBRATION.

Only slightly smaller was the subtitle: Suicide Bomber Kills 38, Wounds 147, at Victoria Embankment in Westminster.

Saleh would read the story, but for now he was satisfied with his good friend's compliment. He smiled at Ahmed.

"Khalid was one of the faithful, Allah be praised," Saleh said.

"He will be rewarded in heaven," Ahmed replied. After a pause he added, "We have another assignment for you."

"Whatever the Brothers require," Saleh said with a slight nod, still basking in his mentor's approval. He was surprised that another mission would follow so soon. He'd spent the previous three weeks in London preparing Khalid and his support team for the last mission, and three weeks before that planning and selecting his team. Still, he was hesitant to ask.

"What is this one?" he asked anyway.

Ahmed looked briefly at Saleh before returning his eyes to the traffic ahead, his expression unreadable. Then he smiled broadly through his heavy beard. Unlike Ahmed, Saleh had been required to shave his beard for his overseas missions, so he was pleased that the latest style favored a little facial hair—it allowed him to have a few days' growth. With his light skin and easy grasp of the Queen's English, he was able to move freely around Europe. And his assumed name, Samuel, led many people to assume he was Jewish, which made him laugh—when it didn't make him angry.

"You have performed flawlessly on your assignments, Saleh," Ahmed said. "How many students did you recruit for the camps? Twenty-seven? And you supported Rashid's team on quite a few successful missions. You have demonstrated that you know how to plan a mission and lead a team."

Saleh had been raised in Saudi Arabia, in one of the Wahhabi training camps, along with children from around the Arab world. That he had pleased his instructors was evident when, at age seventeen, he was sent to England to study at Cambridge and to observe for himself Western decadence. With nearly unlimited funding from the Brothers, he immersed himself in the culture—fast cars, alcohol, and women. But despite appearances, he'd never doubted the teachings of his youth for a moment, and only once questioned his own actions. Even then, he'd rationalized away his concerns without much effort. After all, he'd been sent to England to understand why the United States was referred to as the Great

Satan, and why she and her Western allies were called godless. After experiencing the temptations of decadence for himself, he understood all the better why Westerners needed to be destroyed.

Called back from England after three years, Saleh had been given small assignments, and then gradually larger ones, taking messages and packages to Brothers in Islamic centers around the world. Eventually, he'd been assigned to Rashid's team in England, which recruited local Arab youths for the Wahhabi training camps. Then he was assigned to set up communication networks for young people returning to England from the camps—what they called sleepers. Having proven himself to be a resourceful and dedicated organizer, Saleh had been sent back to Cambridge, recruiting sleepers for suicide missions. His assignments had increased in size and complexity so that now, at age twenty-nine, he had completed two successful missions of his own.

Ahmed had stopped talking. Saleh was disappointed that he wasn't going to say anything about the next assignment, but then Ahmed surprised him.

"This one will be special, the most audacious mission the Brothers have ever planned. They have a lot of faith in you. It is not safe to talk out in the open. You will get the details from them." Then, as he stopped at a light, he turned to face Saleh, grinning broadly at his protégé. "This one will be solo. You are going to Chiapas, Mexico."

4

Amos Two

Twin World—Salt Lake City, 8 June

"Doc, he said he's your son, Michael, but we both know Michael was killed five and a half months ago in London."

"But you said he had a program in his hand," Doc argued, "so he had to have come in through the security checkpoint, and you looked at his ID. Who else could he be?"

"I don't know," JP said, "but until we confirm that he is who he said he is, we need to treat this like any other public encounter,"

"You know, we were never able to verify Mike's death. Maybe he hit his head and wandered off, and only now remembers who he is. And what about that incident in Ogden, Utah last month? Didn't you say the FBI found Michael's DNA at the scene of the blood bank robbery?"

"That's what they said," JP replied, "but they also admitted that DNA testing has been wrong before. Anyway, I'm responsible for your safety. You need to let me do my job."

As they approached the door to the room where JP had left Michael, JP held his arm out to stop Doc from entering. "Officially, your son died five and a half months ago in London."

"Okay, JP, do your job, but once we confirm he's my Michael, you let me enjoy the moment. My son has come back from the dead, and I only have a few minutes before I have to get back to Buck. I'm part of the show tonight."

JP entered the room ahead of Doc and faced Mike, who stood and tried to look around JP at Amos Two, or "Doc", as the agent had called him.

"Mike," JP said, "I need to confirm a few things before I can allow you to talk to Doc."

"What would you like to know?" Mike asked, nervously.

JP noticed Mike's nervousness. It didn't necessarily mean anything. Being around famous people, and especially those with their own security detail in tow, made some folks nervous. It was one factor he had to consider.

"You came through the security checkpoint, right?" When Mike hesitated, JP went on. "We can check the video to confirm that, so you need to be truthful."

"Tell them 'yes'," Terry said in Mike's ear. *"I can get you out if we need to."*

"Yes," Mike said.

JP had been bluffing. They had video coverage, but he wasn't going to take time to check it. Doc had a deadline. He was just testing Mike.

"May I see your ID again?"

Mike handed JP his driver's license again and JP turned to show it to Doc, who studied it for a moment.

"Everything looks correct," Doc said.

"Where have you been for the last five and a half months?" JP asked.

Mike just stared at JP.

"Something's wrong here," Terry said. *"Something must have happened to Mike. They're too surprised at your presence. Pretend you don't know, like you've had amnesia, or something."*

"Sorry, sir," Mike said, "but I can't tell you. I don't know."

"That's it, JP," Doc said, convinced that Mike had been hit on the head in London and wandered away from the explosion with amnesia. He shouldered his way past JP to face Michael. "I'll take it from here," he said. "Why don't you wait in the hall and I'll call if I need anything?"

"Yes, sir," JP said reluctantly. He handed Mike's ID back to him, and left the room, closing the door behind him.

☢

"Is it really you, Michael?" Doc asked. "We thought you were dead."

Mike thought Amos Two would rush to him to give him a hug, but he didn't. Doc looked so much like his dad—except that his hair was shorter, like he had been getting regular haircuts. It was all he could do not to give Doc a crushing embrace and cry on his shoulder; but Doc's restraint made him cautious.

"What happened five and a half months ago," Mike asked cautiously.

"A terrorist detonated a bomb in London that killed your mother and sisters. Until now, we suspected you were also killed." Mike was startled. Was Doc saying that his whole family had been wiped out by the terrorist bomb? How could he even function? And, that meant Mike would *not* find the rest of the family in the twin world.

"You didn't know," Doc said, likely guessing from the reaction. "We thought you were caught in the explosion, too, but you must have hit your head and wandered off, not remembering what had happened."

"That's unbelievable," Mike said, tears coming to his eyes as he thought about losing his dad, and how painful it would be to have lost the whole family. "How are you able to stand it?"

Mike heard Terry's sniffle in his ear. So, he knew that Terry understood what Doc had said and must be feeling it, too. This was going to be more difficult than he'd imagined.

"I've lost a lot of sleep over it," Doc said. "When did you remember who you were?"

"Be careful," Terry warned. *"Start slow."*

"I saw your name in the paper and knew I had to see you," Mike said, sniffling himself.

"Can I have a hug," Doc asked, opening his arms.

Mike rushed to him and gave him that tearful embrace.

"How I've missed you," Doc said wistfully.

"I've missed you, too," Mike said, then realized he probably shouldn't have said that. Doc thought Mike had just recovered from amnesia.

Doc held him at arm's length and studied his face.

"You're just as I remembered, only half a year older," Doc said, choking on his words. "Look Mike, I have to get back to the meeting. Buck wants to show me off again." Doc smiled. "Are you hungry? I'll have JP get you something to eat; anything you want."

"D-dad," Mike struggled with the word, wanting Doc to be his dad, but knowing he wasn't. When Doc stopped and looked him in the eye, Mike continued. "I need to tell you why I'm here."

"You came to see me, right?"

"There's a very important reason."

"Can it wait?"

"I suppose, but when you hear what it is, you're going to want to know more."

Doc frowned. "Are you really my Michael?" he asked suspiciously, then laughed. Michael had a tendency to be overly-serious, which sometimes seemed melodramatic. Doc took a step toward the door and Mike feared he would miss his opportunity.

"I am Amos Blund's son, Michael. Everything I've said is true, except the part about having amnesia."

"Careful, Mike," Terry said.

"I need to tell him the truth, and we don't have time to beat around the bush," Mike said.

"Who are you talking to?" Doc asked. "Are you hallucinating? Do I need to get a doctor?" Doc took another step toward the door.

"Doc, can you give me five minutes to explain?"

Doc looked at his watch. "Five minutes," he said.

Mike pointed to the chairs and they both sat.

"I wasn't in London on New Year' eve with the rest of the family," Mike said. "For the last year, I've been in the Preserve, an underground retreat that you and your partner built and stocked to survive for thirty years."

Amos's face looked calmer than Mike thought it would, but he could see Amos calculating inside. "Have you been under medical care since the accident?" Doc asked.

"I thought you'd have trouble believing this, so I've brought evidence." Mike sat casually with his hands resting on the table, so Doc raised an eyebrow in question.

"Do you know Terry Stephens?" Mike asked.

"I know the name."

"Did you, at one time, think of building medical devices?"

"Yes, but most doctors do. They want to invent something to make their job easier."

"And your idea was to build a machine that would look inside the human body, non-intrusively, to diagnose medical conditions. You even had a name for it. You called it the Observer."

Doc looked surprised, as if the name and device had never been shared with his son.

"Your mother must have told you about it."

"No Doc, I helped you build it. It exists, and it works, beautifully. Not only as a medical device, but as a gate to another world."

"That's enough," Doc said, and started to rise. "I don't know what kind of game you're playing here, but I've heard enough. I'm going to get you some professional help."

"Here I come," Terry said in Mike's ear.

Suddenly, a circle appeared just to Mike's left and grew until it was about six feet in diameter. Mike watched Doc's face as a man about Doc's age, but a little shorter and stockier, stood in the middle of the circle, smiling at Doc.

"Hi Amos," Terry said. "I'm Terry, your partner in our world."

Doc's mouth opened and shut several times, as though he were trying to decide what to say. He didn't move for a moment, and then almost missed the chair when he tried to sit again.

"What kind of parlor trick is this?" Doc finally asked. There was a table and shelves behind Terry, and clear and distinct definition of the boundaries of the circle. Mike watched Doc, knowing how his mind must be struggling to figure out what he was seeing.

"Amos—Doc—we are visiting you from a parallel world, by means of the Observer, which you invented and the three of us built." Terry said. He waited, but Doc didn't or couldn't respond, so he continued. "We are on a parallel course with your world. Our world has just gone through global thermonuclear war and we believe yours is headed there. There are some things we've learned that we think will help you. And, perhaps, there are some things that you can do to help us. Are you willing to listen?"

There was a knock at the door and JP spoke.

"Doc," he said, "the president is asking for you. Are you about finished?"

Doc shook his head, likely trying to make sense of what he was seeing. Mike was still there, but the gate was just winking out of existence.

"Just a minute, JP," Doc said. "I'll be out in a minute. Mike, what just happened?"

"Doc—I'd like to call you Dad—we need your help. We have a crisis in our world and need your expertise. Will you help us?"

"How is any of what you're telling me possible?"

"I don't know, but it is. Somehow, maybe when you had to make a decision between staying with medical research or going into government service, two timelines were created. In our world, you invented and patented medical prosthesis, created the Observer, built the Preserve and invented a mini nuclear reactor to power the Preserve for over thirty years. There's a lot more I can tell you, but it looks like we're out of time."

Doc looked at the door. The gate opened again. Mike got up, disappointed, and turned toward it.

"Wait," Doc said, his voice frantic. "I need to know more. I need to figure out what just happened—how you came to be here, how Terry was standing in the middle of the air. And, I can't lose you again. How did you even get in here? Was it through that hole in the air?"

"Yes. I guess I lied about that, too," Mike said.

"You can't leave that way. I couldn't explain it. Wait here a minute." Doc hurried to the door and opened it a few inches. "JP, give me your mobile phone."

"Sir?" JP questioned, pulling his phone out of his shirt pocket. "My secure phone?"

"I need a way for Michael to contact me. You can get another one." He took the phone and closed the door. He opened the phone and looked at it. "I'm on speed-dial number one," he said. "Call me in two days and I'll know my schedule. We can decide where to meet. Can you get to Washington, D.C.?"

"No. This is the farthest we can travel from Logan Canyon."

"Okay. I'll find an excuse to come back to Utah tomorrow or the next day. You'll call me day after tomorrow?"

"Yes," Mike said and nodded.

"Then give me a hug and JP will get you to the front door. I have no doubt you'll find your way from there."

They hugged, Mike squeezing Doc as hard as Doc did Mike, then Doc was gone.

5

Jose Mendosa

Old World—Detention Facility, 11 June

Jose Mendosa, El Jefe of the Los Zetas drug cartel in Mexico, had been captured days earlier in his hacienda in a small village near Chiapas, Mexico and brought to a high security detention facility in Virginia, where CIA agents questioned him about his role in the building of a nuclear bomb and smuggling it into the United States. At first, he denied any knowledge of the events, but as the CIA worked with him, laying out the penalties for drug smuggling and distribution of drugs to minors, Mendosa softened up.

"I admit that we made a business agreement with an Arab to help assemble a bomb in exchange for weapons and protective body armor," Mendosa said, "but he swore the bomb would not be functional, that its purpose was only to scare the United States into releasing 217 Islamist freedom fighters from illegal incarceration."

"Are you familiar with terrorist activity globally, and in particular against the United States?" the interrogator asked.

"Of course," he admitted. "I watch the news."

"Then you have seen the suicide bombers, with their vests of dynamite?"

"Oh yes. A terrible thing, especially the way they use women and children. It is cowardly."

"So, if you disagree with their tactics, why did you agree to help them?"

"It was a business deal and I am a businessman, nothing more. He had something I needed and I had something he wanted."

"Which was proximity to the United States and a way to smuggle something into the country, is that right?"

"Of course," Mendosa said, "but I did not expect them to detonate the bomb."

"Of course not," the interrogator said. "It was just a business deal."

"Correct."

"So, how did you get the bomb into the United States?" a second agent asked.

Mendosa considered denying that he had helped smuggle the bomb, or lying about it, but realized he had already given too much information away and could not take it all back, so he cooperated with the agents and told them about the million-dollar, single use submarine that he had used to deliver the Arab and his bomb to the South Carolina coast. He even admitted that he worked with a small, independent boat owner to transfer the bomb to shore, but claimed he had no knowledge of whose boat was used, since he used an intermediary for the deal.

After several hours of questioning, the CIA could get no more information out of him, without resorting to torture, so they locked him up and hoped they would have another opportunity to talk to him.

6

A New Bill

**Twin World—The White House, 16 January
(five months earlier)**

President Buck McCormick sat at a desk under the spotlights in the Rose Garden, preparing to sign into law sweeping new legislation aimed at stopping terrorism around the world. He wished that they'd turn off the lights, because they were making him perspire, even on this cold January day. he'd asked his Chief of Staff, Eric Epstein, to have them turned off.

"Sir," Eric said. "You see the media representatives in their heavy coats and muffs? You don't like being cold, more than you don't like being hot. I suggest we leave the lights on. Besides, you can see better with them on."

Buck grumbled for a few moments, then looked up and smiled for the cameras. A stack of folders sat on the desk to his left, each one embossed with the seal of the President of the United States, and containing a copy of legislation designed to punish governments found to harbor terrorists or to sanction terrorism by providing funding, facilities or weapons technology. The language in the legislation was flexible enough to allow the president to determine, at his sole discretion and with very few restrictions, who to punish and what the punishment would be, including anything up to and including blocking all financial and other aid to the offending country. It was an unprecedented move by Congress, made possible by public sentiment in response to the deaths of

Lillie Blund and her children.

An equal number of pens, also stamped with the presidential seal, formed a row on his right. Each had been tested to ensure that they worked, so there would be no embarrassing moments for the media talking heads who were primed for this event.

Key members of Congress from both political parties stood behind the president, many of their legislative aides were visible in the background. Media representatives stood behind a yellow rope in front of the desk, at a distance that White House security felt was safe, out of sight of the cameras and ready to ask questions if and when the opportunity came.

Buck looked around, smiling for the cameras, but mostly watching faces. He was good at reading people, and what he saw was a mixture of hope and pessimism. Surveys said that most of the citizens of the United States wanted—no demanded—government action to stop the bombings; they were tired of the violence and death. But some special interests, those who would lose money from reduced government spending, were vocal, and in some cases violent, in their opposition to this move.

Checking the sky to confirm that an incoming snow storm still held off, Buck continued looking around. He noticed Doc, to the left of the media, his body turned away from the podium. Doc was looking around too, his face a mask. Their eyes met and Doc nodded once, then continued scanning the crowd.

"They're going to try to sabotage this legislation," Doc had said at breakfast earlier.

"What can they do?" Buck had asked. "The bill has been passed by both the House and the Senate, and I'm signing it into law in an hour. After that, only the Supreme Court can stop it from becoming law."

"Senator Stenger looks like a haunted man, like he's getting a lot of pressure from his political backers and party hacks. If he fails, they could muddy his reputation and replace him with someone more controllable. I think he's becoming desperate."

"Okay," Buck had sighed, "I'll trust you on this. Keep an eye on him."

"He may have help by now. As you said, it's too late for him to do anything by himself. I'll watch the paper trail to make sure nothing happens to the bill after it's signed."

"What could happen? There are multiple copies and the key points of the legislation are well known."

"It's just a gut feeling," Doc had said, rising as Buck pushed aside his breakfast dishes and stood to get ready for the signing meeting.

"Of course."

☢

Doc watched a smiling president open the first folder from the stack, pick up the first pen on his right, and sign his name with a flourish. He closed the folder and set it on the forward edge of the desk, then handed the pen to the Speaker of the House, a member of his party and a strong political supporter. He repeated the process eleven more times, each time handing the pen to a man or woman behind him, seven members of his own party and five from the opposition.

Doc studied the president, the press, and especially the politicians, to see if he could spot anything out of the ordinary. They had been through this process twice before in recent months, once on a trade bill and again on tax and medical insurance reform and nothing untoward had happened.

Finally, the last copy was signed. A political aide placed the stack of folders in a briefcase, and hurried away. Her abruptness, and the suddenness of her appearance and departure, set off alarm bells in Doc's head. He turned to JP, the head of his security team, standing behind him.

"Follow that aide," Doc said. "She's supposed to deliver those folders to Jen, the president's secretary. If she doesn't, I want to know where she goes. Take someone with you."

He ran a hand through his hair and shook his head. How had he gotten himself into this position, questioning everyone's motives and running surveillance? All he'd ever wanted was to be a surgeon, with free time to pursue his dream of inventing medical devices. He knew that's what he'd be doing now, if Buck hadn't pressured him to "serve his country" by joining Buck's political machine after he'd won a Senate race nine years earlier.

Doc had met Greg during high school and they'd become close friends. Greg went on to serve in the military, then played football while earning his law degree from Ohio State. That was where he picked up his nickname, Buck, by playing linebacker for the Buckeyes. Then he went into politics. Amos had paid his way through engineering, then medical school, finally becoming a surgeon. They had been best man at each other's weddings and godfather to each other's children. Then Greg had hounded Amos to use his brilliant mind to advise Senator Gregory 'Buck' McCormick. In the end, Amos couldn't resist the charismatic Senator. Now, he was special advisor to the president of the United States, designing policy, negotiating with foreign diplomats and hobnobbing with politicians on both sides of the aisle.

He had to admit that they'd made some remarkable changes—improvements, he told himself—in the federal government, and Greg always gave Amos most of the credit, privately and in public. But he often wondered where he would be and what he would be doing if he had chosen to stay with medicine.

JP and Digs followed the aide, at a discrete distance, through the West Colonnade into the West Wing. She turned left past the Cabinet Room toward the secretary's office, but instead of turning left into the office, she followed the corridor to the right and continued to the far west end of the hall, near the elevator. Her heels, clicking on the tile floor, provided cover for their quiet footsteps.

The men waited around a corner long enough to hear her enter the elevator. They heard the swish of the elevator door that told them it had closed. JP peeked around the corner and watched the elevator signal its decent. Then he led Digs down the adjacent stairs to the basement. JP cracked open the door on the bottom landing and listened for the aide's clicking heels. She exited the elevator and turned right, away from them, toward the Situation Room at the end of the hallway. He thought that might be where she was going, but she stopped, rapped on a door, then entered a video conference room and closed the door behind her.

JP and Digs slipped into a room across the hall to wait, in case she dropped off the briefcase and left immediately. They didn't want to be in the stairwell, in case she chose to take the stairs back up to the main floor. After a few moments, she exited and returned to the elevator. When they heard the elevator door close, they waited a few more moments, then approached the video conference room door. JP motioned for Digs to follow him into the room and spread out, left and right, with their Glock 19 handguns out and ready. It was understood that he would take the lead and do the talking, if needed.

When they entered, they found Senator Stenger and two other men sitting at a small table, opening folders containing the signed copies of the legislation and, apparently, dismantling them.

"What's the meaning of this?" Senator Stenger bellowed indignantly.

"Senator," JP said, "it looks like you've been caught. Everyone, please place your hands on the table where we can see them. You're all under arrest."

All three men complied immediately.

❂

"Go right in," Jen said pressing the buzzer to release the door lock. She picked up her red pen and went back to studying the papers on her desk. Doc and JP entered the Oval Office, to find Buck rising from his desk to meet them.

"Buck," Doc said as he shook hands with the president, "you know JP . . . Ty Morgan, the head of my security team."

"How are you JP?" Buck asked.

"I'm fine, sir," JP said.

"Excellent. Was it JP who found the culprits?" he asked Doc.

"Tell him what you told me," Doc told JP.

"It looked like they were taking the signature page off the original copies and replacing the body of the legislation with their own version, sir," JP said.

"I don't suppose anyone has had time to compare the versions?" Buck asked Doc.

"Too soon," Doc said, "but both stacks are now in the possession of the Attorney General, and a photocopy of each has been delivered to the Speaker of the House, the President of the Senate, and, of course, Jen. It looks like she's already halfway through her copies."

"And it was Stenger?" Buck asked.

"Yes, sir," JP said. "Senator Stenger and two of his aides."

"Good. That will take him out of the picture for a while."

"Sir," JP said, "they broke enough laws to be thrown in prison for a long time."

"We'll see," Buck said. "Right now, I'm only interested in getting that legislation through the Supreme Court review and getting it implemented. With Stenger out of the way, maybe we have a chance."

7

The Bargain

Twin World—Chiapas, Mexico, January 15

"The vests and automatic weapons have arrived, as promised," Jose Mendosa said. "Why did they take so long to get here?"

"We had to be very careful," Saleh said, "that the Americans would not find them. That would have ruined our deal and probably revealed our plans."

"And what are your plans? I mean, what is it you expect me to do in exchange?"

"As you were told earlier, we will bring bomb components here to be assembled, then you will help us get the bomb into the United States, undetected."

"What type of bomb is this?"

"It will look like a nuclear weapon, and you will treat it like one, but that will only be for show. We want the United States to think we have an operational explosive and plan to set it off in Washington, so they will release our brothers." In reality, Saleh expected to build a real nuclear weapon and detonate it in Washington, but he was afraid to tell El Jefe the truth, for fear El Jefe would refuse to cooperate. After all, the United States was Mendosa's biggest customer for illegal drugs.

Within days, El Jefe would use his new vests and automatic weapons to virtually wipe out the Gulf cartel and take over the drug trade and infiltration routes, from Matamoros into the United States. Then he would look for an undiscovered route to use to carry the 'fake' bomb into the United States.

8

Doc's Visit

Twin World—Logan, Utah, 12 June

"Michael?" Doc asked when Mike answered the phone.

"It's me," Mike said, sitting on a bench in First Dam Park at the mouth of Logan Canyon, in the twin world. He had been alternately sitting and pacing for the last ten minutes, while Terry had attempted, through the gate opening over his shoulder, to reassure him that Amos Two would come around and cooperate with them.

"Are you in Salt Lake?" Doc asked.

"Logan," Mike said. "What do you want to do?"

"I want you to explain everything you told me two days ago, but I don't want to do it over the phone. Can we meet tomorrow in Salt Lake?"

"Yes. Where?" Mike's anxiety spiked, worrying about this meeting possibly being a setup.

"*Mike,*" Terry said in his ear, "*stop acting so nervous.*"

"I have a reservation at the Grand America hotel. You remember JP?"

"Yes."

"I should arrive at the hotel about eleven a.m. JP will wait for you in the lobby and bring you to me. Will that work?"

"That's fine. I'll give you a few minutes to settle in, and be there about eleven-fifteen."

"And bring that gate-thing and Terry with you, okay?" Doc asked, chuckling.

"Yes, sir," Mike said, trying to stifle his own laughter. That sounded just like his dad, which helped him relax.

Old World—The Preserve, 12 June

"Mike," Terry said as they sat in the lab a few minutes later, "you need to convince him to come to the Preserve. He needs to see the videos of the war and listen to the recordings. That's the only way we'll convince him to help."

"Have you selected some videos to show him?" Mike asked.

"You convince him to come. I'll worry about what to show him."

"Okay. What's going on with the Outcasts?"

"You know as much as I do. They brought Justin's wife to the valley, all of the Garden City people have been vaccinated, and they're still working on building the shelter. They named Sheryl's baby Lisa Beth. The baby's healthy and immune to smallpox. What else? Oh yeah, we're using up water faster than we should, because the water we're giving the Outcasts isn't being recycled."

"What can we do about that?" Mike asked in alarm. He'd never had to worry about things being out of balance, because Amos and Terry had set up the Preserve to be self-sustaining, as long as everyone was inside.

"I'm working on it. I wish your dad was here. I need his brain."

They were both silent for a few moments, Mike missing his dad and assuming Terry missed him as well.

Twin World—Salt Lake City, Utah, 12 June

Mike entered the lobby of the Grand America hotel and noticed JP immediately. He was out of uniform, in khakis, a button-down dress shirt and sports coat, probably concealing a handgun; but the dark glasses were the give-away. They met at the elevator and JP held out his hand, smiling.

"Nice to see you again, Michael," JP said.

"Thank you," Mike said, shaking the offered hand, surprised that JP's handshake was casual and firm, rather than crushing.

"I hope I have a chance to get to know you better," JP said as he pushed the button for the top floor and the elevator began to move. "Your dad hasn't stopped talking about you since we met the other day."

"I'm sure his memories are better than the reality," Mike said with a nervous laugh, realizing that Doc had a penthouse suite that the public was probably paying for.

There was another Secret Service agent outside the elevator door and two more at the door to the suite, who stayed at their posts even after Mike and JP had passed.

"Michael," Doc said and hurried over to greet him with a hug. "I worried that you wouldn't come."

"*See,*" Terry said in Mike's ear.

"Why wouldn't I?" Mike asked. "I was the one who contacted you, remember?"

Doc laughed, a familiar sound that tugged at Mike's heart.

"Yes, you did," he said, "and I'm glad you did. I want to know everything you can tell me about where you've been."

"Where I've been," Mike said, realizing immediately that this was a coded message, since Doc probably hadn't told JP about their prior conversation. He likely still believed that Mike had just recovered from amnesia, stemming from the accident in London.

"Let's go in the bedroom," Doc said, "and JP can watch our backs from out here, okay son." Another coded message, a way to get JP out of the conversation.

"I'm good with that," Mike said. He wanted to add 'Dad', but was afraid he couldn't say it without stammering, and that would be awkward.

As soon as they were alone, Doc became serious.

"Terry, are you there?" he asked, then waited for Terry to show himself.

"Right here, Amos," Terry said as the gate opened next to the bed, a few feet away from where Mike and Doc stood. Terry sat at a worktable in a wooden chair with a wall of video monitors behind him on the wall.

"One of you please tell me everything," Doc said, motioning for Michael to sit in the chair at a small writing desk, while he sat on the edge of the bed.

Terry laughed. "So, you believe us?" he asked.

"I don't know what I believe. Either you're amazing magicians and liars, or you have some fantastic technology that I want to know about. Who's going to start?"

"Do you want to tell him?" Terry asked, turning an open palm to Mike.

"Where to start," Mike said with a sigh. "Okay, we lived in Logan, Utah for as long as I can remember. We moved to a new subdivision and that's where you met Terry, because I pulled his daughter's pigtail at school." Terry chuckled and Doc smiled.

"Terry lived on the next street over and you and Mom took me over to apologize. Instead of being punished by you or chewed out by Terry, you two discovered that you had the same interests. You shared ideas and eventually became partners in designing graphite composite medical protheses. Then, you had this brainstorm to build a machine that would look inside the human body without surgery or other intrusive methods, for diagnostic purposes."

"You were the brains of the partnership," Terry interjected, drawing Doc's attention, "and I was the mechanic who figured out how to implement the plans."

Mike thought, from Doc's restlessness, that some of this rang true. "You remember some of this, don't you?" he asked.

Doc continued to stir, then finally spoke.

"We did live in Logan and we did move into a new subdivision on the west side of town, but we didn't stay long. When Buck pressured me to serve on his committee, you were only eleven or twelve years old, and we moved to Virginia."

"So, something happened in my life as well," Terry said.

"What do you mean?" Doc asked.

"We're convinced that your world and ours are parallel worlds, and the reason you didn't invent the Observer in your world is because we never met and never became partners. But the reason we never met and became partners is because Mike never pulled Katie's pigtail, or I never moved into the neighborhood."

So, there was another mystery that needed to be solved. Mike became distracted thinking about it.

"What else, Michael?" Doc asked, drawing Mike's attention.

"You started selling your patents to raise money. You bought property—a small valley actually—in Logan Canyon, and named it Aspen Valley."

"A whole valley?" Doc asked.

Terry chuckled, but didn't speak.

"By the time you were ready to build the Preserve, I had graduated with degrees in engineering and geology, and was able to help. We used dynamite to blast out a cave, then coated the inside of it with gunite, then wired it for LED lighting. We used sixteen-foot diameter corrugated steel pipe, split lengthwise, to make the rooms and the hallways in between. We made garage and passage doors out of graphite composites to look like rock, so they would be hidden. We used pressure pads for light switches—"

"Wait," Doc said, holding up both hands. "I don't know anything about graphite composites, or corrugated steel pipe, or . . ."

His voice trailed off as he looked at Mike, who was grinning. "You did all that?" he asked.

"Those were among Mike's contributions, Amos," Terry said. "He hasn't told you about his discovery with the Observer."

"You say I built the Observer, and it worked as a diagnostic tool?"

"Yes, we built it," Terry said, "and yes, it works, but we'll get to that in a minute. First, Mike needs to tell you about the construction site."

"In Aspen Valley?" Doc asked.

"No," Terry laughed. "At the Weber State campus in Ogden."

"I didn't think I could get more confused," Doc said, "but if that's what you're trying to do, you've succeeded."

"I'll explain," Mike said. "The first thing we discovered with the Observer was that we could see things at a distance. So, instead of trying to look inside the body, we tried to see how far away we could see. We followed the canyon road all the way to Ogden."

"This was with the gate?" Doc asked.

"Well, no," Mike said. "At that time, we were projecting an image on the wall of the lab in the back yard in Logan."

"So, it wasn't a gate, it was an image."

"We thought it was an image, because that's all we saw in the lab."

"Amos," Terry said, "how about letting Mike tell it in his own way. I think it will become clear."

Doc nodded.

Mike sighed. "Once we got that far—to Ogden, that is—we knew there was a medical center under construction on the east side of the campus, so we tried to find it, but we couldn't. It just wasn't there. We were confused."

"You were confused?" Doc said with a snort. "Now you know

how I feel right now."

"Anyway, we got interrupted by the terrorist threat and had to move the Observer to the Preserve."

Doc jerked upright, feeling his pulse quicken. Visions of an explosion in London came involuntarily to his mind. He looked from Mike to Terry and back.

"What terrorist threat?" he asked.

"We'll get to that," Terry said. "Go on, Mike."

"You . . .well, Dad in our world . . . was among the last to arrive at the Preserve, days before the deadline."

"What deadline?" Doc asked. This was too frustrating. Why didn't they get to the point?

"We'll get there," Terry said.

"In my lifetime?" Doc asked.

"Be patient, Amos. This is important."

Doc stopped speaking, but his mind was filled with terrorist threats and bombings that he had witnessed or succeeded in stopping. He hated the fact that neither he, nor the U.S. government, had been able to stop them all.

"After Dad arrived at the Preserve, Terry and I showed him what we had discovered. We weren't seeing our world, or at least, not in the present time, and we couldn't tell where or when the image we were seeing existed. The way we had discovered it was when I studied the control panel we'd built and noticed that it didn't match the schematic we'd drawn. So, we built another control panel to match the schematic. In the process of demonstrating the difference to Dad, he noticed the image was not projected on the wall, like it had been in the lab in Logan. Because the lab in the Preserve was a different size than the one in Logan, the image was free-standing in the air, and you could see something different on each side of the image. Literally. We could walk around the image projected in the air, and our view would change depending on which direction we were looking. We became convinced that we were seeing a different time or place when we sent the image to the valley surrounding the Preserve. With one control panel we could see the exposed cliff, the way it is now. With the other panel, there were trees blocking the view of the cliff, like we were looking at the past or the future."

"That's incredible! I may have to see this thing! So, what convinced you that it was a gate instead of an image?" Doc asked. He was starting to understand what they were telling him, and the information was almost more than he could comprehend. This was all background for how they had discovered the gate. But why was the discovery of the gate important, unless it explained why they were here and what they wanted from him?

"We discovered it was a gate when a rabbit, then a mouse, came through what we believed was only an image, into the lab from the valley," Terry said. Mike looked at him, as if to say 'let me tell it.' "It's okay Mike," Terry continued, "we need to move faster, so we can get to what's most important."

Terry motioned for Mike to continue.

"Once we knew it was a gate, we were able to look for the answer to the first question, that is: what time or place were we looking at? We learned that we were looking at a twin world—a parallel world of some kind. We found the date on a newspaper, and determined that everything else was the same, like language, currency, and so on. The only difference was the timeline. That construction site in Ogden baffled me until I discovered that the site excavation had started in our world seventy-two days after it had started in yours. We started calling it the twin world, and the gate became the Gemini Gate, or the door between twin worlds.

"I wanted to know if we existed in the twin world, but Dad didn't want us to contaminate *your* world or to potentially harm ourselves by going through the gate. He wanted us to stop worrying about the twin world and focus on the medical application of the gate, which we had really ignored up to that point.

"Then I did something stupid," Mike admitted, with a look at Terry. "I went through the gate and it shut down behind me." Mike stopped talking and looked at Terry again.

"Didn't you just open it up again," Doc asked, after waiting impatiently for a few moments for Mike to continue. That's what Doc thought he would have done. What was he missing? Why did Michael say it was stupid? He understood the caution the other Amos, in the other world had shown, but this sounded too tempting, even to him.

"I did it behind Dad's back, at night, with only Katie to back me up. The electrical charge from my sinoatrial node changed the settings and Katie couldn't reset it without knowledgeable help, By the time she got Terry into the lab to rescue me, I'd been beaten by three bad dudes. They nearly killed me. It took months to recover."

Mike looked truly humbled to have to admit his mistake. Doc felt a surge of pride for Mike's maturity.

"And Katie is?" Doc asked.

"My daughter," Terry said. "Now Mike's wife."

Doc smiled. He was truly happy for Mike, in addition to being proud of him. "I bet she's a beauty" he said.

"She is, and I'm lucky to have her," Mike replied.

"So, you learned to control the gate," Doc said, trying to get Mike to continue.

"Actually," Terry said, "It was also Mike's idea to learn how to program the gate to remember where it had been and create jumps between locations. We can now jump from one location to another anywhere between the north end of Bear Lake and Salt Lake City. We had to tweak things a little to improve stability at that distance, but we've learned a lot in a year's time."

"Amazing," Doc said sincerely. If what they were saying was true, and he was beginning to believe it was, this was phenomenal technology.

"We've also learned how to disconnect this side of the gate and send it out of the Preserve," Mike said.

"What does that do for you?" Doc asked.

"It has allowed us to use some of the people living in the radiation-contaminated valley, to run errands for us in Garden City," Mike said.

"Hmm," Doc said. "so you don't have to go out and get exposed to the radiation."

"Exactly," Mike said. "Then you believe us?"

"How can I not believe it? You're sitting here in front of me. What else?"

There was a knock at the door.

"Doc, what do you want to do for lunch?" JP asked through the door.

Doc wondered how he would explain the gate and Terry's presence, but when he looked in that direction, they were gone.

"Why don't you order room service for us, so we can keep talking?" Doc asked.

"Sure, Doc."

"Thanks." When Amos looked back at Mike, he felt his heart skip a beat. Terry was there again, right where he'd been moments before.

"That's hard to get used to," he said, chuckling and shaking his head.

"There are a few other things we need to tell you," Terry said with a straight face.

"This sounds serious," Doc said.

"It is," Terry replied. "Let me take it for a few minutes, Mike." Mike nodded.

"In June of last year, Al-Qaeda issued a threat indicating they had a nuclear weapon and would detonate it in Washington, D.C. It turned out that they did have a bomb, assembled in Mexico and smuggled into the country, and they discharged it as promised. Because of Amos's relationship with the president, Greg McCormick, he had more information than the president was sharing with the public. We were able to leave Logan and get to the Preserve before the deadline, which was July fourth, by the way."

"We just experienced the terrorist attack," Doc interrupted, frustrated and not trying to hide the anguish in his voice. He was too embarrassed by his failure to protect his family. He looked at them and bowed his head before speaking again. "But it was in London, not Washington, D.C."

"At the Embankment, on New Year's Eve, right?" Terry asked.

Doc had already told them he lost his Family in a terrorist attack, but their reference to Washington confused him. "How did you find out?" he asked, looking up sharply. "Did you see it in the papers? Did you know that Lillie and my children died in that explosion?" Doc fought to control his emotions. This was too much. They didn't—couldn't—understand his pain.

"No, Amos, we experienced that one in our world, too, although your family was here in Logan at the time instead of in London. Al-Qaeda is planning another one, this one nuclear, for July fourth."

Doc didn't know how to respond. "Another one? Nuclear?"

Terry continued. He explained the sequence of events following the Al-Qaeda threat, each new revelation making Doc's burden heavier.

He explained the search for the bomb in Mexico, along with North Korea's and Russia's roles leading up to the deadline.

He described President McCormick's delivery of a stern message to the UN General Assembly and the promise to retaliate against Russia and North Korea if Al-Qaeda's threat was real and carried out.

Terry outlined the events of the July fourth and the subsequent nuclear exchange with China and Russia, the bombs that destroyed so much in the western United States and Hawaii, and the death and destruction they'd caused.

"Couldn't the president have used conventional weapons to retaliate?" Doc asked.

"Amos tried to convince him not to retaliate with nuclear weapons; but the president believed our enemies would not stop threatening us unless we showed strength."

During a brief respite in the monologue, JP knocked on the door and delivered sandwiches, salads, fresh fruit and drinks for Doc and Michael. Terry disappeared for the few minutes that JP was in the room, then reappeared and continued talking. Mike offered Terry half of his roast beef sandwich, which Terry accepted and seemed to relish, since meat was scarce in the Preserve.

Then Terry continued. He described the expansion of the war to the rest of the northern hemisphere, including the bomb dropped on Hill Air Force Base, and explained how the president had worked with allies and the Saud family to identify Al-Qaeda and ISIS strongholds and weapons stashes, then bomb them.

Terry described the upheaval in nature as the explosions caused earthquakes, then tsunamis and volcanic eruptions.

He explained the president's decision to bomb the CDC and

other Level 4 containment facilities, and the release of the mutated smallpox virus.

He described the chaos that had resulted from the collapse of the electric power grid and the spread of waterborne diseases due to the lack of clean water. He explained that Amos had traded the design of his mini nuclear reactor in exchange for enough vaccinations for everyone at the Preserve, including the Outcasts.

"A mini nuclear reactor?" Doc asked.

"Yes, it's been working for a year already," Terry said, "and should continue to provide power for at least thirty, and maybe as long as fifty years."

"I had some ideas about a mini reactor," Doc said, "but I didn't even tell Lillie about it. So, who are these Outcasts and how did the virus spread all the way to Utah?"

Terry explained Amos's warning to the president to contain the viruses, the president's failure to do so, and the escape of the virus from the Johns Creek shelter near Atlanta, Georgia.

"I'm not sure I can tell you this next part without breaking down," Terry said, "but I'll try. Several of our neighbors in Logan figured out what we were doing and insisted that they be allowed to join us in the Preserve. One of the neighbors, Jason Carlson, only came out of fear and desperation after his eldest son died in an auto accident."

"There was a Carlson family living next door to us in Logan, but I didn't know them well. The father never seemed to be at home."

"That fits," Terry said. "He was loud and obnoxious and a problem from the start. He didn't like the regimentation of life in the Preserve and spent most of his time trying to find a way to escape. When he found a way, he went to Garden City and met up with the Outcasts, who had traveled all the way from Atlanta. He must have decided life in the Preserve was better than on the outside, because he convinced some of the Outcasts that it was his creation, and that they should help him win it back by force. During a gun battle in the valley, which Jason started, intent on taking over the Preserve or destroying it, Jason was killed . . . but so was Amos." Terry stopped talking, and his face betrayed his struggle to restrain his emotions.

"There must be more to that story," Doc said, quietly, attempting to show sympathy for their loss. "I would think that Amos would have been prepared for that emergency."

"There is more," Mike said, "but it needs to wait. There are other things we need to tell you."

Doc had been following the story, with all of its complexities, but was totally unprepared for the other Amos's death. He didn't know what to say.

"That's why you're here," he finally realized, "because *your* Amos died and you need something."

"You're correct in part," Terry said. "We also have something to offer you. We have audio recordings of conversations between *our* Amos and Greg McCormick, revealing the locations of all the Al-Qaeda and ISIS hideouts, weapons stashes, the location of the site in Mexico where the Washington, D.C. bomb was assembled and how it was smuggled into the country, the names of the viral scientists who created the mutated virus and, out of stupidity, allowed it to escape containment. We have the name of the nuclear engineer who Amos entrusted with the design of his mini reactor. We also have a copy of the conversation Amos had with that engineer, containing complete instructions for building the reactor. Most important, we believe your world is on a path to repeat our disaster, unless you stop it."

Doc was shaken. "What makes you think I can do anything

about it? We've been fighting the terrorists for years and seem to be losing ground. They're getting bolder and more threatening all the time."

"Amos, you are the only person in your world who has the intuitive knowledge and is in a strategic position to stop global thermonuclear war, and don't you doubt it. We'll give you access to everything we have, all of our audio and video files. You can come to the Preserve through the gate, to watch and listen. You can take copies of anything you want."

"And what do you want in return?" Doc asked.

"Not much," Terry said. "First and foremost, we want you to believe us, and to realize that you have the capability to make the difference in your world. Second, we have a dying world and no way to save it. With almost one hundred percent of all electronics dead, fried by EMPs, we can't even build the electronic components we need to clean our drinking water. We need some brilliant minds to solve that problem for us. In your position, we think you can gather the resources to solve it."

"Is that all?" Doc asked sarcastically.

"Almost. Third, our people are dying from radiation poisoning, disease and starvation. We need you to find a way to counteract the effects of radiation on soil, water, air, and people."

Doc stared at Terry in disbelief. "Do you know what you're asking?"

"I do, Amos. I've been your partner for over sixteen years. You are, without a doubt, the most brilliant man I know. Lillie might have you beat, because she's also sensitive, but don't try to compete with her."

Doc wanted to laugh, but at the mention of Lillie, he almost fell apart. He agreed with Terry; she was the life in his world, and since her death, he had been a shell of a man, filling the void she'd left by trying to solve all of the world's problems. Well, he'd just been handed the biggest challenge of his life and he was balking at it. As he thought about it, he realized that he did have access to brilliant minds that might be able to solve some of their problems; and he definitely needed the information they'd offered.

Doc looked at his watch, then went to the door. In his peripheral vision, he saw the gate wink out.

"JP," he said, opening the door a foot, "how much time do we have?"

"We need to leave in ninety minutes, if you want to make our scheduled departure; but you're on Air Force One, so the airport will hold traffic until you're ready to leave."

"What drinks do we have?"

"The only non-alcoholic drinks are Coke, Diet Coke, Sprite and bottled water."

Doc looked at Mike and raised his eyebrows.

"Sprite," Mike said, pointing at himself and grinning. Doc guessed that soft drinks were one of the things Mike missed, living in the Preserve. "Coke," Mike added, pointing with his thumb to the spot where Terry had been

"How about a Coke, a Sprite and two bottles of water?" Doc said.

Digs was already getting the drinks out of the fridge, so he handed two to JP and carried the other two himself. They handed the drinks over to Doc, who passed the first two to Mike.

"Give me seventy-five minutes uninterrupted, then we'll leave. Does that work?"

"Anything you say," JP replied, then Doc closed the door and locked it. When he turned around, Terry had returned, and had an open can of Coke in his hand and a smile on his face.

"We won't tell Becca and Katie about this, will we?" Terry

asked Mike conspiratorially, making Mike snicker.

"Okay," Doc said, "I'm ready to go. I want to see as much as you can show me in seventy-five minutes."

Terry set his drink on the table behind him and picked up the portable control board.

"Stick your arm through the gate so I can calibrate it to your nervous system," Terry said. "I expect it won't be much different from Amos's." Doc pushed his arm through the hole while Terry fidgeted with the controls for a moment. "All set. Step through."

9

Revelations

Old World—The Preserve, 12 June

Doc stepped through the gate, cautiously, not knowing what to expect, and felt the tingling that Terry had mentioned—the electrical interference of his SA node on the gate. Mike followed him through, then Terry shut down the gate and set the control panel on the table.

"Amazing!" Doc said, looking back and watching the gate close down. "And you say this is a different world."

"We call this the old world," Mike said, "and your world the twin world."

"Well, I'll be . . ." Doc said. He noticed the video equipment on the wall and table directly in front of him, that he had seen through the gate, but when he looked around, he was surprised by the size of the room.

"Wow," he said. "This is what, a lab?"

"This is the lab," Terry confirmed, "and this box on the table is the Observer."

"It looks so simple. A few dials and buttons and a projection window."

"Yeah, well, the circuitry is on the inside," Terry chuckled, "And it's complex."

Doc looked around the room, focusing on the few items that were visible. They kept a clean shop.

"All of our equipment is in the closets over there," Terry said, pointing, likely guessing at what Doc was thinking as he looked around. "Let's go next door, to the office, and we'll give you a tour of the Preserve."

Taking Terry's comment literally, Doc hesitated. "You don't want the others to see me, do you?"

"I spoke figuratively, Amos. We have some photos on the office wall that will show you what the Preserve looks like."

The office was also larger than he'd expected, but he was getting used to being surprised by Amos, his otherworldly counterpart. There was a large desk in the middle of the room, with six folding metal chairs in a semi-circle in front of it. Two small photos sat on one corner of the desk and a satellite phone sat in the middle. One wall held several more TV monitors, and recording equipment, and another was covered with framed, eight by ten photos, which Terry approached. Most of them were taken from above.

"This one," Terry said, pointing, "is a computer-generated plan view of the Preserve. It shows the layout of the rooms and the tunnels joining them. The garage is at ground level, inside the mountain, here, with an elevator down to the house level. These two," he continued, pointing to two more pictures, "are pictures of Aspen Valley, directly above us, before and after the trees were cleared. They were taken from the same spot on the cliff above the garage. This one," he pointed to the next photo, "shows the cliff face after the trees were cleared."

"So, the aerial views were taken from the top of the cliff?" Doc asked.

"Correct. These pictures," he pointed to the next few pictures as he explained, "show phases of the construction. In this one, you can see some of the holes dug for the rooms and tunnels. In this one, some of the corrugated steel pipe has already been set, about a foot, in concrete, and welded to the adjacent sections."

"That's a big crane," Doc said. He was still trying to visualize the size of the Preserve.

"The steel sections aren't really heavy, but they're large. This one, like most of the rooms, is sixteen feet across and forty feet long. This picture shows concrete being poured over the steel pipe, and the next shows the revegetation of the surface after the rooms were covered with soil. We didn't plant trees because the rooms are only a few feet below the surface."

"And you say you bought the valley, built the preserve and stocked it, from the sale of patents?" He asked Terry.

"We did," Terry said. "We've had a busy few years." Terry took a few minutes and told Doc about some of their inventions—mostly medical protheses—and Doc was impressed.

"Amazing!" Doc said. "That's quite an accomplishment. So, how big is the Preserve?" He wandered back to the image showing the Preserve's layout.

"The living area is about eighteen thousand square feet. The supporting structures, like the medical center, gardens, lab, office and storerooms add about twenty-four thousand more square feet, and the Preserve is spread out over about two acres."

Doc did some quick arithmetic in his head. "That's compact, considering everything you've said is in here."

"We had a structural engineer help us with the design and construction," Terry said, with a smile at Mike. "The rest of the photos show the inside of some of the rooms, the hospital, library, classroom, exercise room, bedroom and community center. Unless you have questions, we'll show you some video of the war." Terry turned to the equipment against the other wall.

"Which is Lillie's room?" Doc asked, still looking at the layout. He couldn't resist. "Just curious" he added, self-consciously. His mind had been on Lillie ever since they'd shown him the layout of the Preserve.

Terry walked back to the layout image and pointed to the room farthest from their present location. "We're here and she's here," he said, with his expression neutral, then returned to the video equipment.

Doc didn't know what Terry and Mike would think of his question about Lillie. He wasn't sure why he had asked. He had a life in another world and might not ever meet her.

"Is this equipment redundant of the equipment in the lab?" he asked, to change the subject.

"Actually, no," Terry replied. "The equipment in the lab is connected to monitors in the valley, all of which were damaged during the fire caused by the nuclear explosion at Hill Air Force Base. Most of them still haven't been repaired or replaced, because of the high radiation level outside. This equipment is connected to satellite and other forms of communication, most of which quit working during the war. Whether they were damaged, or still work, we don't know. Even the government quit broadcasting after a few weeks."

Terry turned on a TV and a DVD player, removed a DVD from a slim case and slipped it into the player. He looked at a list of notes on the inside of the jacket and fast-forwarded it to a specific spot on the recording. When he hit 'play', the image showed Ambassador Daniel Porter, standing at a rostrum, introducing the president of the United States, Gregory McCormick.

"That's Daniel Porter," Doc said.

"He's the U.S. ambassador to the UN," Terry said. "You know him?"

"He has the same job in my world," Doc said. "So, was this taken at the UN?"

"Yes," Terry said. "At a special session in June of last year."

Greg McCormick stepped to the microphone. Terry fast-forwarded the DVD to where McCormick accused Saudi Arabia of birthing Al-Qaeda, then again to where he accused Russia of supplying nuclear weapons technology and materials to Al-Qaeda and North Korea, then to where the Chinese member of the UN Security Council warned McCormick not to fire missiles at Asia. Doc winced at the remark by China, realizing that their stand put the U.S. in a difficult position.

Terry put that DVD away and slipped another one in. The first scene was of the explosion in Washington, D.C. and the death of a helicopter news crew covering the event. In the next scene, Doc could see missile silos opening and missiles exiting their silos, while a female reporter explained that these missiles must be headed for North Korea.

"North Korea got their long-range missiles to work," Doc thought out loud, closing his eyes and shaking his head.

"With a little help from Russia," Terry said.

The next disc showed a clash between the military and looters in the streets, an out-of-control crowd at an airport and a flood of cars and trucks, all headed in one direction, south, taking up all lanes of the highway.

"That was at the border with Mexico," Terry said, then forwarded to a video of the night-time sky from a satellite, with missiles flying generally east and west across North America, looking like falling stars. Terry then forwarded to a scene of the Stratosphere Hotel in Las Vegas, with a giant mushroom cloud in the background that caught up to the hotel and destroyed it and everything around it.

"I've seen enough," Doc said, "and based on what I know, I believe you're right. My world is headed in the same direction. Can you give me the information on the Mexico bomb and the terrorist hideouts? I'm going to try to do some investigating."

While Terry got the video recordings for Doc, Doc took Mike's shoulders.

"Mike, I'm proud of you, for being brave enough to approach me. I don't know how, but we're going to do something to prevent a similar catastrophe in my world. Keep the phone close. My name, Doc, will show up if it's me. If it's anyone else, don't answer it. Okay?"

"Okay, Doc, and thank you for believing."

"I do believe, and I'm going to remember my part of the bargain. I don't know how, but I'm going to try to figure out solutions to your problems. Thanks, Terry," he added as he took Terry's DVD. "Now, Mike, we need to go back."

"Wait," Mike said. "What do you want us to call you?"

"Feel free to call me Doc. That's what everyone else does."

"But your name is Amos, right?"

"It is, and I won't be offended if you call me Amos, or Dad, or Amos Two, as I heard you say one time. Regardless of what you call me, I'll know you're talking to me and not someone else."

"Thanks, Doc," Mike said.

"Thanks, Amos," Terry said at the same time.

Twin World—Salt Lake City, Utah, 12 June

"Mike, thanks again," Doc said as he slid the DVD into his briefcase. "You've had a difficult year."

"No more so than you," Mike said, standing awkwardly a few feet away. He hadn't expected to feel so attached to Doc. He'd been tongue-tied for most of the last hour and had appreciated Terry taking the lead at the end.

Doc turned and took Mike in his arms, giving him a quick hug. "I can have JP walk you out or you can wait five minutes and go with us to the lobby."

"I'll go with you if that's alright."

"It surely is," Doc said, picking up his briefcase and a jacket off the bed. "Let's go.

They hugged again in the lobby, then Mike watched Doc and his security detail enter a limo and drive away. Mike was so grateful for Doc's support that he nearly cried.

"Can I help you?" a hotel employee asked Mike from behind.

Mike tried to answer, but choked on his words.

"Wasn't that 'Doc' Blund, advisor to the president?"

Mike nodded, then turned to the front door. "It was," he said quietly. Then he walked away, not trusting himself to carry on an intelligent conversation with his emotions so close to the surface.

10

Military Intelligence

Twin World—The White House, 11 April
(two months earlier)

"What do you have for us, Tom?" Buck asked his Director of National Intelligence, Thomas Mitchell.

"All of our intelligence sources in Mexico have gone silent, Buck," Tom said. Buck had gotten attached to the nickname that Doc had given him and had given Tom and his other senior level advisors permission to use his nickname when they were meeting alone as the Panel.

The Panel was a secret group of senior advisors that had been authorized to find and kill suspected terrorists, including American citizens, following the 2001 terrorist attacks. The panel had been reorganized under each successive president. He was meeting now with the Panel to discuss their efforts to track Al-Qaeda activities around the world.

"What does it mean?" Buck asked.

"Only speculation sir, but after the Los Zetas drug cartel virtually eliminated the Gulf cartel a couple of months ago, and opened a channel to the border for moving drugs, we suspect it means that the Los Zetas uncovered our sources and eliminated them, or that they've gone into hiding to avoid discovery. It leaves us pretty much blind along the border."

"So, what about the rumor that Al-Qaeda has an agent in Mexico?"

"Before our sources dropped out of sight, they all swore their information was accurate," Secretary of Homeland Security Charles Dickson said. "An Arab is working with the Los Zetas cartel to build a bomb. It's still a rumor, since we haven't found it or anyone who's seen it. I've been receiving satellite images of the area along the border, but the cartel must know our satellite pass-over schedule because we've seen no sign of their activity. In addition, last week an asset in Russia said he's convinced Al Qaeda is trying to deliver bomb components to North Korea."

"Thanks, Chuck," Buck said with a sigh. "Keep looking." Chuck nodded. "Jim, what's the military doing?"

"The Navy boarded an Iranian cargo vessel headed for North Korea last week," Secretary of Defense, General James Seymour said. "They're looking for those bomb components. They didn't find anything that wasn't on the manifest."

"And Iran complained to the UN about our interference," Secretary of State Cyril Hutchison added.

"Great," Buck said in frustration. "So, we have rumors that Russia sold nuclear technology to Al-Qaeda and that Al-Qaeda is assembling a nuclear bomb in Mexico. And we have a rumor that Al-Qaeda sold one or more nuclear warheads to North Korea and that Russia is shipping them east to be assembled onto the ICBMs that North Korea is currently testing in the Sea of Japan. But there's no evidence. Is that correct?"

"Buck, every intelligence asset we have is looking for a bomb," Tom said, "but there's still no sign of it."

The only member of Buck's secret panel that hadn't spoken was Doc Blund, who sat quietly, mentally analyzing what it all meant.

"Doc," Buck said, "give me some good news, will you?"

"Sorry, Buck," Doc said, "nothing to add. But here's a question for you. What if the Los Zetas are building the bomb in Chiapas instead of Matamoros? That's where they have their headquarters, isn't it?"

"It is," Buck replied "Jim, add satellite coverage of Chiapas. Anything else Doc?"

"Just a thought. If Russia was sending parts to North Korea, how would they ship them? It comes to mind that the Trans-Siberian Railway goes from Moscow all the way to Vladivostok, which is a short hop to North Korea."

"Would they put a bomb on a passenger train?" Buck asked.

"Why not?" Jim asked. "The worst that could happen is that it would go off, killing a few—or even a few hundred—civilians. Moscow would just make some excuse about an engine malfunction, or something"

"Jim?" Buck said.

"I'll get eyes on it right away." Jim said. He picked up a phone and spoke into it.

"Anything else you can think of?" Buck asked Doc.

"One thing. London said they heard a name, Samuel Smith. Supposedly, he had something to do with organizing the attack in London on New Year's Eve."

"Tom," Buck said to his DNI, "run Samuel Smith through all the databases and see what you come up with. If he's in the country, I want to know where he is and what he's doing."

"Yes, sir," Tom said.

"Anything else, Doc?" Buck asked.

"Not that I can think of."

"Anything else, gentlemen?" Buck asked. There were no further comments.

11

Doc's Team

Twin World—The White House, 13 June

"I'm meeting with the president after lunch," Doc said. "What do you have for me?" He sat at the side of the table away from the door, while his team members sat on the other three sides. Their assistants and staff members stood or sat around the room. They were in an office in the West Wing identified for special advisors, which had been given to Doc and his team. Technically, his team members were assistants, staff members, and contractors; but he felt they would be more proactive and productive if he treated them as equals—team members—even though they understood what he'd done.

An outsider watching their meetings would think that they didn't take their roles seriously; they sat or stood or walked around and raided the refrigerator that Doc kept stocked with sandwiches, non-alcoholic drinks and fresh fruit—that is, until they started talking. They still moved around the room casually, although quietly, but they were all intelligent, dedicated soldiers in the war against threats to the United States, and it was obvious in the way they worked on the issues and problems that they were asked to handle. They took their jobs seriously.

Two of his team members had been with him since his days as an advisor to Buck in the Senate, Dr. Nicholas James, a nuclear scientist, and Dr. Brian Chalmers, nuclear medicine. The others had been picked up along the way, as Doc had identified needs and the best resources to fill the needs. He had realized, early on, that Buck had predicted his success correctly. People had stood in line to have a chance to work with him. His reputation and theirs improved each time he made a decision or took action, and several former team members had gone on to fill other important government positions.

Each of his team members gave a report on the tasks that Doc had given them. Their normal tasks mostly involved assessments of global nuclear and conventional arsenals; the probability for aggressive military action, and the participants and probable outcomes; the potential for regional alliances and their impacts; and the types and strengths of weapons being developed by foreign governments.

This meeting was going to be different. When they'd finished with their reports, Doc took a deep breath and told them what he had in mind.

"I've been thinking a lot about the potential for a nuclear detonation on U.S. soil, and the impact that would have on the infrastructure and population," he said. Several of his team members nodded their understanding. The threat of a nuclear attack had been on everyone's minds since North Korea had resumed testing their ICBMs and Al-Qaeda had advertised that they were in the market for nuclear weapons, months earlier. "Now I want to do something about it."

Normally, when they met, they made a list of tasks on the whiteboard, prioritized them, and divided them up, with each team member selecting the one or ones they wanted, or Doc assigning them to team members based on their individual specialties. The remaining tasks would be assigned randomly. In that regard, this meeting would be no different. What would be different was the type of assignments they would be given. In the past, most of their tasks involved assessments or cataloguing of available information. Occasionally, they would generate information that the president, military, or other government departments could use to take specific action. Today's list would include research into new solutions.

"Let's make a list of the potential causes, impacts, and corrective measures related to a nuclear attack," he said. They did, with Doc adding to the list when his team missed something that he thought was important, or that Terry had asked him to research.

The list included:

1. convince a nuclear power to share their technology or components,

2. find a way to assemble a nuclear weapon and get it into the U.S.,

3. prevent missiles from reaching the U.S., including Hawaii,

4. be prepared to evacuate or shelter-in-place entire cities

5. protect the power grid from EMPs or develop an alternative power supply that is immune to EMPs,

6. provide clean water and food to major populations,

7. prevent the spread of airborne and waterborne diseases,

8. counteract the effects of radiation poisoning.

"Wow," Chalmers said when they'd exhausted their ideas, "that's a different kind of list than we normally end up with."

"Are those things even possible?" James asked. "I mean, can we find a way to counter the effects of radiation poisoning?"

Doc studied the list, pretending to consider how they should prioritize the items, but he already knew what the highest priorities would be. He stood and placed a number one next to 'protect the power grid from EMPs or develop an alternative power supply that is immune to EMPs'. Then he placed a number two next to 'counteract the effects of radiation poisoning'. Number three went to 'prevent the spread of airborne and waterborne diseases.

"Why those particular priorities, Doc?" James asked. "Wouldn't the logical priority go to preventative measures, not curative?"

"Those look like the most difficult tasks," Dr. Sterling Pattersen said. As one of the best virologists in the country, he would likely be on the teams responsible for those tasks.

"Good questions," Doc replied. "Nick, in this case, the military or other departments are already worrying about the preventative measures, but I'll bring them up to the president anyway. Sterling, we need to tackle this because they *are* difficult, maybe impossible, but I believe this team has the best shot at solving them." There were nods around the table as they considered Doc's comments and his confidence in them. "I want Nick to handle the power grid, Brian to take radiation poisoning, and Sterling to tackle diseases. Any objections?" There were none.

"The rest of you can join one of these teams or pick one of the other tasks to work on. Let me know what you decide. Sterling . . . all of you . . . don't be surprised if you're needed as a team member or resource for more than one of these tasks. Now, I need to copy the list and get to my meeting, but I want to meet with each of you after you've documented your thoughts. Let me know when you're ready."

The meeting broke up, but Dr. James stayed until the others had left.

"What is it, Nick?" Doc asked.

"My wife introduced me to a young nuclear scientist the other day that I want to recruit," Nick said. "Her name is Dr. Chandra Robertson. She works for the NRC, but is disillusioned by the amount of regulation forced on industry. She thinks we could generate power much cheaper than we do. When you included 'developing an alternative power supply that is immune to EMPs', I thought of her. May I speak with her about this task?"

"Excellent suggestion, Nick. Determine her level of ability and interest and see if she knows other like-minded scientists." Doc remembered Terry mentioning something similar and decided to give Mike a call.

After Nick left, Doc tried to call Mike, but he got an error message. Mike had JP's phone, but was in the old world, while Doc was in the twin world. He realized then, and mentally chastised himself for not realizing it sooner, that they must have to be in the same world for the cell towers to connect the call.

☢

"Come in, Doc," Buck said, a few minutes later. Doc entered the Oval Office and took a seat on a couch near the president's desk. "What's the latest?"

"I just met with my team and gave them new assignments," Doc said. "Since you already have the Defense Department and Homeland Security trying to prevent a terrorist attack, I changed my focus to one of *'what do we do if they succeed in detonating a bomb in the United States.'*"

"Let's not even go there," Buck said. "We have to find and stop those bombs."

"Hear me out, Buck. Just suppose that Russia is doing all the nasty things we think they're doing. What if the terrorists have a bomb in Mexico and we can't find it in time to stop it, or if North Korea gets a nuclear warhead and successfully mates it to one of their ICBMs? What are we going to do about it? Are we going to retaliate against Russia and North Korea? Is China going to come to the defense of North Korea? Are we going to start a global thermonuclear war?"

"Heaven forbid," Buck said.

"Would you like to know what I think we should do?"

"Always. You're the analyst, the advisor that gives me the advice to keep me out of trouble."

"If I've ever given you good advice before, you need to hear what I have to say today and give it your greatest consideration."

"Go ahead, Doc," Buck said with a humoring smile.

"Perhaps our allies could help us make a list of Al-Qaeda and ISIS hideouts and weapons caches."

"That's a pretty short list right now."

"Only because Israel isn't sharing. I'd include Saudi Arabia, too."

"Why would Israel or the Saud family share that kind of information with us?"

"Convince them that the threat is real and help them understand the impact it could have on the world, including their countries, if we don't stop the terrorists."

"Okay, Doc, but you may have just earned yourself another trip to the Middle East."

Doc sighed. He should have guessed that it would be thrown back at him.

"Cy," Buck said, speaking to his Secretary of State, who was in the room with the other members of Buck' secret panel. "Will you set up a meeting with the UK, France, Israel, and Saudi Arabia? Highest priority. And make sure they consult with their advisors, to get the most complete and most recent information available?"

"On it," Cy said, making a note on his tablet.

"Okay, Doc. What else?" the President asked.

"I think you should then set our military satellites—milsats—to watch those sites for activity, and be prepared to go before the UN General Assembly and threaten Al-Qaeda's co-conspirators with retaliation if they don't stop the bombs," Doc said.

"That won't make any difference. Russia thinks we're weak and won't retaliate. Allowing Al-Qaeda to set off a bomb in the United States will prove it, since we *won't* retaliate, unless there are no other options."

"You have to make them believe you will."

"How?"

"I'll have to think about that," Doc said. He had a couple of ideas, but needed to work through them.

"What else?"

"Test the missile defense system. Make sure no foreign missiles can survive long enough to reach U.S. territory, and that includes Hawaii."

"That's not a bad idea. We haven't tested any of those missiles in years. How do we know they'll work? We don't know what improvements China has made to the designs they stole from us, so we should find out. What else?"

"Be prepared to evacuate the government to bunkers that have been overhauled and will outlast nuclear fallout."

"You mean update them with new technology and emergency supplies."

"Yes, including long-term power supplies."

"Like extra generator fuel, right?" Buck asked

"I'm working on an idea that may help there," Doc said. "Perhaps something else will be better than fuel. I'll get back to you on that."

"Okay, do you have more?"

"Yes. Protect the national power grid from EMPs."

"You know we've been working on that with industry, hardening new construction as the utilities have funding."

"But not fast enough. Threaten to cut off subsidies and discounts unless they do more, faster. Give them deadlines. While you're at it, make them standardize repair and replacement parts. We should also create an in-house capability to build parts, especially those big transformers. Right now, there's no incentive to stockpile parts, so we need to have the ability to build them in-house."

"That could be expensive," Buck replied. "Who would decide on a timetable for compliance, which parts to make the standards, and who would pay for the obsolete parts?"

"Use up the parts and replace them with standards. If you want, I'll hire someone we can trust to do it."

"You've got it," Buck said with a smile. "Anything else?"

"Find a way to protect water supply and treatment. That could be taken care of by hardening the national power grid, but there may be other things we can do for water treatment plants and distribution systems. We have to be prepared to prevent the spread of waterborne diseases."

"Doc, have you estimated how long all this would take and how much it would cost the taxpayers?"

"Can you tell me how much time we have before we need them?" When Buck just stared at him, Doc figured the president was thinking the same thing he was. Al-Qaeda could be very close to having a bomb.

"I haven't, Buck, but it can be done. Authorize me to hire the resources and I'll get it started."

"Consider it done, Doc. How soon can you get back to me with an answer?"

"I don't even know all the questions, Buck. I've already assigned the power grid problem and waterborne diseases to my team members. I've also assigned a couple of items that we haven't discussed."

"Do I need to know about them?"

"No reason not to tell you, since you're paying our wages," Doc said, smiling. "We're going to look at airborne diseases and a way to counteract the effects of radiation poisoning."

Buck whistled. "You've pulled out all the stops, haven't you?"

"I figured that if *you* can't stop the bomb, *I'm* going to have to cure the world," Doc said, forcing a smile. He was trying to appear lighthearted; but he had seen evidence of what their world might look like in a few weeks. This was not a lighthearted moment. He wasn't prepared to tell Buck his real reason for wanting to solve all of these problems; but thought this was the best way to get it started.

14 June

Doc stopped Sterling Pattersen in the hall and handed him a sheet of paper.

"Sterling, these are the names of some researchers at the level 4 facilities in Georgia and Maryland that are working with the Smallpox virus. Will you make some discrete inquiries into what kind of research they're doing and what progress they're making?"

"Sure thing. Why?" Sterling asked.

"I have an idea of what they're doing, and I don't want to see it get out of control. Thanks."

"Nick," Doc said, stopping Nick Chalmers just leaving the office a few minutes later. "Will you put out some feelers for people to help with the power grid problem?" he asked.

"Already started," Nick said. "Did you have some specific skillsets in mind?"

"Yes, we need people to figure out how to speed up our effort to harden the national power grid, and protect water treatment plants and distribution systems."

"I'll modify my request and send it out again," Nick said.

"Thanks. One other thing. Back in the 50s, we didn't have microchips built into every process and system. See if you can find a water treatment plant design and electrical substation design that don't require microchips, along with someone to set up a manufacturing facility to build parts, including power transformers."

"You got it."

15 June

Doc was listening to a morning news report while he shaved. There was so much to do, that he found himself sleeping on the couch in his office more often, rather than going home to his condo. After Lillie had died, he'd sold his house in Virginia and bought a flat in Washington, D.C. that was closer to the White House. He didn't want to waste time travelling back and forth.

A reporter had just broken into the news with a special report. "The United States has received an ultimatum to release two hundred and seventeen Islamists who are being detained in three U.S. penitentiaries. There's irony in the July fourth deadline," she said, looking at her co-anchor. "We're switching to Washington now."

☢

The scene on the TV switched to a striking woman in her thirties, with short brown hair and an expensive pantsuit. As she stood behind a podium, straight-faced and alert, she looked into the camera amid a cacophony of voices calling "Ms. Appleton" repeatedly. There was a banner at the bottom of the screen that read: "Lisa

Appleton, White House Press Secretary. Al- Qaeda threatens a nuclear incident in the U.S. on 4 July. Press conference with Lisa Appleton."

Ms. Appleton invited several questions, then turned the meeting over to President Buck McCormick, who addressed the entire country. "My fellow citizens, those of you safely in your homes, as well as those abroad, constantly in harm's way. The United States has, for close to two and a half centuries, been the strongest and most secure nation in the world. Amid global crises, we here at home have enjoyed near uninterrupted peace and prosperity.

"In recent years, cowardly terrorists have attempted to disturb that peace, as with the attacks in New York, Virginia, and Pennsylvania in 2001 and most recently last New Year's Eve in London. The United States, in cooperation with our allies, have countered this threat at home and abroad, through a vast intelligence network and with significant military action. That intelligence network now assures us that, although our enemies would like nothing better than to detonate a nuclear weapon on U.S. soil, they, as yet, do not have the means to do so. Rest assured that we are doing everything in our power to track the source of this threat and eliminate it."

"The threat is just like Mike said," Doc thought out loud. "I need to listen to Terry's tape again so I know what happens next."

☢

Doc's first appointment of the day was with Dr. Chandra Robertson.

"Why me?" she asked, when Doc told her he wanted her to build a radical new nuclear reactor to protect the electrical power grid.

"I have it on good authority," Doc said, "that you are one of the brightest up-and-coming nuclear scientists at the NRC."

"That's really funny," she said. "Who would say such a thing? I'm only two years out of school and I disagree with many of the practices of the NRC. I can't think of anyone who would give me that kind of endorsement. Most of my management think I won't last another year before I'm run off."

"The comment didn't come from the NRC," Doc said. "Take my word for it. What do you know about my technical background?"

"Some of my professors at MIT think that you are one of the most innovative thinkers in the scientific community. I've read some of the papers you wrote when you were on the Senate committee on science, and think your ideas about nuclear energy are revolutionary."

Doc was flattered, but tried not to show it. "Well, Dr. Robertson, you have been chosen to help revolutionize the nuclear power industry." Doc handed her a disc. "This disc contains a set of instructions on how to construct a mini nuclear reactor that could last for thirty years, or more. The president wants your thoughts on this information."

"Thirty years. Wow! That would be amazing. I'd be happy to," she said. "When would you like my report?"

"Is tomorrow too soon?" he asked.

"I have no idea. I'll listen to the tape and let you know. Tomorrow, this time?" she asked.

"That would be great," he said. "And Dr. Robertson, please don't share this information with anyone else. This is between you and me, at least for now. When someone else needs to know, I'll be the one to introduce you."

"A secret. That's fine with me. I'll do my best." Doc realized he'd given Dr. Robertson an incredible assignment, and had put a great deal of trust in the young woman. He was sure she felt intimidated. Hopefully, Mike and Terry knew what they were talking about.

16 June

"What do you think, Dr. Robertson?" Doc asked.

"Please call me Chandi," Dr. Robertson, said. "I listened to the recording and read the documents that were suggested. I've drawn a diagram of the reactor as instructed on the tape."

"And what do you think?" Doc asked again.

"I think it's the most exciting thing I've heard in my entire career, which hasn't been that long; but I'm prepared to proceed."

"Excellent. Do you have any questions?"

"I had some, but they were all answered on the recording."

"I'll warn you," Doc said. "Previously, someone tried to second guess this design, and it ended badly. Please don't allow anyone to change the design. Contact me if anyone tries, or if you have any questions. Here's my mobile number if you need to contact me."

"Now what?" she asked.

"I'm putting you in touch with Dr. Nick James. He's my expert on nuclear energy. He's going to help you get the materials and resources you need, and find you a place to build them."

"Them?" she asked.

"Yes," Doc said. "Once you figure out how to build these reactors, you're going to build and install them as fast as you can, all across the country. You can work with Nick to set priorities for where to install them."

"Nick," Doc said as Nick James entered the office a few minutes later, "this is Dr. Chandra Robertson."

"Chandi," she said, holding out her hand for Nick to shake.

"I look forward to working with you," Nick said. "I've heard about this mini reactor and I'm excited to see it work."

"Me too," Chandi said.

She left with a bounce in her step, already planning what she needed.

❂

"Doc," Sterling Pattersen said as he entered Doc's office, "did you know that those scientists at the CDC are trying to change certain properties of the Smallpox virus?"

"I did," Doc said. "What have you discovered?"

"They're trying to make a less virulent version of it. Why would they want to do that? We had it wiped out. Why would they want to modify it unless they expected it to come back?"

"What do you think? Will it come back?"

"Not unless they release it. They should leave well enough alone. In fact, they should destroy their samples, like the World Health Organization recommended on two separate occasions."

"What do you think we should do about it?"

"I recommend we go in and confiscate their samples and have them destroyed."

"Will you put that in writing, as a formal recommendation?"

"I will if you want me to."

"Do it."

12

Accidental Release

Twin World—VECTOR, Koltsovo, Russia, 15 June

Dr. Sergei Sergeyevich stepped away from the ticket window, having just purchased rail tickets for himself and his associate and younger brother, Dr. Viktor Sergeyevich at the nearby train station. They had an improvised plan to take the vial, which Sergei carried carefully in his hands, generally west, toward Moscow, not sure what else to do. Viktor trailed behind his brother nervously.

"Be careful with that," Viktor said. "You should have hidden it somewhere safe."

"It is safe in my hands," Sergei said. "There is nowhere safer."

"But you cannot carry it around forever. It is glass, and could break and release the contents."

"That would be bad," Sergei agreed, "since we do not know exactly what the virus is capable of. I just need to get it on the train, then we can find a place to hide it until we get where we are going."

The two doctors had left the level 4 research and storage facility for contagious viral, biological and other agents—the State Research Center of Virology and Biotechnology (VECTOR)—in Koltsovo, Novosibirsk Oblast, Russia, hours earlier. From there, they had gone straight to their flat in Koltsovo to pack a bag, pocket their savings, and buy train tickets. Sergei had received a message from his counterpart at the CDC in the United States, Dr. Thomas Strang, notifying him that presidential advisors had been to the CDC and were making noise about destroying their experimental Smallpox samples. Sergei had agreed with Dr. Strang, that they should try to protect the samples from possible destruction by the World Health Organization in order to continue their research. Sergei still didn't know where they could take the virus that had the safety and security measures needed to protect the public from an accidental release, not that they intended to allow its release. So, for now, he intended to keep it with him and leave VECTOR. Viktor had reluctantly agreed with the plan, since this research had become his life's work; he didn't know what he would do without it.

Once on the train, Sergei wrapped the sample vial, in its protective, sealed cryo-container, in his cotton jacket and stashed it in an overhead bin, then tried to allow his mind to enjoy the ride. They both looked out the window, admiring the Ob River as it floated alongside the tracks in places, and talked about Moscow, where Viktor had never been. Sergei told him about the onion domes, the museums, and other grand structures; the old and the new intermingled in an amazing skyline.

The train stopped every few minutes to pick up or drop off passengers. Eventually, as their train car filled up, people sat in their compartment, placing coats, hats and other objects in the overhead bins. The first time someone set a package next to Sergei's coat, he looked at Viktor with concern, stood, and checked on the vial. Satisfied that there was plenty of room in the bin, he relaxed. When a group of noisy, rowdy teenagers entered and began pushing each other playfully, he became concerned again and checked the package again. The package next to it had been pushed closer but there was still room.

"If you are concerned about it," Viktor said, "maybe you should put it in your lap."

"No," Sergei replied. "The container is strong and there's plenty of room in the bin. I think it is safer there." Satisfied that no harm had come to the container, he relaxed again.

When night came, Sergei and Victor placed coats behind their heads and slept in their seats. In the morning, they ate cheese and crackers that Viktor had brought with him, washed down with tepid bottled water. They continued talking, in particular about what they would do once they arrived in Moscow and where they would go.

"You should check the package again," Viktor said hours later, glancing at the overhead bin. Sergei looked around, wondering if Viktor had seen something that made him nervous, but the only people nearby were an older couple sitting on the bench opposite them. Nevertheless, he decided to check on the package. He stood and looked in the bin. Sometime during their trip, his jacket had been pushed into a corner of the bin and other packages had been piled in next to it. Sergei knew that the cryo-container was strong and he was sure the vial had been protected, but he decided to check it anyway.

Lifting his jacket down from the bin, carefully, he could feel the container wrapped inside; it felt secure. Unwrapping the cotton cloth carefully, he thought he felt a damp spot on the cotton, but dismissed it. It wasn't until he studied the container that he noticed the crack in the clear glass of the cryo-container and saw, through the glass, that the vial of liquid inside had broken, with the liquid from the virus sample filling the bottom of the container. Somehow, the package had been jostled hard enough to crack the container and break the vial containing the Smallpox virus sample.

Sergei spun around to look at Viktor, certain the panic he felt inside filled his eyes. Upon seeing his brother, Viktor's eyes matched the new terror filling Sergei. They didn't know how virulent this virus was, since it was an experimental sample. Suddenly remembering the damp spot on his cotton jacket, he located it again and touched it with his finger. Viktor watched, silently. Had the virus leaked out of the container? If so, would it become airborne just from exposure to the air? By evaporation? Had he just contaminated himself by touching the wet spot on his jacket? He turned the container in his hands, looking for the crack again. Sure enough, there was the crack and there was a drop of liquid on the outside of the container. He almost wiped the drop off the container with his hand, then stopped himself and wrapped the container back in the cotton.

"It has cracked, hasn't it?" Viktor asked. "Are we in trouble?"

"Yes, a crack," Sergei replied. "I do not know how serious this is, but I do not want to keep the sample now. We must find a way to dispose of it."

"What should we do with it?" Viktor asked. "We cannot just throw it in the trash or out the window. What about the river?"

"I do not know," Sergei said. "I do not think that is a good idea. What else?"

Viktor shrugged. "Leave it on the train?" he asked, the question betraying the fact that Viktor knew that was a bad idea.

Sergei gave him a dirty look. "Maybe we should take it back to the facility" Sergei said.

"That might be the best idea," Viktor said, "but we are now a whole day away. Even if we go back, what do we do with it in the meantime? How virulent is it?"

"I do not know, but we better try."

They got off the train at the next stop and bought tickets back to Koltsovo, for a train leaving in two hours; they had just missed the previous one.

Sergei suspected that he was already contaminated, if it were possible to become contaminated from the leaky container, so he sent Viktor to buy food in the station, while he sat on a bench on the platform to wait. A young woman sat next to him, initially ignoring him, but soon turned and began flirting with him.

"What is your name?" the woman asked, casually.

"Sergei."

"Hello Sergei, where are you going?"

"To Koltsovo." Sergei knew he was being short with the woman, but this was definitely a bad time.

Sergei had been told he was attractive by several of the women scientists at the facility, but this was the first time, in a long time, that he had been hit upon by a woman. Her timing couldn't have been worse.

"That is such a long way," the woman said. "I am traveling that way also. Perhaps we should get to know each other better."

Sergei shrugged his shoulders, trying to convey his disinterest in the woman, but she was undeterred. After a few moments of casual flirting, during which time Sergei continued his attempts to ignore her, the woman reached over and brushed a lock of hair from Sergei's forehead. "You are such a handsome man, Sergei."

Her fingers lingered on his forehead, then she moved them back and ran them gently through Sergei's hair. With her other hand, she reached down and clasped Sergei's hands. Sergei could take no more. He had to stop this.

"You must stop this," he said, as forcefully as he dared given the possible fragility of the woman.

Before the woman could respond, a large, muscular man approached, clasped Sergei's shirt collar, and lifted him to his feet.

"Are you molesting my girlfriend?" the man demanded.

Sergei tried to determine the best response, but quickly decided this was a setup, probably to get money from him. He got his feet under him, planted them firmly, then tried to display more confidence than he actually felt.

"I am not molesting your girlfriend," Sergei said boldly. "I have asked, even demanded that she leave me be, but she would not. Take the woman and leave before I summon the police."

The man shoved Sergei, causing him to lose balance and fall hard upon the bench which he had so recently vacated. Thankfully, Viktor appeared at that moment.

"What is going on here?" Viktor asked.

"They're trying to rob me," Sergei said loudly, trying to, and successfully attracting the attention of passers-by. The large man swung a fist at Sergei and caught him on the chin, forcing his head back. Sergei's reaction was to swing his right hand back at the man, to defend himself. Sergei's right hand held the jacket wrapped around the container holding the virus sample. Sergei heard the container break and watched the liquid soak the cotton, forming a large dark spot on the jacket.

Sergei's chin, neck, and head hurt, but there were more pressing, and urgent matters to contend with now. He closed his eyes for a few moments to let his head clear. When he reopened them, he stared into the face of a very angry man, who had pulled his fist back in preparation to take another swing.

The swing was cut short as a whistle blew, announcing the imminent arrival of station security. The man dropped his hand to his side and turned, walking away briskly; but not before Sergei noticed the moisture on the man's cheek, likely from where he'd been hit with the jacket. If Sergei was correct, the man had just been contaminated with the virus.

13

Radiation Cure

Twin World—The White House, 15 June

"How's it coming, Brian?" Doc asked Brian Chalmers, his nuclear medicine specialist.

"I've been researching the problem of radiation poisoning and the problem of radiation contamination to air, water and soil as a single problem with a medical solution," Brian said. "I'm tackling it similar to the way we're approaching the cancer problem. Have you been keeping up with those advancements?"

"I've heard some things," Doc said. "How does that relate to radiation contamination?"

"First, let me tell you about cancer research. About two years ago, medical researchers began experimenting with a radical new cancer cure called CAR-T—chimeric antigen receptor T-cell therapy—that has since cured certain types of cancers at a rate of between forty percent and eighty-one percent of patients in different clinical tests. It involves genetically engineering immune T-cells in the blood to recognize and attack the cancer. It's FDA approved, but the treatment is so new that there's still a huge learning curve on post-operative treatment. But the cure seems to be real and complete.

"I figured that if we could find something that would use the body's own healing capability—something like the T-cell—we could engineer it to attack and/or repair the cells. damaged by radiation."

"That sounds promising. Have you found anything?" Doc asked.

"My wife, Toni, has been looking at it with me and talking to her associates at Montefiore. They have several ideas and have begun some research in their off-duty time."

"Excellent! What about the environmental contamination?" Doc asked.

"We've decided that the least expensive method for air and water cleanup is filtering. A filter medium is already commercially available. It's expensive, but what isn't these days? Soil cleanup is more complex. We're thinking about saturation, and if we can work it out, it might be an alternative for filtering air and water, too."

"Keep me posted, Brian." Doc said.

16 June

"Nick, how's your project coming along?" Doc asked Nick James, his nuclear scientist.

"Chandi and I met with power industry representatives yesterday, after talking to you, to discuss priorities for hardening the power grid. A couple of industry reps took the action to begin building a comprehensive and prioritized database of power needs, while Chandi and I work on building the mini reactor. I think we'll have more fun than they will."

"No doubt. Anything else?" Doc asked.

"My wife, Sharon suggested that she could introduce a bill in the Michigan House of Representatives to fund the research in her state. She thinks that other states may feel as strongly about helping as she does."

"Good idea, Brian. I'll pass the suggestion on to State and see if they want to spearhead a fundraising effort."

"Sterling, any more on the Smallpox research?" Doc asked.

"Just that they've sent me all their research notes and I'm going through them to see what might go wrong. Anything you want me to watch for?"

"You can look for anything that relates to side effects of the changes they're introducing or that indicates that survivors could remain contagious after the virus has run its course."

"Is that what we're worried about? That's a pretty serious side effect."

"That's what I need you to find out. Anything else?"

"Cy sent me a report out of Russia that suggests their Smallpox sample may have escaped containment," Sterling said.

"How did it happen?"

"The researcher working with it took it out of the facility and the vial broke. They must have been notified by the CDC that we were making inquiries."

"Then let's confiscate the samples in the U.S, before something similar happens. Okay, people, grab a donut on your way out. I can't eat all of those."

14

The Guest

Old World—The Preserve, 17 June

"Tell me about the UN meeting," Doc said after they'd repeated much from their previous meeting and he'd given them an update on his progress with their requests. Mike and Terry expressed enthusiasm for the progress on radiation treatment and told him what they knew about the confrontation at the UN, focusing on President McCormick's challenges and the other delegates' responses. "How do we convince Russia and the others that we're serious?" Doc thought out loud, not expecting an answer. Mike surprised him.

"Maybe the only thing they'll understand is a demonstration," Mike said.

Doc thought about that. "You mean, show them that we know where they are and that we can take them out at will?" Doc asked.

"That should do it, don't you think?"

"We aren't usually that aggressive," Doc said, "But this is an unusual situation. I'll think about it. Terry, can I have copies of the video clips you showed me the other day? I need to make notes and see if we've covered everything that could go wrong."

Terry already had a disc prepared and handed it to Doc. "So, is everything going according to plan," Terry asked Doc.

"You've been a great help," Doc said, "but I did receive one surprise. A report from Russia said their Smallpox sample has been released. What should we do about that?"

"We need to get you some vaccinations from the president or the formulation for the vaccine," Terry said.

"That's what I thought," Doc said. "Can I just call him and ask for them?"

"You can," Terry said, "or we can call for you. Whichever you prefer."

"I've got some other things to do, so I'll put it on my list of things to do. I need to go now."

Doc was finished asking questions and gathering his things to leave.

"I need a favor," Mike said slowly, "but I'm afraid to ask."

"Ask away, Mike. I'll do anything within my power to help you. I hope you know that."

"It's about Mom," Mike said, making Doc stop and look him in the eye.

"What about your mom?" Doc asked.

"She's moping around here like a sick puppy," Mike said. "She took Dad's death really hard, and hasn't recovered." Doc thought that described him as well.

"I think if she saw you," Mike continued, "she'd straighten up and look to the future again."

"You may be right," Doc said, "but I don't know if that's such a good idea, Mike."

"I agree," Terry said. "What are you thinking Mike?"

"I just want Mom to be happy again. I want her to be herself, to take an interest in what's going on with her family."

"That's a noble cause, Mike, but I don't see how seeing me would have that effect on her. I have to go back to my world and she belongs here."

"Then you don't want to meet her?" Mike asked.

"Mike, I'd love to meet her, but how do you know she'd want

to meet me?"

"If she *does* want to meet you, will you agree to see her?"

"Of course, Mike. If that's what you want; but only if Lillie wants it, too."

✦

"Mom," Mike said, once he got his mom to open her bedroom door and talk to him, "I have a surprise for you."

"What is it, Michael?"

"I want you to get cleaned up and come out to meet someone."

"I'm not in the mood, Michael. Can it wait? Hold on, what do you mean 'meet someone'? I already know everyone here."

"It's a surprise mom, and when would be a better time? You haven't left your room in days."

"It's been hard," Lillie said. "You know that."

"Yes, I do. But this guest my change all of that."

"I've already met everyone," Lillie said, frowning.

"You remember that you gave me permission—or rather Dad did—to search for ourselves in the twin world?" Mike asked

"Yes," Lillie said. "Have you found one of us? Your father? That's who you were looking for, wasn't it?"

"Yes, I was looking for Amos Two, and I've found him!"

"I don't want to meet him. It would be awkward. He has a life in his world and I have mine in this one. What good would come of us meeting each other?"

"I want you to stop moping around like your life is over. Like Dad said, you should look to the future. Why not meet him? It might liven up your day. He's so much like dad."

"I'm sure he is, but he probably has a wife and family that he needs to get back to, and he doesn't need to waste time talking to me."

"He's single, and he's probably lonely, just like you. His wife, Lillie, in the twin world, also passed away. I'm not asking, or even considering that the two of you would hit it off or something. But you could be friends. Come on, Mom. Just come and meet him."

"You're not going to let this go until I agree, are you?"

"As chairman of the board, I'm giving you forty-five minutes to get cleaned up and report to the Lab."

"That's not really within the powers of the Chairman of the Board, Michael. But nice try. Assuming I agreed to this, though, would I talk to him through the gate?"

"No. You can talk to him face-to-face."

"He's here? In the Preserve?" Lillie asked, becoming upset. Her face registered her shock. Mike nodded. "How dare you invite him to the Preserve without my permission," she said. "You set this whole thing up to embarrass me, didn't you?" she asked, then started fussing with her hair and looking around like she was looking for a mirror. "I'm not presentable."

"Seriously mom. You think I would *try* to embarrass you? What I'm *trying* to do is *not* embarrass you. That's why I said you should get cleaned up, and look presentable. Becca is here to help."

"I probably don't need help," Lillie said, walking over to a mirror. She stood there for a moment, looking at herself, then spoke again. "Okay, send Becca in."

Mike opened the door to let Becca in. "Take what time you need," Mike told Becca as she slipped past him into Lillie's bedroom. "I'll keep our guest busy until you get Mom to the lab."

☢

"How many people work for you?" Terry asked Doc, while they waited for Lillie. Moments later, Mike watched Lillie slip quietly into the office, and take a seat near the door. Doc was facing away from her, and clearly hadn't heard her come in.

"I have three direct reports and between twenty and thirty specialists that report to them." Doc said.

"And all of them are technical people?"

"Scientists and engineers, yes"

"Doc," Mike said, pointing in Lillie's direction, "Let me introduce you to my mom, Lillie Blund."

Doc spun around so fast that Mike was surprised he stayed in his seat. He focused on Lillie and a huge grin split his face. He hesitated a moment, studying her face, then walked casually over and stuck out his hand to her.

"It's a pleasure to meet you Mrs. Blund. I feel like I've known you for a long time." They shook hands, Doc holding onto her hand so long that she started to blush. If he noticed how sickly she looked, and Mike guessed he had to notice, he chose not to mention it, probably so that he wouldn't embarrass her.

"It's a pleasure," she said with a simple smile. "Welcome to my home and please call me Lillie"

"It's a beautiful home, Lillie. Terry and Mike have been showing me around and sharing some of its secrets with me. Your husband must have been a very creative and intelligent man." Doc said with a smile.

"Oh, he was," Lillie said, Mike watched his mom and Amos Two talking. Their polite conversation continued a bit longer, and Mike thought he could sense a bit of flirting from Amos Two. His dad, Amos One, had flirted with his mom almost constantly, so Mike wasn't surprised to see Amos Two doing the same. Mike wondered whether either of them felt any guilt about flirting with another person's spouse. Logically, that would make sense; but there certainly wasn't any rule—morally, ethically or legally—preventing two single people from getting to know each other better in that way.

"Excuse me," Doc said, "but I need to get back to the office. I have so much to do. It was nice meeting you, Lillie. Thanks for the information Terry and Mike. Mike, are you coming back with me?"

"I'd better," Mike said, standing to follow Doc back to the lab, where the gate waited to return them to Salt Lake City.

After Mike and Doc had gone, shutting the door behind them, Terry turned to Lillie.

"I think you enjoyed that little visit," he said. Lillie became instantly defensive. She knew this wasn't a set-up, but she felt guilty—well, not guilty exactly; but certainly a bit strange and confused—by the way Doc had behaved, and about the way she had been attracted to him.

"I hope you got that out of your system, Terry, and we won't see a repeat performance."

"What do you mean?" Terry asked, smiling.

"He has his world and we have ours. You don't need to play matchmaker, because it won't work. We'll all end up disappointed and unhappy."

"I'm not playing with you, Lillie. And Mike isn't either. We weren't' trying to set you two up. Doc's obvious flirting was all his own. We were just trying to help you see the world around you. Mike thought you could use a bit of cheering up. But you need to know that our two worlds are tied together in some serious ways."

"What do you mean?"

"His world is headed down the same path as ours. They're just a year behind us."

"Do you mean . . . ?" Lillie started to say, but Terry obviously guessed what she was going to say and beat her to it.

"The terrorists that bombed Washington, D.C. in our world last July, have threatened a fourth of July attack this year in the twin world. And they already attacked London, just like what happened in our world a year earlier. But in the twin world, Amos Two's wife and children were killed in the London bombing."

Lillie gasped, then covered her face with her hands. Her body shook.

"Oh dear," she said. "That poor man."

"We're trying to help Doc prevent war, in exchange for some scientific research that might help us," Terry explained.

"What can we do to help them?" Lillie asked, speaking in a hush, as if afraid of being overheard. Her emotions were on the brink, not only from meeting Doc, but particularly from hearing that his family had been killed in a terrorist attack.

"We've already shared what we know about Al-Qaeda, North Korea, Russia, China and the Los Zetas drug cartel. Hopefully, they can act to stop the terrorists before the deadline."

"Will he keep us informed?" Lillie asked,

"I thought you didn't want to see him again."

"This is different. I want to know if he succeeds in saving lives."

"I'll let you know if he contacts us again."

"Terry, how did he know we were here and know how to contact us?"

"Mike found him and spoke with him."

Lillie listened intently as Terry gave her what felt like an abbreviated explanation of their trip to the twin world and "Doc's" previous trip to the preserve.

"So, he's already been here before today?"

"Yes, and he's seen most of our technology. He's quite impressed with how brilliant he is, in both worlds." Terry smiled at his own joke.

Lillie became pensive, thinking about what she'd heard, but left the office in a good mood, already planning to do her hair and nails. Doc's visit had been good for her, as Mike had suggested it would be.

18 June

"Mom," Emily said, appearing surprised when Lillie showed up for breakfast. "H . . .how are you feeling," she stammered, obviously at a loss for what to say. "You're looking more animated."

"Pretty good, actually." Lillie said, smiling at her daughter's unease. "How are you doing running the house?"

"Everyone's doing fine. We're maintaining—well, holding steady."

"Great. Do you need any help?" Lillie asked, hoping Emily would say she had everything under control.

"If you want to help, Mom, I'm sure I can find something for you to do"

"Actually, I'm not looking for something to do. If you've got it under control, I'll leave well enough alone."

"I've got it, if you have other things you want to do."

"Good. I want to go to the exercise room and try to get myself back in shape. I'll see you later," Lillie said, as she sat down to eat what would be the most food she had eaten in one sitting in many days.

"Hi Mom," Mike said, as Lillie was trying to leave the dining room. "Do you have a few minutes?"

"Of course, Michael," she said. She followed him to the lab, where Terry was doing something with the observer.

"Mom," Mike began, "do you have any questions?"

"Questions about what?" she asked.

"About anything. About my trips to the twin world? About

Doc? About what we shared with him or what we asked him to do?"

With each new question, Lillie shook her head. When Mike was finished, she said, "No, Michael. I told Terry that, as long as you two agree, you can do whatever you want. I seldom questioned your father in these matters, and I'm not going to start with you."

"You're not even curious?"

"Of course, I am. But I trust you to tell me what I need to know when I need to know it, like when you invite a visitor from another world to the Preserve." She looked at Terry as if asking him to confirm her position.

"She's right Mike," Terry said. "We just need to be careful to notify her when what we're doing affects *her* world." She nodded.

"Now, is there anything I need to know?" Lillie asked.

"Yes, Mom," Mike said. "I love you. I'm glad you felt strong enough to face Doc yesterday. It tells me that you have the resilience that I always thought you had. I was afraid that you'd given up and didn't want to be part of our adventure anymore; but Doc thought—hoped really—that seeing him might help motivate you. I'm happy that you're back. You *are* back, aren't you?"

Lillie realized that Doc's thoughts and feelings about her must have stemmed from a belief that he would know her best. If Doc had been married to Lillie Two for as long as she was married to Amos, it seemed that Doc would know her almost as well as Amos did.

"Mike," Lillie said, "Don't turn this into an experiment, with me as your guinea pig. But, yes, I'm through feeling sorry for myself. I've joined the world of the living again. Now, tell me you're not inviting him back to disrupt our routine again."

"Actually, Mom, he's probably coming back today. He and Terry have an agreement to share technology. I told him he's welcome to come anytime."

"Then you better decide how to break it to the others, so they don't have a heart attack when they see him. It's probably best if you keep him away from me, though."

"Mom, is it possible that seeing Doc helped you make the decision to get out of your funk?" Mike asked.

She was certain that it had, but had to be careful how she expressed herself to Michael. He might think he should push Doc on her.

"It was nice seeing him, but I think it was just leaving my room and doing my hair that changed things. It wasn't specifically seeing Doc that did it," she said.

"He's a good-looking man," Mike said, "and he likes you. You couldn't have missed that."

"I agree, Mike." She said, placing her hands on her hips and staring at Mike. "He is good looking, like my Amos; but Amos is dead and I can't imagine there ever being another man in my life. I'm too far past that time in my life, and Doc and I are from different worlds." Then she dropped her hands to her sides, turned, and left the room.

15

Pandemic

Twin World—Koltsovo, Russia, 18 June

Sergei and Viktor had spent several days trying to overcome the effects of smallpox. Although they hadn't known what to expect, they had known it was coming when they started to feel sick, fighting off high fevers. The illness, including sores and resulting scabs overtook them both.

Around their apartment complex, many people were sick; but it wasn't isolated there. News from Moscow talked about the detention of several people at various train terminals. People were suffering from fevers, and the hospitals in those areas were filling up. Local authorities reported that at least forty or fifty people had been exposed, but the numbers would certainly rise as the virus continued to spread.

Authorities had finally figured out where the disease had originated and were trying to figure out what to do about it. Sergei and Victor were afraid to admit their role, for fear of the consequences.

16

Allies

Twin World—The White House, 20 June

"I have Ministers Theresa May of the UK, Eduard Philippe of France and Benjamin Netanyahu of Israel on the line," the operator said. "When I hang up, you'll have them."

"Thank you."

There was a click on the line as the operator hung up. Brief greetings were exchanged and the president thanked the ministers for making themselves available.

"Under the circumstances, Greg," Prime Minister May said, "we all need to be available for each other. What news do you have?"

Buck told them about his efforts to locate the bomb in Mexico, to identify the Al Qaeda strongholds and weapons caches, and to stop Russia from shipping bombs to North Korea, then addressed his current thinking about convincing the Russian government and their industrialists to stop selling weapons to Al-Qaeda. "We're prepared to take the offensive to try to stop them," he said. "I've asked my secretary of State, Cy Hutchison, to call an emergency session of the UN and we're preparing a convincing argument for them that we'll present at the UN general assembly meeting. Can you help us identify their hideouts and weapons caches?"

They spoke for a few minutes about options, and the potential impacts of nuclear detonations and EMPs on their countries and regions. They agreed that the terrorists had to be stopped, regardless of the cost. They compared lists, prepared by their advisers, of suspected Al-Qaeda strongholds and weapons stashes, and came up with a list of thirty-two probable sites in Iran, Syria, Libya, Algeria, Afghanistan and Pakistan. They discussed the activity at ports on the Caspian and Black Seas, adding four more sites in the Russian provinces to their list. Minister Netanyahu identified another thirteen suspected ISIS hideouts which they all agreed should be added to the list. Doc compared their list against the one Terry had given him and saw that they matched exactly. Good! He wouldn't have to show Buck Terry's list and try to explain where he got it.

"Doc," Buck began "what was the outcome of your two-day trip to Saudi Arabia?"

"King Salmon assured me that he is doing everything within his power to stop the terrorist activities in the region, but that he can't upset the rest of the Saud family by being more involved with the allied plans to go after the terrorists."

They debated the most likely reaction from Russia and other countries with nuclear weapons, then considered whether to warn the governments of the world that they were prepared to take the offensive, if necessary.

"Not bloody likely," Minister May stated emphatically. "Let's hope we catch them all napping."

When they finished talking, Buck summarized their plan.

"We'll verify all forty-nine sites using satellites, and show the world what we know. It will be revealing some of our technological capabilities, to let them know how we located them, but I'm prepared to do that if the plan has a chance of succeeding. We'll prepare shelters for our populations, in case there's a backlash from our enemies."

"Good," Minister Philippe responded. "I will recommend that other concerned European Union states also prepare shelters to protect their people from the terrorist threat, without tipping our hand."

While Minister Philippe was speaking, the president raised his eyebrows at his advisers, in effect asking for their agreement. He got thumbs up and nods of agreement across the board.

When Minister Philippe finished, Buck asked the three world leaders if there was anything else they needed to consider.

"Do you believe that your presentation to the UN will prevent whatever it is that Al-Qaeda has planned?" Minister May asked. "What if they have sleepers in each of our countries, already in place to carry out their threat with more nuclear weapons?"

"Those are good questions, Theresa. We need to keep looking and coordinate our intelligence, just in case."

"Agreed. It's a good plan. Let's hope it's good enough. As for whether or not my presentation will prevent all-out war, we'll have to judge that after viewing the presentation. We're still putting the final touches on it," he said, nodding to Doc.

"I agree," Minister Netanyahu said. "Can you give us an idea of what you plan to do?"

The president explained a little about the presentation he planned to make, without giving away the details, then soberly thanked the leaders and bid them God-speed, ended the call, and turned back to the men in front of him.

"This looks good Doc," Buck said. "I think we're ready for the UN. We just need Jim to get the military in position for the dem-onstrations."

21 June

"Buck," Doc said, "I need to go back to Salt Lake City to conclude some business. It could take me a few days. Do you have everything you need for the UN meeting?"

"What's this business you suddenly have in Salt Lake. You haven't had assets there for years."

"That's about to change. I'm looking at buying property and building a home. You remember that Utah is my home state, right?"

"Are you planning to leave me? We're not finished yet, you know."

Doc felt obligated to Buck, to finish what they'd started. No, he wouldn't leave until he'd wrapped up what he was doing for Buck. He owed him that much. "We'll wrap this up before I change gears, Buck," He said

"Glad to hear it, Doc."

Old World—The Preserve, 21 June

"Terry," Doc began "are you interested in forming a partnership for medical research, like you had with Amos?"

"Whenever you're ready, Doc. After we spoke the first time, I took the liberty of copying our partnership agreement, in anticipation that you would be interested in reinventing some of our patented designs for use in your world."

"Fantastic, Terry. That's exactly what I have in mind. In fact, if you're willing, I'll cut through the red tape and have you give me the contact information for the bidders on each of the patents."

Terry pulled a manila folder about two inches thick out of a drawer and handed it over. "Here's the agreement, along with some of the patent applications and contact lists," he said. Doc opened the folder, removed the partnership agreement off the top of the stack, and prepared to sign it.

"Don't you want to read it first?" Terry asked.

"Why?" Doc asked. "Have you suddenly become untrustworthy?"

Terry sputtered, trying to form a response. Then just shook his head.

Doc signed the agreement and handed it back to Terry, smiling teasingly at Terry's obvious discomfort, then stuffed the folder into his briefcase. "I've hired a patent attorney in Salt Lake. I'll turn these over to him to get the process started."

"Why the hurry?" Terry asked.

"I've contacted the owners of Aspen Valley in the twin world and made offers to buy the land. There's more than one parcel, so I have to deal with two owners. I need the cash to close the deals."

"What are you thinking?"

"I'm going to build another Preserve."

"Why? You're welcome to come here anytime."

"I know, and I appreciate it, Terry, but I have a couple of ideas for improvements, and one of them requires me to coax Lillie out of her shell."

"You know she told Mike that she doesn't want to see you again? 'You have your world and she has hers,' were her words."

"I'm not surprised, but I know Lillie. She won't be able to resist."

17

New Revelations

Twin World—Salt Lake City, 21 June

"Mike, I've set up an Email account and internet access for you," Doc said. "Here's the information. Of course, just like the phone, you'll only be able to contact me if you send the email from *my* world, not your own."

"I already have your phone. Why would I need email?"

"Things could get crazy around here in the next couple of weeks. We need a backup for contacting each other. Now, tell me about Amos's relationship with the president."

Mike and Terry took turns explaining everything they knew, including the fallout Amos and Greg had over the Smallpox vaccinations and Amos's last accusing words to the president.

"Not what I was hoping to hear," Doc said. "I want to get information from Greg, but it may be impossible if they had a falling out."

"They were friends for a long time, as you know," Terry said. "I wouldn't be surprised if Greg is still hopeful of getting information from Amos, so he may still be willing to talk."

"I'm still surprised you never told President McCormick about Amos' death in your world. What was the reason for not telling him?"

"We thought it would take away our advantage," Terry replied. "It was so difficult to get the president to give us vaccinations and cooperate regarding not trying to find Aspen Valley and the

Outcasts. If the president knew Amos was dead, he might feel he has carte blanche to come looking for us and we would lose the negotiating power we currently have. We can't risk losing it."

"Thanks, Terry. We'll make sure that whatever I say with the president in your world keeps things straight. I don't want to upset the status quo."

"Thanks, Doc," Terry said. "You're still planning to move to Utah and open a medical practice?"

"Really?" Mike asked, interrupting. This was the first he'd heard of it.

"Really!" Doc said. "I've purchased five acres on the West side of Logan, for a homestead, and I'm going to purchase Aspen Valley, a little more property than you have, so I can make a couple of improvements."

"Can you tell us about your plans?" Mike asked.

"Let's leave that for a surprise. If I can keep my mouth shut long enough, it will still be a surprise, anyway."

Twin World—The White House, 22 June

"Doc," Nick called as Doc hurried down the corridor.

"What is it Nick?" Doc asked, stopping abruptly. One thing Doc's team members could count on was that, no matter how busy he was, and he was usually in a hurry from one emergency to another, he would always take time to listen.

"Chandi has completed six mini reactors," Nick said, holding a mobile phone up to his ear. "They've been tested and are ready to go online."

"No problems or complications?" Doc asked.

"We had one question, but she listened to the recording again and got the answer. The chairman of the NRC insisted that he be allowed to oversee the construction and verify the design, but

Chandi asked Buck to talk to him and that was the end of it."

"Perfect. Are you ready to turn it on?"

"Chandi is in the water treatment plant with the technicians and will turn it on when I give her the go-ahead."

Doc had heard about the disaster when the reactors were turned on in Amos's world and it would eat him up inside if Chandi got caught in that; but he had implicit faith in Amos's instructions, so he gave them the go ahead. "Do it."

Nick already had Chandi on the phone and told her to proceed. Doc could hear her excited voice from several feet away as the machinery began to whirr in the background.

"We have power," Chandi shouted in the background a few moments later.

"That's great, Chandi. I'm with Doc right now," Nick replied

"Tell her, congratulations," Doc said. "Go ahead and install the others."

"We have go-ahead on the others," Nick said. "Why don't I meet you at the deli for a quick bite to eat, then we'll head over to unit number two? Okay, see you in fifteen."

"Okay Doc," Nick said. "I'll get back to you if we have any trouble."

"Thanks Nick. Good work!"

Doc decided to check in on his other staffers, so that he'd have the latest updates on all important areas of their plan, just in case he ran into Buck. Brian was in the office. He'd just returned from the South Pacific, where he'd been working with the military to test the effects of his radiation cure. He'd picked a location where he knew nuclear testing had been performed during the fifties and sixties. They'd used a helicopter to saturate the sand, and filters on the air and water. The monitors and gauges showed marked reductions of radiation contamination in all three mediums.

"Perfect!" Doc said. "Can you get me a written report?"

"Almost finished." Brian said. "I'll leave it on your desk. However, keep in mind that this is only the first test. We're planning on doing more."

"Great. Thanks, Brian." Doc said. Sterling was just hanging up the phone. "Sterling, what's your status?"

"That was my contact at WHO. They agree we should destroy the Smallpox samples. Unfortunately, the samples at VECTOR, in Russia, have disappeared, but the researchers, brothers who've been working with the virus for years, were located. They didn't have the samples anymore."

"Do they know where the samples are now?" Doc asked.

"The government found the brothers at their apartment and quarantined them. They have an outbreak near Koltsovo, which they suspect was caused by the brothers, so they're quarantining everyone in the area until they can figure it out. It is believed that the samples are somewhere in the area, but the brothers aren't talking. I wouldn't be surprised if they've hidden the samples intentionally as leverage to protect their lives. Who knows what the Russian government will do to them once they turn over the samples."

"Thanks, Sterling. I'll tell the president."

Doc knew he needed to speak to the president, Greg McCormick, in the other world. He needed the vaccine formulation. But talking to the president, in another world, made him nervous. It was time though, and he hoped Mike and Terry could help.

Old World—The Preserve, 22 June

"The government is headed to shelters," Doc told Terry as they stood in the office, discussing patents, "probably early next week, before the deadline. Buck is working with Jim Seymour, his

SecDef, to determine who to include and where to send them. Once we're inside, we won't come out until the deadline is passed, assuming a positive outcome. If there is a bomb, and if it goes off, you know as much as I do."

Lillie exited the hospital giftshop dressed in her candy-striped outfit. She carried a flower arrangement that had been ordered over the phone for Mrs. Thompson in room 714, who was recovering from surgery. Before she reached the elevator, a good-looking intern entered the hallway in front of her and walked in her direction. "Hello, Doctor," she said, exaggerating both words, trying to be flirtatious.

"Hello, yourself," he replied, grinning when he saw who it was.

They had never been introduced, but had seen each other around the hospital for the last few days. She didn't know who he was, and didn't know his name, but she wanted to meet him. She thought he was handsome and was developing a crush on him like she'd never had on any man before.

Lillie woke from her nap, remembering this dream because she'd had it many times since that long-ago day when she'd finally worked up the nerve to talk to Amos. Within days of meeting in that hospital hallway, they were in a serious relationship that never cooled. It had been the beginning of an exciting ride that had led them to the alter and a long and happy marriage. She was as beautiful as he was handsome. Their courtship had become the talk of the hospital and the only question on people's minds was how long it would take for them to tie the knot.

She had called him Doc until she'd learned his name, and had continued to call him "Doc" until he'd finished medical school and opened his medical practice. It had become a term of endearment.

Her mind wandered and she wondered why Amos from the

twin world went by Doc instead of Amos—she was certain his name was Amos. Maybe his wife—Lillie—had always called him Doc. Or, maybe he had started going by Doc after he went to work for the president, to remind him of his roots. That had to be the other Lillie's doing. That's what she would have done if she had been in that situation.

What a strange thought, looking at Doc's life from the perspective of Doc's wife. What would that life have been like, married to an advisor to the president, travelling all over the world, trying to solve global problems? But that had ended badly for *that* Lillie and her children, when they'd travelled to London last New Years' Eve.

She realized that she had to get past these thoughts, knowing they would only cause her discomfort, or worse.

"Lillie," Terry said through her bedroom door.

"What is it Terry?" she called, realizing that it had been Terry's call that had awakened her from her daydream.

"Doc would like to have a word with you before he leaves. Can you spare a minute?"

Great timing, she thought, as Doc's image popped into her head. She knew it was Doc's image in her head because of the shorter haircut. "What does he want?" she asked.

"Just to see you again."

"Oh, alright. I'll be out in a minute." She'd told Mike and Terry she had no interest in seeing the man again. But she realized that she really did want to see him. It confused her. Why did she want to see him? Either way, she would. Maybe it would help her figure it out.

Doc was waiting just outside her bedroom, in the common area of her bedroom wing, standing, not sitting.

Doc took a couple steps toward Lillie and took her hand.

He held it in his while he spoke to her. As she looked into his eyes, she realized that her daydream, the one that had always been about Amos over the years, this time had been about Doc. It scared her to be subconsciously visualizing herself as Doc's wife. She pulled her hand out of his, interrupting him in mid-sentence and making him frown. He had been telling her that the government in *his* world was going to evacuate to underground bunkers in a few days and that he wouldn't be able to see her again until after the terrorist deadline. She wondered why he thought she would care, but realized that she did; she *did* want to see him again. "I'm going to quit government service, move to Utah and open a medical practice," he said.

"Why are you telling me this?" she asked.

"I just wanted you to know," he said. The way he looked at her said all she needed to know. She'd seen that look on Amos's face many times over the years. It was a look that expressed intense feelings. Love, oftentimes; but not always. Amos had that look whenever he really felt confident in what he was saying or feeling. "Be safe," she said, meaning it.

"I will," he replied. "I'll see you again soon."

"I look forward to it," she said, the words slipping out before she could stop herself. She frowned as he walked away, down the bedroom tunnel toward the community center and the lab. She could hear family members greeting him. The same feelings of unease crept in. She *had* meant it. She wanted to see him again. It terrified her.

☢

"Terry, tell me again about Amos's relationship with Greg Mc-Cormick and why it's stressed today," Doc said.

"Amos and Greg had a long, friendly relationship," Terry said.

"But their relationship became strained toward the end, just before Amos died."

"But Greg didn't know Amos died, right?"

"That's right."

Terry explained how Amos had accepted a satphone from Greg in lieu of joining his administration, how Amos always answered the phone and assisted Greg with whatever crisis he was currently facing; but without having all the facts, Amos had to guess at what was happening in Washington. He explained how that had changed when Greg had failed to take Amos's advice on controlling the viruses at the CDC.

"When the Outcasts showed up in Garden City," Terry said, "and I became infected, Amos wanted vaccinations. Greg was under pressure to solve the energy crisis, and used the excuse of providing vaccinations to us, to try to capture a family member to hold as hostage until Amos agreed to hand over his reactor design."

"I thought Amos gave Greg the design anyway," Doc said.

"He did, but he was so angry at Greg for the threat to the family, that he failed to control his temper, something rare with Amos, and just about killed their lifelong friendship. Now, Greg thinks Amos refuses to talk to him because he's still angry."

"Did Amos refuse to talk to him?"

"Not exactly. Amos was shot about that time and could no longer come to the phone. Mike and Lillie have stalled him ever since, so nothing has been resolved between them."

"Do you think if I called Greg," Doc asked, "it would smooth things over?"

"Well, we've kind of assumed you would, based on your comments earlier. But I'd like to know to what end?" Terry asked. "Amos can't have an ongoing dialogue with Greg, since he's dead."

"But I can," Doc said. "Is it okay with you if I call Greg to confirm some details? Who knows if there will come a time when we really need him? We should leave that path open."

"I like your thinking," Terry said, "but that goes without saying, since we've been partners forever."

"Speaking of which, are you still willing to be my partner and let me get rich from your prosthesis designs?" Doc asked.

"You're just planning to use the funds to build another Preserve, aren't you?" Terry asked.

"If I don't spend it all, I'll invest it for us."

"Then nothing's changed. Here are the rest of the designs," he said, handing over another manila folder full of documents, "and a copy of the partnership agreement. You're still planning to return to Utah and hang your shingle?"

"I am, but I've got some loose ends to wrap up in Washington, so I don't know how soon."

"Lillie may not understand you placing Washington ahead of her," Terry said with a sly smile.

"Lillie doesn't think she's on my radar at all," Doc replied.

"Is she?" Terry asked, "on your radar, I mean."

"Absolutely, Terry. She's my number one reason for moving back."

"Then you need to let her know, Doc."

They made eye contact and Terry tried to express without words how serious he was. Then Terry told Doc what he already knew, that he needed to court Lillie the way he had when they'd first met. Then she would know he was serious.

23 June

"Mike?" Greg asked when he answered the Satphone.

"It's Amos, Greg," Doc said. He wondered if he could pull this off, pretending to be Amos.

"It's so good to hear your voice, old friend," Greg said. "I wondered if you would ever talk to me again. I figured you hadn't forgiven me for the incident in Garden City."

"It's good to hear you too. I'm giving you a chance to make up for it by giving me some information about the terrorists and events leading up to the war."

"Well, I'm happy to try. I miss you buddy. But I thought I answered all your questions the last time we talked. What else do you want to know?"

"I want details about where the bomb was built in Mexico, how it was shipped, including the route, and how it got to Washington."

"Why do you want to know?" Greg asked.

"Call it professional curiosity. I want to know how the cartel, and the terrorists, think, and what resources they have."

Greg told him about the capture and interrogation of El Jefe, Jose Mendosa, and the information they had received as a result.

"It was assembled at a plantation in Chiapas, Mexico," Greg said. "We have the GPS coordinates if you want them. It was transported to the gulf coast by commercial van and loaded into a mini-submarine, taken around Florida to the waters off the South Carolina coast, where it was transferred to a fishing boat and taken to shore. This is where the facts get a little fuzzy, because it was now out of Mendosa's control. It was loaded into the trunk of a rental car hired by a Samuel Smith—we believe that was the false cover name for the terrorist—and delivered to the person who detonated it in Washington, D.C. Samuel Smith was later tracked by the FBI from the CDC, which he apparently planned to blow up, to his damaged car near Atlanta, where he was killed by a team of Army Rangers after he had contracted Smallpox."

They discussed the events leading up to and including the bombings.

"What do you think would have been different if you'd bombed Al-Qaeda before the deadline," Doc asked.

"If we'd thought to compile the list of terrorist hideouts, and bombed them before the deadline, it would have taken the wind out of the sails of the terrorists; but we still would have had to stop the Mexico bomb to prevent war. I had committed to retaliate against Russia and North Korea, and I don't think that would have changed."

"How are the mini reactors working?" Doc asked.

"After the initial disaster," Greg began. "and with your help, we got it right. We're now building them as fast as we can and have several critical facilities up and running."

"Do you have the formulation for the Smallpox vaccine?" Doc asked.

"We do. Do you have new cases?"

"No, I just wondered if I could have a copy of it. Call it a control copy, in case the original gets lost."

"It's a little complicated, so why don't I have someone read it off to you while you record it?"

"Perfect," Doc said. "I'll give the phone to Mike and have him set it up. Anything else you need from me?"

"Not unless you have a cure for radiation poisoning or a supply of large electrical transformers on hand," Greg said.

"That's a tall order," Doc said, "but if I come across any of those, I'll be sure to share."

They both laughed, Doc thinking about how shocked Greg would be when he delivered on that request.

When he turned the phone over to Mike, Doc was thinking about what else he could share with Buck to help in his world.

Twin World—Salt Lake City, 23 June

Doc spent the rest of the day searching the internet for anything he could find on Terry Stephens in the twin world, deciding that he was impressed with Terry's medical credentials and influence in the scientific community. He discovered that Terry had patents for prosthetics and had written a paper on the need for a non-intrusive medical procedure, but no evidence that he had built anything.

☢

Doc had made his call to Greg from the office in the Preserve and the internet search from the hotel in Salt Lake in the twin world. He had asked Mike to check on him that evening, since he wanted to return to the Preserve before the end of the day. In the lab again, Mike asked what Doc wanted to do.

"See Lillie?" Doc said, without hesitation.

"She's been doing better and I'm convinced it's because of your visits," Mike said. "Terry, do you know where Mom is?"

Terry looked at live videos from the community center, then the kitchen, then the exercise room. "Exercise room," he said.

"Let me see if I can coax her out here," Mike said.

"Better idea," Doc said. "I'll go surprise her."

"I don't know if that's such a good idea," Mike replied, "She might . . ." but Doc was already out the door. He'd studied the floor plans and knew his way around. He greeted several members of the family as he passed through the community center.

☢

Lillie turned to look when she heard the door open. She was dressed in tight exercise shorts and top that showed off her shapely, albeit too-skinny body. She immediately grabbed a towel and threw it over her lap.

"What do you think you're doing?" she asked angrily.

"I wanted to see that you're still as sensitive about your cute figure as you've always been." In reality, he was devastated by her poor appearance, sunken eyes and cheeks. It made him want to take care of her, nurse her back to health.

"It's not cute, and it's not your problem," she said.

"We can fix that," he said casually, as he strolled over and sat on an exercise bike facing her.

"Go away, so I can put some clothes on," she said.

"No," he said.

"Then turn your head"

"No."

She huffed, then stood, and put her jeans and a sweatshirt on as quickly as she could, watching the grin on his face and the twinkle in his eye. He suspected she was probably flattered by his attention. When she was presentable, she took his hand and led him back to the office, where she said good-bye and turned to leave.

"Where are you going?" he asked. "I came here to see you."

"I'm sorry if you wasted a trip, but I need to shower and go help Becca in the kitchen."

"I can wash your back."

"No you can't," she said, walking away,

"That was a little forward, don't you think?" Terry asked, having heard the end of the conversation.

"You never know unless you ask," Doc said. "Tell me about the hospital and what you're doing with the Observer, Terry." They spent some time discussing the Observer, but Doc couldn't concentrate; he kept thinking about Lillie and how starved and tired she looked.

When he returned to his hotel room in the twin world, Doc called Buck on his private line and shared the information he'd picked up from Greg, including the fact that he had the Smallpox vaccine formulation, without giving away his source. He said he would give the formulation to Sterling Patterson. The entire time, he worried that his budding feelings for Lillie were sympathy rather than affection.

"Maybe she's right," he said to himself. "Maybe we're better off staying in our own worlds."

Twin World—The Preserve, 24 June

Doc stayed in Salt Lake City so he could go to the Preserve to see Lillie and Terry again.

"Are you getting anything done, sitting in this hotel room," JP asked. They'd been in Salt Lake for two days now and, as far as JP knew, Doc hadn't left the room. That wasn't like him. Doc was usually on the go all day long.

"I'm making lots of phone calls and taking lots of notes," Doc said. "Go rent a car for the rest of the day. We're going for a ride."

JP looked skeptical, but didn't argue with his boss.

While Doc waited, he called Buck again and reinforced the fact that Al-Qaeda would use nuclear bombs if they could get them. Buck told him that Cy had requested a meeting of the UN General Assembly and gotten it, so they discussed Buck's presentation to the UN in addition to the possible military actions. Buck liked Doc's suggestions and had started getting the information on Al-Qaeda, ISIS, North Korea, Russia and the Los Zetas. They strategized on how to handle the UN presentation and what the SecDef and DNI needed to do to be prepared. Buck wanted him back in Washington, D.C., but Doc said he had run into complications and needed more time in Salt Lake.

After the call, Doc had JP drive him up Logan Canyon to Aspen Valley. On the way, JP wanted to talk.

"Doc," JP said, "I heard a rumor that the president wants you to take an agent with you when you leave government service."

"I've heard the same rumor. I'm thinking that you should go with me. What do you think?"

"You could take any agent you want, and I know there are some agents in the service who have roots in Utah. Why would you pick me?"

"For obvious reasons, JP. I know you best, I trust you, and I think you'd like the assignment."

"Did you know I'm getting married?"

"Congratulations, Utah is a great place to raise a family. But, when have you had time to date?"

"I'm not with you 24/7, you know. I do have a life, barely."

"Do you want to stay in Virginia, rather than relocating to Utah. I can make that happen."

"No. Please don't change anything. We've already spoken about it at length and agree this is a good move for us."

"So, when's the wedding?"

"We wanted to do it before the move, but decided I'd come with you now and she'd join me as soon as she can work out the details. She has a job, family, and friends to consider. I've already called the Logan City office to arrange for a license and a judge to marry us. We just need to set the day and time."

"Turn onto this trail," Doc said when they arrived at the trail into the valley. They drove to the end of the trail, arriving at a cliff face. They didn't need four-wheel drive, but it was close. The trail was rutted and washed out in places.

Doc imagined the opening that Mike had told him about in the rock wall, which Mike had blasted into the mountain using dynamite, to build the garage in the old world. JP looked around quietly for a while, then spoke.

"Is there something special about this area," JP asked.

"There really is," Doc said, "but I'm just beginning to understand what it is." Doc walked the valley, from the highway to the cliff face and all around in between, getting a feel for it and trying to visualize the preserve and everything that needed to be done to build it. He sloshed through a stream and climbed over rotting logs on the ground. He tried to imagine having done this before, as Amos, but couldn't wrap his head around the twin world concept and him existing in both worlds as different people. He thought he should at least have a memory of being Amos in his world. He made lots of notes and several sketches. When he'd seen enough, he called his attorney and left a voice message. He wanted to close the deal.

After they returned to the hotel, Doc waited for Mike to call again. The plan had been for Mike to enter the twin world and call Doc at 7:00 PM.

"Would it be possible to build an Observer that has the medical capability but not the gate," Doc asked, when Mike and Terry finally called.

"I'm sure it is, Doc," Mike said. "I'll look at the programming. What do you have in mind?"

"If it's possible, I'd like to make a duplicate Observer with the gate and have a set of plans for the one without a gate. Let me know if I need to get you any parts or materials. When you've got all that, I'll tell you what we're going to do with them."

In the remaining time before he had to catch his plane back to Washington, D.C., Doc searched the internet for everything he could find on Artificial Intelligence, or AI. He wanted to know if it was feasible to program the Observer to observe patients and recognize symptoms of medical problems from appearances and behavior. He was pleased with what he found and emailed several website URL's to Mike with a request to review them before his next visit, so they could discuss them.

He would explain when they got together again.

18

Preparations

Twin World—Governors' Conference, 25 June

Buck had asked his secretary of State, Cy Hutchison, to arrange a Governors' conference to discuss how to deal with a nuclear emergency. Cy had succeeded in getting the governors of the northeastern states together in one room, with many of the other governors by teleconference. The governor of California hadn't committed to the meeting, so Buck called him personally and put him on speaker, Buck told the governors about the possibility of a nuclear detonation and asked for their support in keeping the public calm.

"We're trying to stop the bomb, but if we don't succeed, you will all have a lot of angry citizens on your hands," The governors had lots of questions, mostly about what the government was doing to stop the terrorists, but Buck was unwilling, or in some cases, unable, to give them any specifics. The one thing he was able to suggest was that each state authorize the federal government, in writing, to send military personnel to assist local police with problem areas.

Following the governors' meeting, Buck held a press conference to announce that he had raised the Defense Condition to DEFCON level 1, imminent threat of nuclear war. Then with his advisors, he planned military actions in Vladivostok, Chiapas, Northern Africa and the Middle East.

Old World—The Preserve, 26 June

"Lillie," Doc said, "I have a surprise for you. Get a jacket."

"Are we going outside?" she asked.

"Yes, in the twin world." Lillie felt healthier and happy. Whatever Doc had in mind, she was ready to listen.

In the lab, Terry had Lillie place her arm through the gate, which confirmed what Doc had said. When Terry was finished, he opened the gate so Doc and Lillie could step through the gate into Aspen Valley in the twin world.

"What about the radiation . . . ?" Lillie asked, before Doc or Terry answered, she realized there wouldn't be radiation because they weren't in her version of Aspen Valley. "Oh."

The trees were a healthy green, the undergrowth thick and prickly. Birds chirped in the trees and a squirrel ran up a tree trunk, across a thick limb, and jumped into another tree. The sky was overcast and it looked like rain. Everything smelled fresh.

"It's wonderful, Doc." Lillie said, suddenly tearing up at the memories of her early years with Amos. "Why are we here?"

"You realize, of course, that we're in the twin world, right?" he asked.

"Your world, yes." She replied.

"No," he said, "the twin world. I don't belong to either world, now. I'm a citizen of the universe. However, I wanted to show you that Aspen Valley in this world is the same one you fell in love with years ago. This is now *your* Aspen Valley and you can do what you want with it."

"What do you mean, 'my' Aspen Valley?" she asked

"Exactly what I said. I bought it and put it in your name. You now own it."

"No. Really, Doc, what did you do?"

"Just what I said. I bought it in the twin world—in *this* world.

I'm going to build a preserve in it—an improved version based upon the design and specifications Mike and Amos drew up. Terry's building another Observer to place in it, so you can go wherever you want, within its range."

She believed him. How could she not? Here they were. He seemed to be a good man, like her Amos, creative, intelligent, resourceful, loving, kind—everything she'd fallen in love with, over twenty years ago. Her face felt flush and she suddenly realized that she had feelings for this man—for Doc. She knew it was against her better judgment to fall for another man—particularly one from another world. But maybe it was okay. Maybe she could become a citizen of the universe, too.

"I really like you, Doc," she said spontaneously, suddenly embarrassed.

"I like you, too, Lillie."

"This is awkward," Lillie said. "What do we do about it? You have your own world and you'll go back to it, then I'll be left alone again."

"I'm sorry Lillie. I have unfinished business in the twin world, and I need to get back to it, to finish it up. Once the terrorist deadline has passed, I'll be able to return and we can make plans."

Lillie's face fell. The terrorist deadline was a huge obstacle. With Doc in the twin world and her unable to ensure his safety, she could lose him in the explosion. Again, she wondered how her feelings for the man had blossomed so suddenly. She was really worried about him. Doc had tried to convince her that they had things under better control in the twin world, but these were terrorists they were dealing with. How could he be so sure?

"Don't go," she pleaded. "I couldn't survive losing you a second time."

"It's going to be okay Lillie," he said. "Are you ready to go back inside?"

"Can we walk a while?" she asked.

"Of course," he said, taking her hand in his. Her hands had aged with the raising of three children, and she wondered whether he would enjoy the touch.

"Let me tell you what I have in mind for improvements in your preserve." Doc said. They walked and talked for a long time, until Lillie shivered; then Doc suggested that thy go inside. He called Terry on his radio and had him bring the gate to them. While they were waiting, Doc raised her hands to his lips and kissed the back of first, one, then the other.

"I love your hands," he said, answering the question she had asked herself.

Back in the lab, Doc stopped to talk to Terry. Lillie frowned, then sat down in a folding chair.

"Is everything okay?" Terry asked.

Doc glanced at Lillie, and she nodded subtly. "I think she's afraid I'll leave and not be able to come back," Doc said. "I've tried to reassure her that the information you've given me will prevent war, but I don't think she's buying it completely." Doc looked at Lillie again and she nodded again. "I wish I could think of a way to convince her."

"Just come back," Terry said.

"That's the plan," Doc replied. "I need to get back to the twin world now, but I wanted to check with you first. Did you receive the radiation remediation equipment that I had delivered to the Logan airport?"

"I did," Terry said, nodding, "and I gave it to Beth to set up in the valley. I'll check with her later to see if she had any problems with the setup."

"Great!" Doc said. "I'll want a regular report on how it's doing, if that's okay with you."

"No problem. I'll ask Mike to have reports ready. When will we see you again?"

"I need to get back and monitor events in the twin world, but I'll return on the fifth and let you know how things went."

"Sounds good Amos," Terry said. "See you in a few days."

Doc walked over to Lillie and she stood as he approached. When he reached out with both hands, Lillie closed the distance and wrapped him in a hug.

☢

"Where do we put this stuff?" Ben asked Mike.

"There are three types of equipment," Mike told the group. He wore a hazmat suit and stood among the Outcasts in the clearing above the Preserve. The Outcasts had agreed to help install the environmental remediation equipment and monitor it. "This is the equipment to filter the air," he continued, pointing to the disassembled framework that housed air filters. "Place it on the east side of the valley, on the trail. That's the direction the prevailing winds come from, so that's where it will be most effective."

Mike pointed to the next piece of equipment. "This equipment is to filter the water. We'll submerge it in the stream, upstream of the pond. The monitoring for both types of equipment need to be placed downstream—or downwind—from the filters. The soil cleaning process is different. It cleans by saturation, so we'll pour it on the soil, then test the soil later. The instructions for setting up and monitoring all three systems are here," he said, handing some pages to Beth. "Once you decide who's going to do the installations and monitoring, let them review the instructions and make note of any questions. We can talk again tomorrow or the next day."

Twin World—The White House, 28 June

"What's our status?" Buck asked his SecDef, Jim Seymour. Jim had spent the last few days moving military assets into the areas surrounding the Suez Canal, the Mediterranean and Black Seas, and the Gulf of Mexico., with air cover for all of them,

"Everything is ready for your UN meeting," Jim replied.

"Has the missile defense system been tested?" Buck asked.

"We took a few missiles, representative of the entire system, to the south pacific test range to test their guidance systems. The ones we tested responded correctly."

"What about the bunkers?" he asked no one in particular. It was HomeSec Chuck Dickson who replied.

"All checked out and upgraded," Chuck said, "including a mini nuclear reactor in each of them."

"The reactors are working properly?" Buck asked.

"Perfectly. Each was checked out by Dr. Robertson personally."

"Thanks, Chuck. Anything else we need to discuss?" Buck asked.

"All set, Buck," Jim said. "We're ready for the show."

"Doc?" Buck asked.

"All set." Doc replied. "Cy arranged for the projector and links to the satellite feeds from the UN assembly hall. Your speech is on the desk in front of you. You may have to adlib a bit, depending on the pushback from the delegates."

"Understood," Buck said. "Okay everyone, here we go."

19

Demonstrations

Twin World—UN General Assembly, New York City, 28 June

Newly appointed U.S. Ambassador to the United Nations, Daniel Porter, moved away from the podium as President Gregory 'Buck' McCormick walked onto the stage and stopped at the lectern. His nervous, ever-vigilant, security detail stayed at the edge of the stage and around the perimeter of the auditorium. President Mc-Cormick turned to look at the president of this emergency session of the United Nations, Peder Jorgensen of Denmark.

"President Jorgensen, esteemed members of the Security Council, representatives of member states, ladies and gentlemen, thank you for allowing me these few minutes to address the General Assembly of the United Nations.

"The United States of America has hosted the United Nations since its inception because we believe in the founding principles that unite us. The United Nations gives all of us a place to air our grievances and a guarantee that we will be heard and treated fairly. In return, as member states, we each have a responsibility to every other state to be fair and honest. When any one state takes advantage of another, the Security Council and general assembly make every effort to level the playing field for the aggrieved state. I'm here today to tell you that some of our members have violated the trust that we place in them."

A murmur spread through the auditorium. President Mc-Cormick knew it was a bold and confrontational statement. The

General Assembly delegates weren't unaccustomed to confrontation—it happened all the time. What probably surprised them was that it was coming from him. He continued.

"The United States security services have obtained evidence that Al-Qaeda does, indeed, have a nuclear weapon, and intends to detonate it within the borders of the United States."

There was louder murmuring now. This was a very specific accusation. The president raised his voice to be heard over the noise.

"Our evidence indicates that Al-Qaeda is using source funding from Saudi Arabia to build a nuclear device in Mexico with the help of the Los Zetas drug cartel. The cartel plans to help Al-Qaeda smuggle the bomb into the United States using a million-dollar, one-time use submarine, from Mexico, across the Gulf of Mexico and around Florida to South Carolina, to be detonated somewhere near Washington, D.C."

The Saudi representative to the UN, seated in the second row of the auditorium, stood, pointed a finger at the president and yelled.

"That is a lie. We do not fund Al-Qaeda and we do not build bombs."

The crowd quieted, likely hoping to hear President McCormick's response. The president laughed bitterly, then spoke quietly, as the noise in the auditorium had diminished to near silence.

"Mr. Halabi, your denial is the lie. You have been sponsoring terrorist training camps and indoctrinating young people in fundamentalist Wahhabi doctrines for years, and everyone knows it. Saudi Arabia *created* Al-Qaeda."

The noise in the room blossomed again. Buck could only hear some of what was being said, but he saw fingers pointing, faces turning red, and general commotion throughout the room. President Jorgensen stood and moved to a position next to President

McCormick. He pounded his gavel on the podium until the noise level decreased to a reasonable level. Then he turned to President McCormick with subdued anger.

"Must you do this? This is highly unsatisfactory."

President McCormick spoke into the microphone again.

"President Jorgensen has asked me if this accusation is necessary. My answer is to all of you. Any state that deems nuclear war as an acceptable means of obtaining its objectives, is a threat to all of us, not just the target of their aggression. Each of you should be outraged by Al-Qaeda's crass ignorance of, or carelessness about, the real harm—the risk that even one nuclear bomb could ignite a global thermonuclear war that will end life on our world as we know it. This is not just ignorance, nor carelessness—it is evil, and from the devil."

He knew using that phrase would incite, at a minimum, all the radical Arabs. He wanted to see the reaction.

The auditorium exploded again, with Mr. Halabi standing, pointing at the president and shouting.

"You are the devil, not us."

The president had to yell to be heard, even with the microphone.

"Mr. Halabi, do you deny that the Al Saud family provided funding to build a bomb for the purpose of detonating it in Washington, D.C.?"

Mr. Halabi was seated again now, so he could use his microphone, but he had to yell as well, his voice barely carrying above the raucous noise in the room. "I have already denied it and I deny it again."

President Jorgensen pounded his gavel on the lectern again, trying to return the auditorium to some semblance of order. President McCormick didn't wait for the noise to subside but spoke over it.

"Then tell me, Mr. Halabi," the president yelled, "why have two thirds of your staff and their families left the United States in the last week, and why do you, personally, have a one-way ticket out of John F. Kennedy International Airport for tomorrow afternoon? Are you afraid to be in New York on Wednesday afternoon? What do you know that you're not telling this international body?"

As he spoke, the noise in the room again rose to a roar. President Jorgensen pounded on the podium again, then asked President McCormick to excuse him and took over the microphone.

"Mr. Halabi," Jorgensen said, "are you lying to this assembly? Does Saudi Arabia intend to detonate a nuclear device in the United States?"

But Mr. Halabi wasn't listening, he had gone pale and was hunched at his desk, talking on his mobile phone. President McCormick grabbed the microphone again.

"Mister Halabi!" he bellowed.

Halabi reflexively looked up, and the auditorium quieted, shocked at hearing the president of the United States screaming. In a quieter voice, the president resumed.

"Since you're talking to the Al Saud family at the moment, you can pass along the rest of my message. If a nuclear device is detonated in the United States, whether in Washington or elsewhere, whether this Wednesday or any other day, we will drop a larger bomb right on Riyadh. In fact, I'll tell the military to paint your name on the side of it, so that King Salmon knows who is responsible for delivering it to him."

Mr. Halabi's mouth hung open. He lowered his phone to the desk and stared, dumbfounded, at the president. But McCormick was done with him. He turned to the Russian member of the Security Council, sitting on the podium.

"Mr. Sokolov . . ." He shook his head. "Mr. Sokolov, where did

Al-Qaeda get the nuclear material to build their bomb?"

The Russian just shrugged, straight-faced, appearing disinterested. President McCormick continued, shaking his head.

"Russia has been supplying arms to the Middle East for years and has a history of selling nuclear material to other countries through the Siloviki—your former KGB, turned mafia, turned industrialists. If we find that you sold nuclear materials to Al-Qaeda, either directly or through an intermediary, like Iran or Syria, we will be very unhappy. What we do know, Mr. Sokolov, is that your country very recently shipped a weapon to North Korea, a country that has insisted that if they could get a nuclear weapon, they would launch it against the United States on one of their ICBMs, which, by the way, they are currently testing again."

The room had gone unusually quiet. Only murmuring could be heard as delegates got on their cell phones to talk to their respective government contacts. Mr. Sokolov smiled, but the smile didn't reach his eyes.

"We have done no such thing," he said into his microphone, then leaned confidently back in his cushioned chair, his arrogance palpable.

President McCormick turned back to the General Assembly.

"In case you didn't hear him, let the record reflect that Mr. Sokolov said 'we have done no such thing'. My response to Mr. Sokolov, and to the Russian president, is: if not, then why did our Special Forces destroy a bomb in Vladivostok last week?" They hadn't, but the president knew the plan was on the drawing board, thanks to information Doc had supplied, and he thought the threat alone would get the desired response. It did.

Sokolov jumped up at that, looked threateningly at the president, and spoke, quietly, but with great fervor.

"You violated Russian territory by sending troops into Vladivostok? That is an act of war."

"An act of war, you say? And you supplying nuclear weapons to North Korea, a state with an unstable head—a man with a God complex—knowing he intends to use it against the United States. that's not an act of war?"

"You cannot prove it was nuclear," Sokolov said.

His slip of the tongue wasn't lost on those seated in the General Assembly room—he had all but admitted that Russia had sent bomb materials to North Korea. Every eye turned to Sokolov, the unasked questions hanging in the air.

"Ah, you are right. We can't prove it was nuclear, yet," McCormick said. "But, you know what? We don't need to. You've just admitted delivering a bomb to North Korea. I'll give you the same message I gave the Al Saud family. If North Korea fires an ICBM aimed at the United States, we will retaliate with even greater force, and we will send a nuclear warhead to the Kremlin with *your* name painted on the side."

"You wouldn't dare. Russia still has a large arsenal of ICBMs."

Sokolov sat down slowly. He didn't look as confident as he had moments earlier.

President McCormick turned to face the president of this session of the United Nations.

"I'm tired of listening to all the lies," McCormick said. He turned around to face the room again. "Ladies and gentlemen, here is my ultimatum. Russia and Saudi Arabia will stop the nuclear weapons that are intended for use against the United States. If they do not show good faith, beginning right now, the United States will attack Al Qaeda, ISIS and any state that we believe is responsible for, or complicit with them. And I may as well say, Mr. Montes," the president looked at the Mexican ambassador to the UN, "that Mexico needs to ferret out the terrorists who are working with the Los Zetas drug cartel. We need you to do everything in your power to stop the bomb. I'm sure you don't want the United States to be forced to send troops into Mexico to handle this."

Montes, seated in the third row of the auditorium, looked like he was going to be sick. The president knew there was no way Mexico wanted the U.S. to send troops across the border.

"Thank you, President Jorgensen," McCormick said, "for allowing me this time at the podium."

He gave a nod to Ambassador Porter, then tuned to leave the platform, headed for his security detail and the exit. His security team was scanning the auditorium for any overt act of hostility. The noise level in the room quieted as Sokolov stood and taunted him.

"Is the United States so afraid of being seen as weak, that you need to threaten to take these illegal actions against peaceful nations," Sokolov asked, "whose only desire is to protect themselves from aggression?"

"You started all of this by sending bombs to North Korea—an enemy to the world," the president said, as Sokolov continued.

"You do not know where to find Al-Qaeda," Sokolov said, "as you have said many times. Unless you have been lying to us."

McCormick returned to the pulpit. "We've been doing our homework, Mr. Sokolov," he said. "Ambassador Porter," he said, "the presentation please." Ambassador Porter spoke into his phone and a huge image appeared on the wall next to the podium, showing a map with the locations of U.S. military installations and temporary staging locations across the world. The presentation had been prearranged, but Buck hadn't known when the opportunity to use it would arise. It now had. Everyone in the auditorium could see it, as it was projected from the back of the room.

"Our military is currently in position in the Suez Canal, the Mediterranean and Black Seas, and in strategic locations in Mexico. Satellites have been monitoring activities at forty-nine Al-Qaeda and Isis locations in several countries. The governments of those countries will arrest and detain everyone at the monitored sites, to be picked up for questioning. If anyone tries to escape, we will attack that site and ensure there are no survivors. Allied troops will search each facility for holdouts."

The image on the screen changed to show a hilly desert with a few palm trees swaying in a light breeze. "This is an Al Qaeda hideout in Northern Africa, which we have been monitoring for the last several days. Perhaps some of you will recognize it, having been there on occasion. Watch." Suddenly, a bright light streaked in from the left and struck the ground in the middle of the image. As the dust began to clear, people could be seen climbing out of a hole to the right of the impact and running away. They didn't get far before more missiles streaked in from both sides and struck the ground all around the initial impact. The people who had been running, all fell to the ground.

The Russian and Chinese members of the UN Security Council stood in protest, as did others in the room, until about a quarter of the delegates were standing.

"That is a violation of our UN charter," Sokolov said loudly.

McCormick ignored the protest. "How about another demonstration?" the president asked, amid random shouted protests. The scene changed to a wooded hillside and a similar attack took place. No one escaped. The protests decrease as the representatives realized that the president was serious.

"We are prepared to continue," the president said, "but I have a better idea. The governments of the countries where these terrorist groups are located will voluntarily inspect each of the target locations, arrest the terrorists, and hold them for questioning. These instructions must be carried out in the next twelve hours or allied forces will take unilateral action. You can contact our Secretary of State if you have questions about the specific locations.

"Any interference by governments will be deemed aiding and abetting terrorists and an act of war. You have twelve hours from right now to give them up for questioning. Any holdouts will be dealt with summarily and the governments protecting them will be struck from our favored nations list." President McCormick looked around the room. A few heads were nodding, others were shaking. But the thing he wanted to see most wasn't happening. Nobody was speaking into their phones to pass along the message. So, he continued, more forcefully.

"If you don't know or haven't heard, the U.S. Congress recently gave me authority, under a new terrorist response act, to deal with terrorists and those complicit with them, in numerous ways, including stopping all financial and other forms of aid. I encourage you to think carefully before challenging me on this, because I am determined to see it through."

McCormick paused and looked around the auditorium again, gaging reactions. Not quite satisfied, he continued. "I can't resist," he said. "One more demonstration." The scene on the wall changed once again as protests were again voiced from several delegates. The new image showed a clearing in a jungle, where a couple of acres of low crops grew. "Anyone in the room familiar with coca and poppies will recognize the plants in this image," the president said. "This is the headquarters of the Los Zetas drug cartel in Chiapas, Mexico. The Mexican government will arrest and detain everyone at that location, which is currently surrounded by the U.S. military."

The president looked at the video of the Los Zetas site. There were five buildings in the background. The camera zoomed in on the center building, a two-story structure covered with rusting corrugated aluminum siding. "We believe there is a nuclear bomb being assembled in this building." As they watched, the door opened and two men pushed a four-wheeled cart out of the building. A cylinder sat between blocks on the cart. People in the clearing started to scatter and the dolly was left alone, momentarily.

"We suspect that that is a nuclear bomb," Buck said. Just then, a missile zoomed in from the side and struck the cart, destroying the cylinder and killing everyone near it. A second missile hit the building in a flash of blinding light. "If anyone doubts our resolve, let me know now and we'll accelerate the schedule. Mr. Montes," the president said, "never mind the message to your president."

"Just for everyone's information," Buck continued, "another bomb is on a passenger train from Moscow to Vladivostok. We haven't attacked it, yet, and we're not planning to, since there are U.S. citizens on the train. However, if the bomb components get off the train, we will follow them and destroy them once all U.S. citizens are out of the way. Any attempt by Russia or North Korea to detain our citizens, will be dealt with. Have I made myself clear?" There were now numerous people with phones to their ears. McCormick couldn't hear what was being said, but assumed his message—or some message—was being passed along.

"Finally," McCormick continued, "any country known or suspected of having nuclear weapons capability will voluntarily either destroy their facilities or make them available for inspection by an allied force of scientists and military personnel. The U.S., Russia and China will open their nuclear facilities and arsenals for inspection by a similar joint team of Russian, Chinese and U.S. scientists and military personnel, for the purpose of cataloguing their inventory. Non-compliance by any party will be deemed an attempt to hide their capability with the intent to use it later for terrorist activity."

The president looked over the audience one last time before leaving the podium. "The clock is ticking," he said. Then he turned to his right and left the podium.

20

Final Preparations

Twin World—White House Situation Room, 28 June

"How do you think that went?" Buck asked as he looked around the situation room at his advisors.

"From the looks on their faces," Secretary of State Cy Hutchison said, "I'd say they understood your message, even if they didn't like it. We're receiving calls already, asking for GPS coordinates."

"Loud and clear," HomeSec Chuck Dickson added.

"It was good to see the silly grin wiped off Sokolov's ugly face," SecDef Jim Seymour added.

"A word of caution," Doc said. "We think we got the bomb that was headed our way. But let's not be too overconfident. I think we should still follow standard procedure for a terrorist threat, until the deadline has passed."

"I agree," Buck said. "Let's implement the evacuation plan today. Cy, has the evacuation of the northeastern states started?"

"It has, sir, but we're talking about millions of people. It will take some time."

"What about the bunkers?" he asked

"Ready, sir," Jim said. "If I have to stay in one of those things, I want to know that it will survive a conflict."

Over the next twelve hours, every terrorist stronghold was either bombed, blown apart from inside or found upon inspection to be the victim of mass suicide. Within three days, every country on the president's list except North Korea signed a treaty, quickly prepared by Doc's team, to allow inspectors into their countries. The next day, the head of North Korea was arrested by his military leaders and a military tribunal convicted him of crimes against the people of North Korea. He was executed by firing squad, then the interim military government signed the treaty, pending ratification by a new government, to be elected in the near future.

In the northeastern States, word went out by radio, TV, and internet, that the government would temporarily relocate entire populations to government facilities upwind— to the southwest—until the terrorist deadline had passed. Citizens were advised to take only what they could carry in their arms, following airport security guidelines—no weapons, explosives, aerosols, etc.—and get to the nearest airport, where they would be loaded onto military and civilian aircraft and relocated. Similar directions were broadcast to large cities that the president's advisors thought most likely to be targeted— Honolulu, Seattle, San Francisco, Los Angeles, Las Vegas, Cheyenne, Denver, Chicago, Dallas–Fort Worth, Houston, Atlanta, Miami, Boston and Washington, D.C. The military facilities wouldn't be as comfortable as staying in a hotel, but there would be food, beds, and transportation home afterwards.

The TSA had little difficulty managing the crowds at the airports. People were constantly reminded that no one would be left behind and there would be plenty of room on the planes. People soon realized that the military cargo planes weren't as comfortable as the jetliners, but there was room for everyone.

There were traffic bottlenecks and vandalism, but nothing that local authorities hadn't handle before.

29 June

"Buck," DNI Thomas Mitchell said, "the name Samuel Smith

popped up on a list of car reservations in South Carolina this morning. I've sent agents to investigate and follow up."

"Is it possible that what we blew up in Chiapas was not the bomb?" Buck asked the room. Only his senior advisors were present and none of them ventured an opinion. "I guess anything is possible," Buck continued. "Tom, see if you can find out when and how Smith entered the country."

"Already checked all incoming flights and ships since the first of the year. If he was in London on New Year's Eve, that's the earliest he could have entered. No record of him entering the country in that time."

"Okay, go back another six months, just in case. Any other ideas?"

"What if," Doc suggested, "he entered the country on a submarine through South Carolina. With or without a bomb he still could have entered the country that way."

"Yes," Buck said. "Tom, send a team to South Carolina to investigate. Do we know anything about his movements after that?"

"You mean after today?" SecDef Jim Seymour asked. "How could we know what he'll do tomorrow or the next day?"

Jim looked startled by his own question. In fact, Doc thought, everyone looked startled. But he thought he knew where to find answers. He excused himself and went to send an email.

Twin World—The White House, 29 June

Doc waited impatiently for Mike or Terry to reply to his email. When the reply came, he barely read it while walking to the Oval Office. Buck was there and Jen ushered him in without checking with the president.

"What is it Doc?" Buck asked, obviously seeing the look in Doc's eyes.

"There might be another bomb. I think there are two possibilities," Doc said. "Either we didn't destroy the bomb and it's on its way to Washington. Or, we got the bomb, but he has a backup plan."

"Sounds reasonable. What do we do?"

"First, put plain clothes agents on the Mall 24/7 to watch for anything unusual. Second, put undercover agents at the secondary target."

"What's the secondary target?"

"That's the sixty-four-dollar question," Doc said. He knew that Smith had targeted the CDC in the Old World, from the response to his email. But that was under different conditions, so it might not be the target here. "Let's ask Tom to have his people analyze it and suggest options."

"We're running out of time here, Doc."

"I understand, but I'll meet with them to expedite the process."

30 June

Doc returned to the Oval Office after meeting with the FBI analysts. They had made a list of the most likely targets that Smith and his sleepers could get to in the time left before the deadline. Of the thousands of possible targets, they had eliminated those that were not high-value targets, leaving only major government and business centers, and places where large numbers of people would be gathered. They had narrowed the list down to the twelve most likely, then prioritized those. At the top of the list was the CDC near Atlanta, then Wall Street in New York City. Others on the list included state capitals, business districts, sporting events and Washington, D.C., again. Washington was already covered, so the president ordered Tom to send agents to the CDC and Wall Street. Any more than that was speculation. He would hold off unless he heard something that changed his mind.

Later that day, Tom told Buck that the FBI had received a call from an unlikely source. "An FBI agent, travelling through Chantilly, Virginia, on a different assignment, stayed there overnight and struck up a conversation with the motel clerk. Apparently, the clerk is a conspiracy theorist and is particularly suspicious of anyone who looks like they might be from the Middle East." Tom started to chuckle as he continued.

"The clerk set up a hidden camera in the lobby months ago, hoping for a chance to catch a terrorist. He took a snapshot of a man calling himself Samuel Smith, who rented a room for the night, then disappeared without sleeping in the bed. The face matches the one in the video from the UK."

"I don't suppose he knew where Mr. Smith was going in such a hurry?" Buck asked.

"No, he didn't; but he gave us a good description of Smith's car, which matches a car on the list from an auto rental agency in South Carolina. I've put out an All-Points Bulletin to all agencies, including transportation departments that might have traffic cameras in the area. We'll try to determine which way he's travelling and catch up with him."

"Thanks Tom," Buck said.

21

War

Twin World—Prime Bunker, 4 July

Nearly everyone, from all branches of the government had evacuated Washington, D.C. Key members of government organizations were headed to underground bunkers, to wait out the terrorist deadline. The president's bunker was referred to as Prime. Buck sat in the situation room in Prime, surrounded by government and military leaders, while others occupied other bunkers spread around the country. Prime was connected to the other bunkers by secure satellite communications and Buck could see the situation rooms in each of the other bunkers through monitors on the wall, eight of them in two rows, with labels under each to identify the principal occupant. SecDef, for the secretary of Defense, Home-Sec, for the secretary of Homeland Security, DNI, for the director of National Intelligence, STATE, for the secretary of State, VEEP, for the vice president of the United States, ENERGY, for the secretary of Energy, NDCP, for the director of National Drug Control Policy, and JCS, for the chairman of the Joint Chiefs.

"How's the evacuation going?" Buck asked his HomeSec.

"We've moved a lot of people," Chuck Dickson said, "but this is a huge undertaking. There are lots of problems, like people wanting to take their guns, but the TSA is handling it very well, considering."

"What are they doing about the guns?" SecDef Jim Seymour wanted to know. "Just curious," he added.

"They're being tagged and stored at airport security. Hopefully, they'll still be there when the people come to claim them."

"Anything else, Chuck?" McCormick asked.

"I'll just tell you right now that we won't have everyone out by the deadline," Chuck said.

"By choice? Or because we can't move them?" McCormick asked.

"Probably a little of both. Las Vegas is a perfect example of people not wanting to leave. There appear to be more people entering Vegas than leaving. The big hotels are booked up for the next several weeks."

"What about the Russian virus?" Buck asked.

"The CDC Director, Anne Lister, sent the formulation for the vaccine to Moscow for them to try. Preliminary word is that they were reluctant to accept anything from us, but the brothers who were responsible for the release volunteered to try it on themselves and they seem to be getting better. Dr. Lister has agreed to keep in touch with them."

"What about Smith, Tom?" Buck asked.

"We've tracked him as far as the outskirts of Atlanta. If he's part of the terrorist plot, and with the deadline this afternoon, he has to be close to his destination. We've notified the team watching the CDC, in case that's his target."

As the terrorist deadline approached—three pm on July fourth—the president and his advisors watched a news report from a news helicopter circling about twenty miles west of Washington, DC. There was no word from any of the teams watching the Mall in Washington, or the teams watching the CDC and Wall Street, and it had Buck worried. He had threatened the Saud family and the Russians with retaliation if a bomb went off. He had no intention of sending nuclear weapons to the other side of the world, but how could the United States back away from a nuclear detonation on home soil and still hold their place as the world protector of liberty and human rights?

At two o'clock, Buck told Tom to notify his FBI teams to evacuate before the deadline, so they wouldn't be collateral damage in case there was an explosion. At two-ten, he notified the Director of Homeland Security, Chuck Dickson, to stop trying to evacuate Washington, and get his own people out.

"What if the terrorists use the next few minutes, after we've left, to plant their bomb?" Chuck asked.

"I won't ask anyone to sacrifice themselves," Buck said. "If a bomb goes off, we'll decide what to do then."

☢

Minutes before three o'clock, Tom tried to get Buck's attention, but Buck put him off. He was focused on the news helicopter and didn't want to miss anything. Three o'clock came and went without incident, to everyone's relief, and there was no missile from North Korea. After fifteen minutes, the reporters moved on to other news, promising to come back to the story if there were further developments.

"Have we received anything from the CDC or other teams?" Buck asked.

"I was trying to tell you just before three o'clock," Tom said.

"What?" Buck asked, looking at Tom's monitor on the wall.

"I received a report from one of the teams on the Mall. When I couldn't get your attention, I recorded it. Listen"

There was static at first, then the voice of one of the FBI agents came through clear and strong.

"This is agent Richard Vogel. I'm standing outside the National Gallery of Art on Constitution Avenue with the Museum curator, Mr. Glen Gatner. He just told us that his security rollcall revealed one

employee unaccounted for, a Mr. Austin Anderson. He sent a team of security personnel back into the building to look for Mr. Anderson and found him in the basement, hovering over a collection of paintings that will go on display next week.

"When they realized that the words he was mumbling sounded like a Muslim prayer, they decided to look around a little. What they found, hidden among the paintings, looks like a bomb. Anderson wore a headset and had a microphone on his lapel. We tried to talk to the person on the other end, but he cut off the connection as soon as we spoke. We've called in a bomb squad, arrested Mr. Anderson and begun interrogating him. All we've gotten out of him so far, as scared as he is, was the word Smith, and we didn't know what that meant, so we called you."

The last thing Buck heard, before the recording cut off, was Tom's voice saying "Well done, thank you."

"What's significant about the art museum?" Buck asked.

"I asked that, too," Tom said. "agent Vogel said that the National Gallery of Art is just blocks from the Capitol and the White House. So, with Anderson's job at the museum, it was a perfect hiding place for the bomb."

After thirty minutes, and no explosion, the president notified everyone in the bunkers that he was officially declaring a non-event and wanted everyone to go home to their families.

"Looks like you did it, Buck," Doc said from the seat on Buck's left, shortly after the announcement.

"You mean, *you* did it," Buck said. "You're the one who had all he ideas for stopping the bomb and the ongoing threat. I just made it happen."

"Either way, I'm glad it's over."

"Is it truly over?" Buck asked. "What about Smith? What assurance do we have that he won't pop up somewhere else? You know we have Muslims all over the world; densely populated in some places."

"You're right, of course, but now you can focus on some of those Muslim colonies, and you know what to watch for."

"You make it sound like you won't be there to help me," Buck said. "Are you planning to bug out on me, just when we have this crisis under control and can focus on domestic issues?"

"You know, Buck, I never planned to work for the government for the rest of my life. I have other things that I want to accomplish. That's never been a secret."

"But, look what we've accomplished together. We make a good team. Think what we could accomplish in another four years," the president said.

"I'll always be available to you, just not on a full-time basis. I'll make sure you always know where to find me." Doc paused, then continued. "I'm not leaving today, anyway. There are still some loose ends that my team needs to clean up. I'll let you know when I'm finished."

"Find Smith for me. Then you can do whatever you want," Buck said.

"Yes, sir."

Twin World—The White House, 5 July

"We've built ten mini reactors and several of them are already on-line at water and wastewater treatment facilities in the downtown Washington, D.C. area," Nick said. "The ones that were in the government bunkers have been relocated to other high priority locations now that the bunkers have been vacated."

"They're all being tested before being installed?" Doc asked.

"Part of the process, per our instructions," Nick said. "Chandi is waiting at unit number ten for my word to turn it on."

"Do it, then."

Nick spoke into his radio. Doc heard Chandi's reply, a hearty, *'Turning it on now.'* Then he heard machinery come to life over the radio. After about a minute, Chandi reported that number ten was at full power and generating electricity, and that the treatment plant equipment had just come online.

"Perfect," Doc said. "Buck will be pleased." Nick handed Doc a paper that showed the planned locations for the first one hundred units, to give to Buck.

"What about the 1950s vintage water treatment plant?" Doc asked.

"The plans are in the folder," Nick said.

"Thanks Nick. What have you got, Brian?" Doc asked.

"We've tried our cure on several different types of radiation-caused cancer," Brian said "with varying degrees of success; but the types that are caused by nuclear fallout appear to be responding well. That's the best we can do without actual patients."

"Great," Doc said, "and I'm glad that we don't have real patients." The real patients are in a parallel world, and they'll be grateful for the cure, he thought.

"Here's a report on our cure, the lab tests, results, and so on," Brian said, handing a thick folder to Doc.

"What about the radiation mitigation treatments?" Doc asked.

"They've been tested in the Pacific and the Nevada desert, with positive results on air, water and soil," Brian said.

"Thanks Brian. Sterling, what about you?" Doc asked.

"The CDC and Ft. Detrick scientists were conducting tests on Smallpox, just as you suspected, and their preliminary results matched the results you questioned. We reported the information to the WHO and they insisted that we shut down the research and destroy the samples."

"Buck agrees," Doc said, "and has directed CDC Director

Lister to carry out the WHO directive immediately. Please follow up with Director Lister and tell me when it's been done."

"What about the Russian plague?" Sterling asked. "Where did you get the cure?"

"Don't you know?" Doc asked. "You discovered it and gave it to Director Lister."

"I did?" Sterling asked. "How and when did I do that?"

"That's the official story," Doc said, "and I'm sticking to it."

"Are you ever going to tell us the truth about it?"

"Maybe, some day. Thanks, Sterling."

☢

Doc reported to Buck what his team members had accomplished.

"Tell me again about the tasks you told your team were your highest priority," Buck said.

"Well, first," Doc began, "we don't want to have to deal with Smallpox, mutated or otherwise, so we needed to stop their research. Second, what we learned about radiation poisoning was from current cancer research. There's a high likelihood that cancer—all cancers—will be defeated in our lifetime, and we may have helped move that forward by finding a cure for radiation poisoning. In addition, our fear of a nuclear accident will be reduced by having a cure. Third, by building nuclear reactors, we've eliminated the need to construct large fossil fuel power plants, which will help reduce greenhouse gases and climate change in the long run; but you may have to do something about the leadership of the Nuclear Regulatory Commission, who won't want to allow the mini-reactors to be used, because they don't comply with current NRC regulations. You may want to remove the entire Commission and place Chandi in charge as Chairperson."

Twin World—Salt Lake City, 5 July

Doc checked his email for a message from Mike. Not finding one, he left one for Mike, telling him he was on his way and what time he expected to be at the hotel, then he caught his prescheduled flight to Salt Lake City. During the flight, he informed JP that the president had made it official. He wanted Doc to take JP to Utah. They had discussed it previously, but now it was confirmed.

"For how long?" JP asked. "I mean, how long would I be in Utah and would I still be employed by the government?"

"Well," Doc said. "I'm planning to retire from government service, so I'm going to stay in Utah. The president said he'll keep you on the payroll for as long as he's in the White House, so you'll keep all your benefits and pay. I'll provide housing, show you all my secrets, and help you find a new job, if required, in the future.

"Sounds good to me," JP said. "Will getting married be a problem?"

"As I told you before, Utah is a great place to raise a family. I'm building a home for you, so I'll make sure it's big enough to raise a family."

"That's wonderful," JP said.

Doc wanted to tell him about the Preserve, but didn't get a chance before the plane started to descend into the Salt Lake City area.

When they arrived at the hotel, Mike was waiting in the hotel lobby, He invited Mike up to his suite. JP preceded them into the suite and checked each room before allowing Doc and Mike to enter. Alone in the bedroom, Doc told Mike that there had been no explosion and that he wanted to save the details for Terry and Lillie. Moments later, Terry opened the gate and stepped through.

☢

"I've told JP that I want him to be here, in Utah, with me, and he agreed," Doc said.

Mike and Terry looked at each other, but neither spoke.

"I would like him to join us here, right now, since there will be no way for me to keep the Preserve that I'm building a secret from him."

Mike looked at Terry again, then nodded subtly. Terry did the same.

"Okay," Mike said.

Doc stood and walked to the bedroom door. He opened it and invited JP into the bedroom.

As JP entered the room, his eyes widened and he reached for his sidearm. Doc reached over and grabbed JP's hand. "There's no need for that, JP," Doc said. "These are my friends . . . You know Mike. Terry is my business partner. But . . . they're from a . . . different place. Let me start from the beginning. Please sit."

JP sat in a chair next to the small hotel table, but his eyes didn't relax. He kept his hands in front of him, as though readying himself for a confrontation with the man in the room who hadn't been there when he'd first checked it out only minutes earlier.

Doc spent the next several minutes trying to give JP a summary of what he had learned over the past few weeks, and asked Mike and Terry to share bits of information as they went along. It was clear, by the expression on his face, that JP was having a difficult time believing what was being said. So, Doc decided that JP needed a demonstration.

"Terry, can you show JP the Gate? Maybe a quick demonstration, too?" Doc asked.

"Of course," Terry replied. "But JP, please be calm. This is likely one of those situations that you have been trained to protect Doc from. It will be strange to you. It will test your patience and your intellect. Please remain calm. There is no danger—to you or

Doc—from what I'm going to show you. Are you ready?"

JP spoke for the first time since entering the room. "Yes," he said.

Terry looked at Mike, then touched some buttons on a keyboard sitting on the dresser next to where Terry was standing. The Gate opened. It's light and energy filled the room briefly, then settled until the ring outlining the Gate barely shimmered.

JP stared, in obviously disbelief. Even seeing it didn't mean believing it.

"It's a gate," Doc said, "to another world, and it's real. I've been through it many times while you stood or sat out there in the living room of this hotel protecting me."

JP looked over at Doc and his eyes lowered, but he still didn't speak.

"No need to be worried," Doc said. "You were still protecting me from everything in *this* world. You had no way to know I was leaving it entirely."

JP looked back up, and for the first time, Doc saw intrigue and interest in his eyes.

"Do you want to try it?" Doc asked.

JP nodded, then stood.

"Come closer," Terry said. "Watch me first." Terry stepped through the Gate, then turned back and spoke to JP again. "I'm still here, as you can see, but if you look behind me, you'll see that the bedroom wall is no longer there. Instead, you can see the lab where the machinery operating the gate sits." Then Terry stepped back through, into the hotel room, and smiled.

"Now it's your turn," Mike said. "Follow me."

Mike stepped through the gate, then held out his hand in a welcoming gesture. JP turned and looked at Doc, then at Terry, then reached his own hand out, tentatively.

"It tickles," JP said, smiling.

"Yes, it doesn't hurt at all," Doc agreed. "Are you ready Terry?"

"Yes," Terry said, "All calibrated."

"Go on through." Doc said.

JP hesitated. "What did he mean by 'all calibrated'?" JP asked.

"We discovered," Doc said, "that the body's nervous system affects the settings of the gate, so we calibrate it to each individual the first time they pass through. Go ahead. Step through."

JP stepped through the Gate, then Doc and Terry followed. JP watched them come through, then looked past them.

"That's really the hotel room through there, isn't it?" JP said.

Doc knew it was a rhetorical question, but answer anyway. "Yes, it is."

"Where are we, again?" JP asked.

"You are now in Logan canyon, east of Logan, Utah, in the Preserve, our underground shelter," Mike replied. "You're also in a parallel world. You're about to meet some of our family and friends, who have spent the last year, living here."

"So, it's like the government bunkers, right?" JP asked.

"Similar, JP." Doc replied. "I'll explain the differences when we have time. But understand that we are no longer in our world, but in a parallel world that is nearly identical."

"I still can't believe it," JP said. "It sounds like science fiction."

"Have you ever known me to lie?" Doc asked.

JP was startled. "No, sir. Never."

"And you will never catch me in a lie. I mean, I would never lie about something this serious. If you will give me the benefit of the doubt, I will show you things that will amaze you. Will you do that for me?"

"I don't get it," JP said, "but I'll listen and try to figure it out."

Several minutes later, seated in the office in the old world, Doc waited for Mike to gather the board, all of whom were anxious to know what had happened. Doc introduced JP to the board, then shared details of the confrontation at the UN. He discussed the gathering of terrorists from around the world, those that were still alive, to Guantanamo Bay for detention. They spoke for a long time about the status of his team's research into radiation treatment, the building and placing of mini reactors, and the excitement caused by the mini plague in Russia, which was already being resolved. Everyone seemed to be excited, except Lillie, who sat quietly. looking down at her hands, folded in her lap. When Doc finished, Becca announced that dinner was ready and everyone left the office except Doc, Lillie and Terry. Mike wanted to stay, but Doc asked him to escort JP to dinner, which he did, reluctantly, probably sensing that something momentous was about to happen.

Doc reached into his pocket and removed a small box. He held it out to Lillie and opened it, revealing a ring with a beautiful, glistening diamond. Then he knelt on one knee in front of her.

"Lillie," he said, "I love you. Will you marry me?"

☢

"You hardly know me," Lillie replied. "We only met a few days ago."

"I feel like I've known you forever, and you know me better than anyone in this world."

"That's probably true," she said, "but you're just going to go away again, back to the life and people you know, to the commitments you've made. Then where will I be?"

"Lillie, I've already told the president that I'm through, but that I'd be available to consult, like Amos did with Greg in this world."

"See. You'll disappear the next time he calls you with some new crisis that he needs you to resolve."

"Lillie, I promise . . ."

"I know you," she said, interrupting him. "You can't resist a challenge. You'll take off and leave me wondering if I'll ever see you again."

"I already have a challenge," he said, "convincing you that I love you and want to spend the rest of my life making you happy."

"But you're telling me you're going to spend your time in the twin world, so you can answer Buck's calls. How can we be together if I'm in this world with my family?"

"We'll work it out," Doc said. "Please Lillie, marry me."

"I'm sorry, Doc, but I need a better commitment than that. Don't talk of love, show me," she said, quoting a line from her favorite play, *My Fair Lady.*

Doc ran his hand through his hair in a move so familiar to Lillie, that she choked up. Doc looked at her, concern etched into the lines of his face. Then he stood and took her in his arms. "I'm sorry, Lillie, I didn't mean to upset you."

"No, Doc," she said, starting to lose her resolve. She did love this man. "You did nothing wrong. I just don't know if I can handle your lifestyle."

Unfortunately, Terry picked that exact moment to try to sneak past them to the door. He didn't make it.

"Terry," Doc said, "does she know what I've done for her world?"

"She does, Amos," Terry answered. "She knows about the radiation treatments we're conducting on the air, soil and water in the valley. She also knows about the treatments we're planning to conduct on the Outcasts, to cure them of radiation poisoning. Unfortunately, she also knows how much you've done for the twin world that makes you indispensable to them, which doesn't help your case with Lillie."

Doc looked back at Lillie, emotion in his face. "I'm sorry Doc," Lillie said, pulling away from him, "I'm just not ready."

"Lillie, I want to take you to the twin world to see some doctors, where you can recover properly."

"No Doc," she said. "I can recover here."

"What do I need to do to convince you?" he asked.

"Come back to me," she said, then stood up and left the room.

☢

"Here are the plans for a modified Observer," Terry told Doc after Lillie had left. "What do you plan to do with them?"

Doc tried to fight back the sting of Lillie walking out on them—on him. There was still time for their relationship. Now he needed to focus on the task before him.

"Once you have the one with the gate built, I want to place it in the Preserve in the twin world. The plans for the one without a gate are going to Terry Stephens in the twin world."

"Very good," Terry said. "He will appreciate that, based on what you gave me to read about what he's done and what he wants to do for medicine in the twin world."

"Is Mike around?" Doc asked.

"I think he's waiting for us outside."

Doc opened the door to find Mike standing just outside the lab. "Mike," he said, picking up a folder off the desk and handing it to Mike. "Here are my notes on artificial intelligence. I'd like you to review them for accuracy, then consider what it would take to program the Observer to observe patients and recognize symptoms of medical problems from appearances and behaviors."

"Seriously?" Mike asked, thumbing through the stack of legal lined paper, a folder filled with notes. "I've read about AI and there doesn't appear to be consensus by researchers on whether or not you can actually build intelligence into a machine."

"What I read," Doc said, "tells me that the problem is that they can't agree on the definition of 'intelligence'. All I want to do is add 'external observations' as one additional factor in our ability to diagnose medical problems."

"I'll see what I can do, Doc."

"Thank you."

☢

Terry looked through the sensor on the cliff. The Outcasts were gathered in front of the cliff, apparently waiting for him.

"Is everyone present?" he asked.

Beth looked up, but Terry knew he couldn't be seen. He hadn't opened the Gate in their direction.

"We're all here," Beth said, "and we've installed the equipment you delivered to the clearing, according to the instructions that Mike left us."

"Do you have any questions?" Terry asked.

"We've assembled it, set it up where Mike suggested and started operating it. We've read the instructions for how to read and report results. We don't have questions yet. Is there anything else?"

"Did you have any trouble dividing up the responsibilities among yourselves? You don't need to worry about one person doing more or less than their share. There will be other projects in the future, so everyone will have something to do."

"This is Justin," Justin said, "and I have a question. It looks like we should start the soil treatment in the clearing above the Preserve, where we've decided to plant a garden. Is that a good idea?"

"That's a great idea," Terry said. "Start the water treatment on the stream and pond. Start the air treatment upwind of the valley, so it cleans the valley air first."

"That's what we're doing," Beth said. "Where did this technology come from, anyway?"

"Some scientists working for Doc in the twin world did the work for us," Terry replied "It's been tested in the South Pacific and the Nevada desert."

"You wanted to know who was going to do what, right?" Beth asked.

"Yes, if you've already installed everything, I just need to know who's going to report readings to me."

"Let's say for now that Ben will gather results and report them," Beth said. "If that becomes a problem, we'll reconsider."

"Great," Terry said. "New subject. We have the scientists' research on radiation treatment for the human body. We want to begin treating all of you for radiation exposure. Let's work out a schedule for bringing each of you into the hospital for a short treatment each day. Let's start tomorrow morning at 9:00, and we'll go fifteen minutes apart. I'll send the gate to the valley every fifteen minutes to pick up one person and return the previous one. Any questions?"

22

Terry Two

Twin World—Salt Lake City, 10 July

Doc entered the exhibit hall in the Salt Palace Convention Center in Salt Lake City in the twin world, while he studied the program of the day's events. He saw that Dr. Terry Stephens was scheduled to speak in room 104 at ten thirty. It was only nine twenty, but he decided to go to room 104 to see if Terry was hovering nearby. From what he knew of the Terry in Amos's world, he thought this Terry would be nervous enough to want to get a lay of the land before he had to stand up in front of people. This event was advertised as a state of the future in medical research and Terry's topic was The Future of Graphite Composites in Medical Protheses.

Sure enough, Terry was sitting on the edge of a table outside the lecture hall, studying his notes. He looked up as Doc approached.

"Aren't you . . . ?" he began, but Doc cut him off before he could finish.

"I am," Doc said, "and you're Terry Stephens, if I'm not mistaken."

"No mistake," Terry said. "What can I do for you?"

"It's not what you can do for me," Doc said. "It's what I'm going to do for you."

"What do you mean?" Terry asked. "The government doesn't owe me anything."

"I'm not here representing the government, Terry. May I call you Terry? I've read so much about you that I feel like I know you personally."

"You can call me anything you want, but what are you talking about?"

"Do you remember when you lived in Logan years ago?" Doc asked.

"Of course. You lived a street over from me, right? Does this have something to do with Logan?"

"Yes and no," Doc said. "In another life, I think we could have become good friends, maybe business partners. We have so many interests in common."

Terry looked confused. Doc wanted to tell him the truth, but the truth might be too difficult for Terry to accept, even as brilliant as he was. Doc had to handle this a different way. They discussed Terry's research and accomplishments, then Doc got serious.

"I've heard from my sources that you hope to find, or invent, a non-intrusive medical diagnostic tool," Doc said. "Is that correct?"

"Yes! I've dreamed about it for years. There's got to be a better way. I just can't figure it out."

"Well, Terry, I have a surprise for you. Consider this a reward for all you've done for the medical profession." Doc reached into his jacket pocket, lifted out a DVD in a slim case, and held it out to Terry.

"What's this?" Terry asked, taking the DVD hesitantly.

"This is what I call the Observer. The design and schematics are there. You just have to build it."

"Wha . . . ?" Terry stammered.

"Don't question the gift. Just accept it. Build the Observer and change the medical world."

"But If you've already invented it . . ." Terry said.

"You won't find any reference to it in any medical journal, and nothing in the patent office. It's yours to keep and do whatever you want with it. Get rich, give it away, I don't care. Just don't mention my name or try to give me credit for any part of it."

"Why? Why are you doing this?"

"I like to think, Terry, that if we'd been partners for the last few years, we'd have invented this together. This is my gift to you as my partner that never was."

Doc held out his hand and Terry shook it, but still looked bewildered. Then Doc walked away without staying for Terry's lecture.

Old World—The Preserve, 10 July

"Lillie, what's wrong?" Becca asked from across the breakfast table. "You were making such good progress. Today, you're acting like you have no energy and no will to go on." Lillie was pushing food around on her plate, but not eating. "Is there something wrong with the food?"

"I'm sorry, Becca. The food's fine. I'm not sleeping well and I have no appetite. Maybe I need a nap."

"You just got out of bed. You don't need a nap. Maybe you need some exercise, something to get your blood pumping."

"Maybe later."

"Maybe you need a boyfriend," Becca said, smiling mischievously "That might get your blood pumping."

"I don't need a boyfriend. Why would you say such a thing? I'm too old, anyway." Lillie knew that Becca had met Doc, and assumed she was referring to him. Her smile gave her away.

Terry, who was sitting quietly next to Becca, eating his breakfast, obviously couldn't resist speaking up. "Doc asked her to marry him a few days ago and she turned him down."

"He what?" Becca asked, staring at Terry, "And you what?" she added, turning her stare on Lillie.

"Nobody else knows," Terry said, looking around to see who might be in hearing range, but they were alone in the room. "Let's keep it to ourselves for now."

"Lillie, he's the best catch in this or any pond," Becca said. "He even warms my blood, and I'm happily married."

Twin World—Salt Lake City, 10 July

Mike got Doc's email late. Doc was already waiting for him and Terry at the hotel, but easily accepted their apology.

"That's fine," Doc said. "I just wanted to know how the radiation remediation equipment is working in the valley." The Outcasts had been measuring and keeping track of the readings twice a day since they'd installed the equipment. Terry had brought the log along with him and opened it now for Doc to see the readings.

"Very good," Doc said. "The measurements for water and soil look like they're following a bell curve, decreasing as there's less radiation to remove, but the air samples look like they're all over the place."

"I plotted the air readings against wind velocity to see if that was a factor," Terry said. "It appears to be. The higher the wind, the higher the readings. It's as if the wind moves the radiation around and brings more into the valley."

"That makes some kind of sense, doesn't it?" Doc asked.

"I suppose," Terry said, "but I don't want to have to clean up the entire western U.S. before we have clean air in the valley again."

"Let's keep watching it to see if it trends down over time," Doc said.

"Agreed," Terry said. "I believe it should. Are you ready to go to the Preserve?"

"I'm not going today," Doc said.

"Why not?" Terry asked.

"You've given me what I wanted."

"What about Lillie?"

"She doesn't want to see me. She's decided that she doesn't want me in her life."

"Baloney!" Terry said. "She's been moping around all week. Can't sleep, can't eat, she misses you something terrible. She just won't admit to herself that that's the problem. She needs you and you need her."

"I need her, alright, but she doesn't think she needs me. I've got a few more things to do here then I'll check back with you."

"Fine," Terry said. "We'll watch for your email. How goes the sale of the patents?"

"Excellent," Doc said. "I've purchased Aspen Velley and have enough coming in to complete the Preserve. Now, I have my eye on land in Logan, a five-acre parcel on the west side."

"Really?" Terry asked. "What do you want all that land for?"

"You met JP. Buck wants me to take JP with me when I leave government service. I'll need a place for him to live. This will be the easiest way to do it. He knows about the Observer, as you know. I'll probably have to let him in on our other secrets. Fortunately, I trust him with my life, so I should be able to trust him to keep a secret."

"Whatever you say. Are you planning to live there too?"

"That depends on Lillie. If I have to live alone, that's as good a place as any. Have you had a chance to review my notes on artificial intelligence, Mike?" Doc asked, quickly changing the subject.

"I have, and they make a lot of sense. The programming looks easy enough. We just have to come up with a table of observable symptoms associated with different medical problems."

"Terry," Doc said, "do you have some medical books that Mike could study that give observable symptoms for different medical problems?"

"I do," Terry said. "You realize that some symptoms are indications of multiple problems, of course. So, the way this would have to work is for the observer to select all the observed symptoms and find the best fit from a catalogue of problems. That's what doctors do anyway."

"Correct," Doc said. "If the Observer can't make a positive diagnosis from its observations, we'll have to conduct additional tests, just like we would if we didn't have the observer."

"This sounds like it could be time consuming, documenting all the symptoms, multiple times, and building a monstrous database for the Observer to select from," Mike said.

"It's a good thing you don't have anything more pressing to do, then," Terry said with a smile, knowing that Mike had lots of other things that he needed or wanted to do, the most important of which was spending time with his wife.

"Take whatever time you need, Mike" Doc said. "This needs to be done right and you're doing us a big favor by helping."

23

Retirement

Twin World—The White House, 11 July

"This is probably the last time we'll meet as a team," Doc told his team members. "Chandi has a full-time job with the NRC and Nick has been approached by the CDC to determine his interest in working for them. The rest of you are free to do whatever you want, since my departure will mean the end of your government service; unless you are approached by someone in the coming days. I suggest that if you don't have a better offer, you consider forming a company to build and install the equipment that we developed as a team. There should be a domestic market, and surely there will be a global market for hazardous waste cleanup at former nuclear test sites. The retro water treatment plants and mini power plants should be in demand in smaller countries and even some larger ones. Use your contacts in the State department and the UN to your advantage. And in fact, I'll be your first customer. I want a complete water treatment plant and a complete power plant, along with instructions for assembly and operation, as soon as you can deliver them to Logan, Utah. You all have my email address, in case you have questions, and I promise I'll respond quickly. Any questions?"

"What are you going to do?" Nick asked.

"I'm retiring to Logan, Utah, to practice medicine and to design medical protheses."

"I don't hear government service in that answer," Brian said.

"Does that mean you're hanging up your presidential advisor tool-belt?"

"It does, Brian," Doc said, "but I'm not giving up negotiating. I have my eye on a cute little lady out there, and it will take all my negotiating skills, and probably all my accumulated wealth, to convince her to marry me. So wish me luck."

Several people in the room chuckled.

"Let me know when you have each of the plants ready to deliver, so I can notify my customer," Doc added.

"So, you're going to make money off this deal, is that it?" Brian asked.

"Actually, I'm considering giving it away for a worthy cause," Doc said, "And, before you ask, no, I'm not giving it to Russia or North Korea in exchange for their cooperation or anything else. It's for a small, private enterprise.

"Keep Chandi close," Doc continued. "As the new head of the NRC, she'll be a valuable ally in your efforts to market to the power and nuclear industries."

"Will we ever see you again, Doc?" one of the women asked.

"Well, if you're ever in Utah, come and visit me. Drop me a note to let me know you're coming, and I'll show you around. Now, unless you have something else, I need to clean out my desk and say good-bye to Buck." And find the terrorist, Smith, he didn't say.

They all said their good-byes, then Doc stood and left the room.

☢

"Hi Jen. Is Buck in?" Doc said.

"He is," the president's secretary said. "He said to let you right in." She pushed a button that opened the door to the Oval Office and Doc entered.

"What's up?" Doc asked.

"Just making notes about our short stay in the bunkers, for my memoirs," Buck said.

"Already planning your retirement, are you?"

"I have to make notes. I'll never remember everything." Buck put down his pen and focused on Doc. "Are you here to give notice? You know I require six months' notice from anyone who quits, don't you?"

"Then consider this my notice from six months ago . . . or fire me." Doc smiled, knowing the arbitrary rules Buck was currently making up wouldn't stick. Even public service employment was "at-will".

"I can't fire you. Your popularity with the public is higher than mine. What will you do out in Utah?"

"I bought land and I plan to practice medicine and design medical devices."

"Yeah. I also heard that you have a girlfriend. True?" Buck asked.

"Well, one of us wants to be a couple. The other still needs some convincing."

"She doesn't stand a chance against your charm, young man. Go get her. What about Smith?"

"My gut tells me he won't be satisfied with his failure in Washington. I think he'll try again, maybe at the CDC."

"I've already asked Tom and Jim to set up protection for the CDC and Wall Street. Anywhere else I should be worried about?"

"I don't know what to tell you, Buck. He could be anywhere, doing anything. It may be best to put out an APB to watch for him."

"Already done," Buck said.

They shook hands, then Buck stood and gave Doc a brotherly

hug When Buck let go, Doc turned abruptly to hide the tears forming in his eyes. He was ready to go, but Buck was as close a friend as he had ever had.

Sitting in a deli a few blocks from the White House an hour later—having paid for their lunch, Doc told Jim and Tom what he suspected about the terrorist, Smith. "I think he's going to try to bomb the CDC," Doc said.

"We have no evidence," Jim said, "so this is one of your gut feelings, isn't it?"

"Good guess, Jim. What can we do about it?"

"Does the FBI want to handle it?" Jim asked Tom, "or should the military take it?"

"I think the FBI can handle it," Tom said, "if you don't mind."

"Just don't let him surprise you . . . or get away." Doc added. "I'm outta here, and I really don't want to have to worry about that guy anymore."

"You can stop worrying right . . ..now!" Jim said. "He's off your plate."

Twin World—Salt Lake City, 12 July

"He's in Salt Lake," Mike said, reading Doc's text to Lillie. Lillie immediately sat up straight, a pleasant look crossing her features. But when Mike told her that Doc probably wouldn't come to the Preserve, her face fell.

"He'd like to go through the gate so he can call Greg." Mike explained.

"Well," Terry said, "we've planned on that, right? Let's get the gate over there and get this over with."

A few minutes later, Mike and Terry stood in Doc's hotel room. Mike held the portable control to the gate. After a brief review of their plan, Doc stepped through the gate into downtown Salt

Lake, in the old world, as he referred to it, and the gate closed behind him.

He had entered the old world on a pile of rubble that was once the Grand America Hotel. Luckily, Mike hadn't dropped him off at the penthouse level of the hotel, or he would have suffered a multi-story fall. Instead, he found himself a few feet above the lobby floor, on a pile of fallen wall and ceiling debris, with the satphone in his hand. Terry had checked the radiation level before letting Doc go through, and gave him a time limit of fifteen minutes before the accumulated radiation would be at a harmful level.

Doc had been to Salt Lake many times over the years and was dismayed to see the once beautiful and majestic city totally in ruins. Looking up State Street, toward the temple grounds and state capital, he could see that almost every building had suffered major structural damage. He found a bench on the sidewalk that wasn't damaged, brushed off the dust and debris, sat, and called Greg.

"Hello Amos," Greg said, answering almost immediately. "What's up?"

"Hi Greg. You asked me to let you know if I ran across a cure for radiation poisoning or a supply of large electrical transformers. I'm here to deliver."

"Right," Greg laughed, clearly thinking Amos was joking. "Why did you really call?"

"I'm serious," Doc said. "You need to get a helicopter out here to pick them up."

"What are you talking about?" Greg asked. "You can't be serious. Where in the world did you get those?"

Doc smiled. He wanted to say, "I had to go to another world." But he didn't dare. Instead, he said "How are the new reactors working?"

"The mini reactors are working well, Amos, and Chandi has

scaled one up to serve a neighborhood of forty-five homes."

"Greg, I really do have something for you, but you need to come and pick it up. A standard military helicopter should be able to lift it, but make sure the crew brings a couple of different types of lifting harnesses."

"What is it?" Greg asked.

"It contains plans for a 1950s technology water treatment and distribution system. It also includes key components that you might not have on hand or be able to locate. It doesn't require microchips and parts are easy to manufacture. Pick it up at the Logan airport. You know where that is, right?" he teased. He thought back on the story Mike and Terry had told him about Greg's failed drops and attempt to capture Amos.

"Right," Greg said quietly,

"There will be three more pick-ups after this one. I'll let you know when they're ready."

"Can you tell me what they are?" Greg asked.

"One will contain prototypes and instructions for building and scaling radiation remediation equipment for soil, water and air. I suggest you deploy the air treatment equipment in the Pacific, on the west coast and your southern border. Then feel free to share the technology with the rest of the world. The soil and water treat-ment equipment can be deployed locally, where needed."

Greg started to speak, but Doc continued without giving him a chance.

"Another package contains plans for a 1950s technology power distribution system to be used with the mini power plant design. It also contains key components that you might not have on hand or be able to locate, like a large transformer."

Greg didn't respond.

"The last package contains plans for a manufacturing plant

for replacement and new components. Each of the packages are addressed to HomeSec, except the radiation remediation equipment, which is addressed to Dr. Robertson."

"I don't know what to say Amos," Greg said. "This is . . .unbelievable."

"A simple 'thank you' would be appropriate."

"Yes, yes. Thank you, Amos. I'm . . . sorry for the way I've acted. I'm sorry for how I've treated you. You're a better man than I am."

"You're welcome, Greg."

Over the next two days, Doc called Greg three more times to notify him of the pickups. Each time, Greg sent a military helicopter to pick up the packages. Greg questioned the source of the technology he was receiving from Doc, and each time, Doc changed the subject. If Doc had his way, Greg would use the technology and equipment to help rebuild the country, then the world. It wasn't purely self-interest, of course; but Doc knew that any improvement Greg could make in the old world would help his new friends. And helping his new friends might help him with Lillie. That was Doc's new dream, and his greatest goal.

24

Another Attack

Twin World—The CDC, 15 July

Saleh was waiting outside the apartment building where he'd been told his contact lived. The contact had already been checked out and cleared, so he didn't have to clear him himself before proceeding.

A few moments later, a young American male exited the apartment building, walking quickly while pushing his arm into the sleeve of a light jacket. Saleh reached across the seat and opened the door. The young man slid into the seat and held out his hand.

"I'm Jackson," he said.

"Samuel," Saleh said, taking the offered hand and shaking it the way he'd been taught in England. "Where's the package?"

Jackson gave him directions to a nearby self-storage facility as they talked quietly. Saleh tried to assess Jackson's frame of mind as they conversed. He had to assess whether Jackson was ready to make the required sacrifice—if not, he was to eliminate Jackson and wear the vest himself.

The explosives were in a suicide vest this time—nonnuclear— and he'd been assured that the vest held enough explosives to breach the protective barriers and release the agents locked deep inside the CDC, but only if he followed his instructions explicitly. They explained which door to use, the path to follow inside the facility, and how long it should take to get there. He knew he might need to use his gun in order to get to his destination, but the knowledge failed to stir any emotion in him. It was important to meet the timetable, and that was his only concern.

When they arrived, Jackson unlocked his storage unit and raised the overhead door. He looked around secretively, likely to make sure there was no one around. As the door opened, Saleh peered into the semi-darkness. Everything was laid out neatly on shelves. Jackson walked over to a shelf holding a bulky backpack, opened the pack, pulled out a vest, holding it up so Saleh could see it from inside the car. The vest was wrapped with sticks of explosives linked together.

"What have you been told about the mission?" Saleh asked after Jackson had climbed back into the car and shut the door.

"I use my power company panel truck to get close to the building. Then I walk in wearing the vest and set off the explosives. You'll tell me where I need to be for maximum impact." He opened a pocket in the backpack and brought out a radio and Bluetooth earpiece. "You get the radio and I get the earpiece. You talk to me all the way in and tell me when it's time."

"Are you prepared to do that?"

"That's what I committed to do."

"But that's not what I asked."

Jackson appeared to think about the question for a few moments before answering.

"I have an okay life. No family, not many friends, a dumb job. I have a girlfriend and we could have a family one day; but yes, I'm ready."

Judging by his experience with sleepers in London, Saleh decided that if Jackson got a little reinforcement to his training, he would be fine. So, Saleh would help him prepare.

"Let's go back to your apartment. We can read the prophet's words and pray."

Jackson nodded, and Saleh put the car in gear.

"Report," Agent Scott said quietly into his headset. As the most senior agent currently in the FBI's Atlanta office, he was in charge of the team tasked with the CDC stakeout. He'd been itching for this type of assignment for years, but had always been beaten out by more senior agents. Right now, however, the most experienced agents were still on their way back from assignments in the capital, helping with the search for the nuclear weapon, or in New York City, looking for the terrorist. If he could wrap this up quickly, it would be a big feather in his cap.

"James, in place," he heard.

"Fredericks, in place. Nothing to report."

"Kearney, in place. All clear."

"Wright, in place. Nothing in sight but a utility truck."

"Okay," Scott said, "report anything, I mean *anything*, that looks unusual."

"Uh . . .Wright here. I took a look at the driver of the utility truck . . ."

He didn't have to specify that he'd used binoculars—it was procedure.

"And?" Scott asked impatiently.

"Maybe it's nothing."

"What *is it?*"

"Well, he's not wearing the usual company shirt. You know, the one with a logo on it?"

"What's he wearing?"

"That's the thing. He's got on a light jacket, but it looks bulky, like he's got something on underneath it."

"Fredericks, get a second set of eyes over there," Scott said as he started to move to the front of the building to see for himself.

"On it," Fredericks said.

"The rest of you, stay put," Scott added, "but keep your eyes open."

"I see him," Fredericks said. "I agree it looks suspicious, and he's headed for the front door of the building."

"Stop him!"

"On it."

"Wait!" Wright said. "His lips are moving. Either he's talking to himself or he has an accomplice."

"He has a Bluetooth earpiece," Fredericks said.

"He must have an accomplice," Scott said. "Stay under cover and look around for possible . . ."

"Got one," Kearney said, interrupting. "My ten o'clock. In a car."

"I see him," James replied. "He's talking into a radio."

"Okay," Scott said, thinking quickly. "Wright, approach the utility guy. Don't let him get inside the building. Kearns and James, close in on the car—without being seen, if possible."

✲

Jackson had pulled into the parking lot, but the parking spaces close to the door had been occupied.

"I'll park in the closest space available," he'd said.

"Not good enough," Saleh had replied. "Park right in front of the door if you have to."

"That will be too suspicious."

"I don't care. You need to get inside quickly."

Jackson had ignored Saleh's instructions and parked in an open stall about six spaces from the front door. He'd casually listened to Saleh's tirade, not always in English, and, he'd suspected, not all complimentary.

"Look, I'm here now and ready to go in. Do you want to argue, or do you want me to get started?"

"Okay, get going," Saleh had said after he'd fumed a bit more.

Jackson had stepped out of the truck, straightened his jacket, and headed for the front door.

"There's someone in the parking lot," Saleh said. "You have to hurry."

"Where?" Jackson asked, looking around.

"Don't stop. Don't look around. Run!"

"Hey, buddy!" a man called as he hurried across the parking lot toward Jackson. "I have a question."

"Don't stop!" Saleh yelled in his ear. Jackson debated taking the earpiece out so he wouldn't have to listen to Saleh. He started moving toward the door again.

"Hey, wait," the man called. He was much closer and was wearing dark sunglasses.

"Shoot him and get inside!" Saleh yelled. Jackson thought Saleh sounded scared, or nervous. The thought crossed Jackson's mind that if he failed in this mission, Al-Qaeda would not let him live. He thought about the gun. If he pulled it out, he could get shot if this guy was some kind of security. If he didn't do what Saleh said, Saleh might shoot him. If he went inside and set off the bomb, he would be dead for sure. In the end, his indecision decided the outcome.

Suddenly, the man was right beside him, his gun pointed at Jackson's chest.

"Keep your hands where I can see them. What are you wearing under your jacket?"

☢

Saleh's whole world was collapsing before his eyes. Jackson had failed him by not following directions, and now he didn't have time to get the explosives and take them inside himself. He could shoot Jackson and the man standing next to him, or he could drive away. Then he realized Jackson knew too much—he had to die. He pulled out his gun and rolled down his window.

"The accomplice just rolled down his window," Kearney said, making Fredericks stop and look in that direction. He caught the reflection of the gun barrel as it pointed out the car window in his direction, so he pushed Jackson one way and dropped the other way, just as bullets started flying. He kept his head down, listening to gunfire from at least three sources. Then a car engine started and tires squealed as a car tried to speed away.

"He's getting away," James said.

"I think I hit him at least once," Kearney added.

"Don't let him get away," Scott said. "Any injuries? What about the utility guy, Fredericks?"

Fredericks had gone to the utility worker as soon as he'd heard the car leave. He still had his gun out and pointed at the downed man, just in case, as he approached. Everyone reported that they were fine. Fredericks was the last to report.

"I'm fine. Just a few scrapes. The utility guy was shot in the head. His pulse is weak. I'm checking to see what he was carrying before I try to stabilize him."

"Good idea," Scott said. "I've called for an ambulance and I'm on my way. James and Kearney, get the car and try to follow the accomplice."

But both James and Kearney were busy. They had run from their hiding places on either side of the getaway car and stood in the middle of the parking lot, side-by-side, legs apart, hands in front of them, holding and firing their handguns at the accelerating car. Each ejected an empty clip, shoved another into their Sig-Sauer 8mm handgun and continued firing into the rear window and tires. The car started to swerve erratically, then jumped a curb and smashed into a power pole, stopping suddenly. Both agents ran to the car, one on either side, and pointed their guns in the windows, before cautiously peering inside.

The driver leaned forward against the steering wheel. He had two bullet holes in the back of his head and another in his right shoulder. The front and back windshields were shattered and there were holes in the dashboard. The driver's handgun was still in his hand, which rested in his lap, and it appeared that he had shot himself in the chest. He wouldn't be taken alive to be interrogated.

25

The Technology

Twin World—Salt Lake City, 15 July

President Greg McCormick, Chandi Robertson, and secretary of Homeland Security, Chuck Dickson called Mike and left a message for Amos to return the call at his earliest convenience. When Doc called them back, the first thing out of Greg's mouth was "Amos, level with us. Where did you get this technology?"

"Most of the technology," Doc said, calmly "can be researched on the internet. The radiation treatment is a spin-off of current cancer research, also available on the internet. As for the radiation remediation technology, I had to be a little creative. However, I can say this with absolute certainty: It works. As for where all the material came from, that's my little secret."

"Come on Amos, where'd you get it?"

"Greg, are you going to look a gift horse in the mouth? I would think that you would have already gotten off the phone by now and started building these facilities."

"Amos," Chandi said, "Do you have a few minutes to answers some questions?"

"Always, Chandi. What do you want to know?" Doc spent an hour answering Chandi's and Chuck's questions about the equipment he'd supplied. Then Doc suggested that they set up domestic manufacturing facilities to duplicate key components. He also suggested that they gather specific technical resources to run the new manufacturing facility and a group to determine what else they might need. He even gave them names of people to locate and hire, including Brian Chalmers, Nicholas James and Sterling Pattersen. Then he told them that if they gave him a list of what else they needed, in the next two weeks, he would try to help.

"I gave you the design for my mini reactor," Doc said to Greg, "and the knowledge to scale it up. Now you have enough parts to equip a manufacturing plant for all the parts you need. Now I'd ask you to spend your energy rebuilding your country and leave my family alone."

"Why are you being so secretive?" Greg asked.

"Not secretive, Greg, just private," Doc replied, but thought maybe Greg could handle the truth, coming from him. *Maybe I'll tell him, sometime,* he thought.

"You'll keep the satphone handy?" Greg asked.

"Of course," Doc replied.

Twin World—The White House, 18 July

Buck left an urgent voice message for Doc, asking him to come to the Oval Office. Assuming the worst, Doc flew to Washington, D.C., and took a cab to the white house. After passing through security, Doc was ushered back to the oval office, finding Buck sitting casually in his favorite chair, as if he hadn't a care in the world.

"Sorry for taking so long, Buck," Doc said, now wondering whether Buck's summons had actually been an urgent request.

"When are you leaving?" Buck asked.

"I was already gone," Doc said. "I was in Utah when I got your message. I've already cleared out my desk. I've sold my flat and my car. I'll catch a plane back to Utah as soon as we're done here."

"I'll miss you, Doc."

"I get the feeling this wasn't an urgent meeting," Doc said. "I flew out here, you know."

"Well, I know that now," Buck replied. "Sorry for that."

"I'll miss you too, Buck, and, as much as I hate to admit it, I'll miss this rat race, too."

"I'm not surprised you feel that way. It kind of grows on you."

"Are you planning to stay for another term?"

"If the people will have me," Buck said.

"What do you mean? You're the most popular president since George Washington."

"Actually; without you, I'll be a nobody. I'll be living off past glory."

"That's not true. You've established friendly relations with all of the important countries of the world. Everyone on my team said they would stay if you needed them. And you've established your credibility."

"And what will you do?"

"Now that I've helped save the world, I'm finally starting the medical research I always wanted to do. That's why I'm spending so much time in Utah."

"Where are you getting the resources to build the large home in Logan, and what are you doing on the property you bought in Logan Canyon?"

"Are you spying on me?" Doc asked.

"Like any good executive would." Buck replied, smiling.

"Hmm. Well, I'm selling patents on my inventions to raise funds," Doc said, "and I have my eye on a gal in Logan whose love I'm trying to buy."

"You haven't had time to invent anything," Buck said.

"Don't tell the patent office," Doc said. "I need the money."

"And who is this lady you're chasing?"

"She's a lot like my Lillie. I can't resist her, but she's not convinced yet."

"Well, she better come around soon, before someone else puts her hooks in you. She'll never find a better catch."

"Thanks for the endorsement. I'll tell her what you said and see if that makes a difference." Doc smiled. He really would miss these conversations.

"Doc," Buck said, "I need you to handle an investigation. There was an outbreak of Smallpox in the Crimea, and Russia accused us of starting it. They've threatened retaliation if we don't drop the nuclear inspections."

"So there *was* a reason you called me here."

"Yes."

"Well we didn't cause a Smallpox outbreak. They let the virus escape from their level 4 containment facility. Their threat is nothing more than blackmail."

"Call it whatever you want, Doc. We have a problem. If we don't resolve it, quickly, it could escalate into a messy confrontation."

Doc was torn. He felt obligated to help Buck, but his budding relationship with Lillie probably wouldn't survive if he left her now and went back to the twin world the first time Buck needed him. She had already accused him of being willing to do just that.

"Buck," Doc said, apologetically, "I've already told my lady that I'm done with the government. If I come back here to help you, I could lose her forever. You'll have to figure this one out without me. Maybe you can call my old team together and have them work on it."

"I really wish you would do this for me," Buck said.

"I wish I could," Doc said. "Maybe I can help without getting personally involved." He was thinking about the cure from Lillie's world that Anne Lister had already given to Russia. He could talk to Anne Lister, but he didn't want to get involved. He would call Sterling Pattersen as soon as he left Buck. Doc stood and turned toward the door.

"So, is that a firm 'no'?" Buck asked, his voice sounding desperate.

"Not a *firm* no, but a probable one. I'll get back to you soon."

"What about Smith?" Buck asked, before Doc could leave.

"Tom can give you the details," Doc said, "but the FBI found and killed him near Atlanta after he tried to bomb the CDC."

"You're sure it was him?"

"Little doubt. In his backpack they found a well-worn copy of the Koran and the car's GPS was set with a map back to the motel where he stayed the night before, the one the FBI said they confirmed with the attendant in the office."

Doc thought Buck wanted to keep him talking, maybe try again to talk him into going back, so he quickly left the Oval office.

"Sterling," Doc said when he had Sterling Pattersen on the phone, "What's the status of the vaccine for Koltsovo?"

"CDC Director Anne Lister said she sent the formulation to the director of VECTOR, but it appears he doesn't know what to do with it. I asked her to have her scientists make up a batch of the vaccine and take it to Russia herself. She balked at the suggestion. She wants to know where I got it. I think she's afraid to be in Russia if there are going to be political problems."

"Tell her you made up the formula. I don't care what you tell her. Just don't let her throw it away. If you tell Buck that I gave it to you, he'll make sure it gets handled correctly and ends up going to the right people."

"Buck just called to tell me he's called a meeting for seven a.m. tomorrow with me, Nick James and Brian Chalmers. Is this what the meeting is about?"

"I'm sure it is. If necessary, ask Buck to talk to Anne and send security with her and her scientists. They should leave as soon as they have a batch made. That's the best way to stop the political stress."

"But she'll want to test the vaccine, I'm sure."

"The only people she has to test it on are in Russia, so she needs to get over there."

"Right. I'll let you know what happens."

"You only need to contact me if there's a problem. Otherwise, I trust you to take care of it."

"Thanks, Doc. I'll do my best."

"I know you will Sterling. Thanks."

Old World—The Preserve, 19 July

Terry called a meeting in the community center and included everyone in the Preserve, and those in the valley by audio and video, which Mike and Chris had mounted on the cliff the previous day wearing hazmat suits. It was a new experience for Chris. He had confided in Lillie that it had made him feel claustrophobic wearing the suit, and made him nauseated; but Lillie knew Chris was excited to do it because it showed that he was being accepted as one of the adults.

"We've been in contact with the twin world," Mike said, "and arranged an exchange of technology, which we're already testing in the valley, with the help of the Outcasts. Preliminary results show that water and soil quality in the valley are improving. The Outcasts should feel comfortable planting in the soil and eating what they grow. It's not too late to plant for this growing season. They're also treating the air, but the improvement is slower, probably because of the air movement in and out of the valley."

"I've never heard of technology that will clean up radiation poisoning," Beth said. "How did we come by this technology?"

"We had some help from scientists in the twin world," Mike admitted. "We exchanged the technology for information about the war. We believed their world was on a parallel path and headed for a similar crisis. They agreed and took steps to avert the crisis, with our help."

"I've been monitoring the equipment you placed in the valley," Ben said. "It's amazing, and it's doing exactly what you said."

Lillie sat quietly at the front of the room. This sounded like something Amos would do, so she expected Doc was responsible; but she was afraid to get her hopes up. She really wanted Doc to come back to her, but she had made it perfectly clear to him that she didn't need him. Maybe he would believe her and go away for real. She hoped not.

"Let me introduce our benefactor," Mike said. "Doc Blund, special advisor to the president of the United States in the twin world." Just then, Doc stepped into the room, followed by JP. Most of those in the preserve had already met him. Lillie had heard some of the kids talking about how they believed he was really Amos, who hadn't died, but had been in hiding, waiting for his full recovery before reappearing.

Rachel ran to him, calling him Dad, and hugged him. "We thought you were dead," she said. He smiled and hugged her back.

"It's good to be back," he said, looking directly at Lillie, who smiled tentatively.

"I need to explain," Doc said.

"Do you want me to?" Terry asked.

"Thanks, Terry, but I think I know enough now to explain." Doc began by explaining Mike's search in the twin world for his dad. He quickly discovered that the Outcasts didn't know much about the twin world, so he backed up and explained the latest discoveries with the Observer.

"Mike found me," he said, "working for the president of the United States. We exchanged stories and discovered that we could help each other by sharing information. Mike and Terry helped the twin world avoid global nuclear war, and I was able to gather the resources to solve your radiation problems—radiation sickness and soil, water and air contamination, which we learned were related to a cancer cure." He answered several questions about the technology and his team of experts who helped him come up with it. Matt, in particular seemed excited about the idea of a cancer cure. Lillie knew that Matt's family had a history of cancer, so she wasn't surprised by his questions or his apparent excitement.

After answering all their questions, Doc introduced JP—real name, Ty Morgan.

"This amazing man is my security guard from the twin world. The president insisted that when I left government service, I take him with me—I guess he thinks I've made a few enemies in the last nine years working for the government. Anyway, I've now told JP all my secrets and he has sworn to protect my life, even at the expense of his own. So he now knows all about the two worlds, the Gate, the Observer and the Preserve."

"Is he going to live in the Preserve?" Rachel asked, eyeing JP.

"I've built a home for him in Logan in the twin world, for him and his family. Yes, Rachel, JP is engaged.

"Now, you're probably wondering about the twin world. How did it come to exist? The best guess Terry, Mike and I have been able to come up with is that when I had to make a career decision nine years ago, there was a division in the time stream. But how it happened, we'll probably never know."

There was suddenly a lot of noise and confusion in the room, everyone wondering at Doc's comment. Lillie watched him carefully as he let the others talk for a few minutes, until they all settled down again to listen.

"Why would that singular event, your career decision, create a split in the timestream and a parallel world?" Chris asked.

"I asked myself the same question. Since I couldn't find any other differences in the twin world—I mean, all the people I know in the government are the same in both worlds—I wondered what made my decision so important. I suspect that my role in the government of the twin world was critical in the solution of several domestic and global problems, not the least of which was stopping nuclear war and reducing the radical terrorist threat. Fate may have known that my presence could make that difference and chose to run with two worlds, to see what difference it would make. Maybe someday, the two worlds will come together again and one of them will wink out of existence. But who knows?

"In the meantime, some of you may be wondering if you exist in the twin world. From my research, I was able to track down all of you, except for the baby born to Emily and Matt and the baby born to Bryce and Sheryl. I believe it's because the families never met each other in the twin world."

Doc explained the explosion in London that took his family and Mike's brave attempt to contact him through his secret service detail. "As Mike said, we exchanged technology, to help the twin world avoid a global war and to help this world clean up its environment."

"What now?" Beth asked. "Do you go back to your world?"

"You didn't call it your world," Ben said. "Why did you call it the twin world, like Mike does?"

"Good questions," Doc said. "Before I explain, I have another surprise for Lillie, Mike, Emily, and Rachel. Will you come with me for a few minutes? The rest of you can be thinking of any other questions you may have. We'll be a few minutes."

The four of them came forward and he led them to the lab, where the gate stood open. He didn't hesitate, but walked through the gate into the valley. The others followed cautiously.

"Is this our world?" Rachal asked.

"Emily," Doc said, "can you tell where we are?"

"We must be in the twin world," she said. "There's no fire damage."

"Correct. What do you notice about it?"

"The trees are missing, like in our world," she said.

"Correct again. What does it mean?" he asked,

"You've built a preserve here, too?" Rachel asked.

"I'm building a Preserve, yes. The earthwork is nearly complete, but the interior is still being worked on, along with a duplicate Gemini gate, a larger medical center for research and radiation treatment, a covered swimming pool, hot tub, steam room, even a larger reservoir. Any questions?"

Lillie watched the faces of her children as they stumbled through understanding what Doc had done, and planned to do in the twin world. She was shocked herself, but tried not to let it show. She was still wary of Doc's presence. She wanted to be with him, but she wasn't convinced he was around to stay.

"What do you mean 'all the earthwork is done'?" Mike asked, finally breaking the silence that had persisted for several seconds.

"Well Mike," Doc began, "Based on the plans you gave me, the crew has cut down the trees, pulled out the stumps, and cleared the brush. Starting at the west end, they've laid out the locations for digging holes, dug many of the holes and trenches, set the steel in concrete, poured concrete over the top and backfilled the dirt. They've completed about seventy-five percent of the underground work and fifty percent of the surface finishing. They're ready to begin revegetation of the surface."

"That's fast work," Mike said.

"We have a large crew," Doc replied. "They're moving so fast, they sometimes have to wait for each other to get out of the way."

"Are you going back to Washington?" Rachel asked.

"What do you want me to do?" he asked.

"Stay with us!" Rachel said without hesitation.

He looked at Emily. "Stay." Emily said after looking at her mother and seeing a reflection of what Lillie could only assume was a tortured look on her own face.

"Stay," Mike said before he could ask.

Doc looked at Lillie, who stirred, but didn't speak immediately.

"What do you want, Lillie?" he asked. "I'll do whatever you say. Stay or go, you say it and it happens, today, permanently. No more waffling."

Lillie looked at each of her children, weighing their wants and needs against her own wishes. In the end, it was no contest. She wanted him, badly. When Amos had died, she was certain there would never be another man in her life, but she had been wrong. Here he was, and he was hers, if she wanted him. All she had to do was say the word. Why was she having so much trouble saying it?

"Stay" she finally said, straitening her shoulders and looking at him boldly.

Doc moved to her quickly and wrapped his arms around her. He pulled her close, but looked her in the eye. Moments later, he kissed her. She threw her arms around his necked and returned the kiss.

"When will it be finished?" Mike asked after a short, fake cough.

"If you want to help," Doc said, "it will be completed much faster. We have the original inventory of the library, the exercise rooms, the bedrooms, kitchen, community center, storage rooms, and so on. I need someone to review and update the list. It doesn't have to be identical, so anyone who wants to help, can."

"I'm in!" Mike said.

Lillie smiled. They were *all* in.

When they returned to the others, there were more questions about where they had gone and what they'd seen. Doc told them he was building a Preserve in the twin world, similar to this one, and that everyone would see it when it was finished. The rest of those in the Preserve, as well as the Outcasts, clamored for their turn to see the valley. He promised that when the radiation was cleaned up some more, he would allow them an extended visit. In the meantime, Doc would deliver more building materials for the Outcasts to work with. He got a commitment from them to continue to operate the equipment in the valley in exchange for being allowed to build homes.

"You still haven't explained why you call it the twin world instead of your world," Ben said, when there was a break in the conversation.

"Thanks for reminding me, Ben. I want you all to understand why I refer to my own world as the twin world instead of calling it my world. I guess, technically, whichever world you're in, the other one is the twin. Anyway, it's because I'm going to ask Lillie to marry me and this will be our primary world." He turned to look at Lillie before continuing. "She turned me down a few days ago, because she worried that I would want to go back to the twin world and she couldn't leave all of you. I've decided to stay in this world and only visit the twin world if, and when, Lillie wants to."

Doc looked at Lillie again, then bent down, kneeling on one

knee. "Will you marry me, Lillie?"

Lillie's eyes teared up, and Doc worried that he might have upset her again. But she soon dropped to her own knees, nodding her head. Then she wrapped her arms around him and sobbed.

Old World—The Preserve, 30 July

"Doc has an announcement," Mike said when everyone was gathered, both inside the community center and outside in the valley. Doc waited for the babble of voices to subside before trying to talk to them.

"Thank you all for gathering," Doc said. "I've been getting lots of complaints that I haven't explained enough about the Preserve in the twin world. So, I'm telling you now that there are a few upgrades over this Preserve. They won't mean a lot to the Outcasts, since you haven't been in this one; but you'll appreciate anyway, that the new Preserve will have a larger, better equipped hospital, where we'll treat the Outcasts for their radiation sickness and handle other medical problems. Matt needs to finish his medical training, so he'll help me and see if we can work on his education. What will make a difference to the Outcasts is a larger reservoir and a way to recycle the water used in the valley. For the rest of you, I've added a swimming pool, hot tub, and saunas, to increase your exercise options, and a few other things. When it's finished, which will be soon, we'll all go there for a vacation of sorts."

Everyone started talking at once, some commenting and others asking questions. Doc held up his hands to stop them.

"Now, I'm open to questions," he said, looking around the community center, "one at a time."

"How long will we be there?" one person asked.

"Will we stay there overnight or go back and forth?" another asked.

"I don't have a swimsuit," Chris said. "Do we go skinny-dip-ping?"

"Would you like that, Chris?" Mike asked. But before Chris could answer, Doc continued. "We'll have answers to all your questions. Right now, I just wanted to let you know what we're doing and see if you had questions or suggestions."

Twin World—The Preserve, 1 September

Doc entered the pool room to find most of the family where he had expected them—in the pool. He'd been to a store in Logan and purchased swimsuits for anyone who wanted or needed one, particularly Chris. He spoke to Rachel, who was closest, lying on a lounge chair beside the pool.

"Rachel, where's your mother?" he asked.

"She just took Emily to the hospital. She's in labor."

"Not your mother, I hope." Doc replied, smiling. He turned and walked away, toward the hospital, leaving Rachel shaking her head in amusement.

☢

"There you are," Lillie said when Doc entered. "I sent Rylee to find you. I see she did." Rylee Parker was their sixteen-year-old, unofficially adopted daughter. She had been with them ever since her parents and brother had died in the auto accident the previous year when they were trying to get to the Preserve.

"Rylee's in the pool," Doc said. "She was standing on the end of the diving board when I saw her last."

Feeling frustrated, Lillie debated saying something about Rylee's infatuation with Zach, Justin's nephew who had joined them from Garden City after the battle for Aspen Valley, but decided that it would be counterproductive. What she really wanted was for Doc to wash up and deliver Emily's baby.

"Emily's in labor, Doc," she said instead. "She needs you."

"Is Matt prepped?" he asked.

"He's getting ready right now."

"I've been coaching him for this. I think I'm going to have him take the lead and I'll assist. It will be good for him. Would that be alright?" he asked.

"I think it would be wonderful," Lillie said. "I'll get my camera and take pictures, so they can remember the day Matt delivered his own baby."

Over the next several hours, they waited, and Emily pushed. Doc was prepared to bail Matt out, if he got in trouble, but there was no need; Matt delivered their baby boy without complications. When he laid the baby on Em's stomach, wrapped in a warm blanket, Em cried.

"My little Matthew," she said. "He's beautiful, Matt. Thank you for this beautiful, baby boy."

"It was my pleasure," he said, his beaming smile obvious behind his surgical mask. "We'll name him *Matthew Amos Green*. Is that okay?"

"Perfect!" she replied, smiling down at the baby who was rooting against her chest.

26

Virus Cure

Twin World—The White House, 20 September

"What's going on in Russia?" Doc asked Buck, after they had exchanged pleasantries for a few minutes. Doc had really wanted to stay out of the conflict in the twin world, but he couldn't help himself. The phone call to Buck wasn't strictly necessary, but he was dying for information.

"Russia is showing propaganda videos of old people and children dying of Smallpox," Buck said, "and telling the world we're to blame. He's telling them that their epidemic is a U.S. plot to kill off their enemies."

"Did you get them the cure that I gave Sterling and asked Anne Lister to take to them?" Doc asked.

"We tried, but they refuse to acknowledge that we would try to help them. They said that it must be a trick, to influence public opinion in our favor."

"I have another idea," Doc said. "I have blood and tissue samples from two babies that have been born immune. Maybe they would like to develop their own vaccine from those samples. They might be convinced to take the samples anonymously and claim that they developed their own solution."

"Well, that's certainly worth a try," Buck said. "The virus has spread all over Russia and into China and other southeast Asian countries. They've got to have significant pressure on them by now to find a solution."

"Anything in Europe or the U.S.?" Doc asked.

"We acted quickly to shut down all air and ocean traffic into the U.S. Europe did the same at our urging, but it might not work, as you can imagine. Sharing all those borders will make it real tough. Other countries followed suit when they saw what was happening; but I don't know how long we can continue that. There are U.S. citizens travelling all over the world and they want to come home to family and jobs."

"Will you send someone out here to get the samples? Then you and your advisors can figure out the best way to approach Russia, maybe through China."

"Why don't you bring the samples and negotiate it for us?" Buck asked, his voice pleading.

"Can't do it, Buck," Doc said. "Sorry."

"Just for a few days?"

"Not even for half a day. I made Lillie a promise." As soon as the words were out of his mouth, he knew it was a mistake.

"Lillie?" Buck asked. "I thought Lillie died. Your girlfriend's name is also Lillie? That's quite a coincidence Doc. What's going on?"

Doc realized there was no way out of an explanation. He'd been considering telling Buck what had happened; now it seemed that he'd let the cat out of the bag. "It's a secret, Buck, but I can see I'll have to tell you eventually. Take care of the virus and we'll talk again in a few days. Then I'll tell you everything. Alright?"

"Alright, Doc. Let me see what I can do, then we'll talk."

Twin World—The Preserve, 20 September
"The Preserve is finished. Have you discussed with everyone where they want to live for the next few weeks?" Doc asked Lillie.

"Everyone wants to stay here, because of the pool, but they

realize we don't have room for all of them."

"Then how will you handle it?" Doc asked. "Draw straws?"

"I won't handle it," Lillie said. "House management is now Emily's responsibility and Mike is the chairman. I told them they could do whatever they wanted, and they threatened to give you and I last choice."

Doc laughed. "Maybe we'll have to stay in Logan," he said.

"Is the house finished? Is that even an option?"

"It's close. Would you like to see it?"

"Of course. You know I want to see how you've decorated it without my help. But what if I run into the other Lillie?"

"Not likely. Remember, I told you she died in London."

"With her children. Yeah. I'd forgotten," Lillie said.

"Let's go take a look.," Doc took her by the hand, leading her to the lab and the Observer. "Before we go," he said, thoughtfully, "let me show you something here." He set the gate for Aspen Valley, above the Preserve in the twin world. When he had it set, they stepped through.

Once in the valley, Doc pointed out what was left of the tree stumps that had been pulled out of the ground to make room for excavation. They had been piled to one side. "That's the last of the cleanup out here," he said. "Revegetation is in progress." The air was cool, and birds chirped loudly in the trees, with summer coming to a close.

"It smells wonderful, Doc," Lillie said as they held hands and strolled across the clearing toward the trees. Her recently improved energy bubbled to the surface, and she swung her arms, as though she had come alive. "Thank you, Doc, for everything."

"You still haven't seen everything," he said, "so maybe you want to reserve judgement."

"Oh?" she asked, wondering what other surprises he had for

her. She was quiet, enjoying the fresh air and loving his company, as they strolled across the valley.

"What are you doing?" she asked suddenly.

"What do you mean?" he asked. "I'm walking through my favorite valley with my favorite lady."

"You're singing!" she said. "What are you singing?"

He was humming *My Endless Love,* recorded by Diana Ross and Lionel Richie in 1981.

"I'm sorry," he said. "I didn't realize I was doing that. I'll stop if you want."

"Oh, no," Lillie said. "You don't have to stop. It just surprised me. Amos used to do that," she said.

"What, sing?" he asked.

"Well, he used to quote lines from his favorite old love songs. I thought it was endearing. It made me feel like he was serenading me. Well, at least always thinking of me."

"So, do you want me to sing or not?" He asked.

"Please continue," she said, turning to face him. She gave him a kiss, and he started humming again.

"Over here," he said as he led her to a spot on the edge of the clearing. He pointed out a foundation for a building about the size of a small house. "This is above your bedroom in the Preserve. It will have an elevator, so you can come up here any time you want and spread out . . . or check the air. I'll show you the plans, but it has a large project room, a luxurious bathroom, large, walk-in closet and everything else you'll need in a she-shed."

"What do you mean, a she-shed?" she asked.

"It's the equivalent of a man-cave. You can do whatever you want in it. You can even keep male servants and no one will know."

"I only need one male servant. Speaking of which, have you thought about a date?" Lillie looked into his eyes.

"It's your decision," Doc reminded her, "We'll get married as soon as you say so"

"Well, I've thought about it a lot. We've waited this long. I'd like to have it on our original wedding date. Would that be alright with you?" she asked.

"Don't want to have to remember two wedding dates, is that it?" he asked, teasing her.

"That's *not* it," she said. "You know I'm sentimental, and Christmas is my favorite time of year."

"Whatever you want," he said. "Christmas Eve, it is. You tell the family and I'll tell the guests." They had already discussed who they would invite. "So, what has Emily decided?"

"About where everyone should stay?" she asked.

Doc nodded.

"Mike helped her figure out how to fit all of the original residents, plus Isaac and Zach—so they can be close to Sydney and Rylee and use the pool—in the new Preserve. The Outcasts will stay in their cabin in the old world—at least for now. Mike will jump them into the hospital each day, for their daily radiation treatment. Ben and the other men want to continue working on the cabin."

"Fine. That leaves the old Preserve basically empty. How are they coming with the cabin?"

"Beth said they have the exterior walls finished and many of the interior walls are up. Mike connected them to our power supply and Bryce is wiring the cabin for lighting with Mike's help. Mike has drawn a plumbing diagram, and is teaching Ben and Justin how to read the diagram, translate it into piping and fittings, and install everything. He said Justin is a natural with blueprints and plumbing. In fact, Justin is asking if he can build another house after they finish this one." Seeing the look on Doc's face she hurried on. "I told him that when the cabin is finished, we can talk about a second one."

"All of that sounds great!" Doc replied. "Ready to go to Logan?"

"Ready," she said.

Doc led her back to the gate and set the Observer for a jump to Logan. He looked through the gate to ensure that no one was watching and took the portable control with him, so they could return when they were finished Then he ushered Lillie through the gate.

They were standing on the sidewalk in front of a long brick rambler. They walked up the flower-lined sidewalk to the front porch. She sat on a porch swing that hung from the ceiling and swung back and forth a couple of times before joining him at the front door. He unlocked the door and pushed it open for her. She hung on his arm, holding tight, and looked into a tiled entry with a full-length mirror on the wall opposite the door. She caught at her reflection and frowned.

"My hair is a mess," she said, lifting her hand to her head. She ran her fingers through her hair, like Amos had done so many times to his own head..

"It's fine," Doc said, pulling her hand back down, "and you're beautiful. Any prettier and you'd make our fancy new home look dull."

"It's beautiful, Doc," she said.

"Can I carry you across the threshold?" he asked.

"Isn't that a tradition for after the wedding?" she asked.

"Do we have to do everything by the book?"

"Yes," she said emphatically. "Everything."

When they entered the living room, he could see JP sitting at the kitchen table, reviewing a stack of papers.

"Hi Lillie," JP said. "How are you feel . . ." He stopped abruptly.

"The question is just fine," Lillie replied. "And I'm doing very well. Thank you."

"That's good to hear. Has everyone gone swimming in the pool?"

"All except you," Doc said. "When do you want to see the new Preserve?"

"Whenever I don't have to be protecting your life."

"Well, you're not doing much of that right now. Why don't you go join the rest of the family? Most of them are there now. And take that lovely lady you dragged out here."

"I don't want to crash the party."

"You're just like family now. I want you to feel like you can go anywhere on my property. You need access so you can pretend you're protecting me."

JP placed both his hands over his heart and cringed. "Ouch, that hurt, Doc."

Lillie smacked Doc on the shoulder thinking JP would take offence at his comment, implying that he wasn't doing his job.

"Sorry, JP," Doc said, pretending to be injured from Lillie's slap. "No insult intended."

"If you're going back there in a few minutes," JP said, "I'll go with you, then. Anna is in the other room. She'd love to go too."

"That works."

27

Re-election

Twin World—The Preserve, 15 December

"Doc, Buck called. He said it wasn't urgent, but asked if you would call him back." Lillie looked at Doc, trying to give him a *do you have to?* kind of look. They were out in the valley in the twin world. Doc was trying to decide if there was anything else he wanted the crew to do before he signed off on the work and paid them.

"I should see what he wants," Doc said. "I can always say 'no'. I have many times lately."

"Can you?" she asked, worried anew that she would lose him to his other life.

"I can, and I will," he said. They returned to the preserve and sat on the couch in Lillie's bedroom. Doc called Buck, with Lillie sitting next to him, their thighs touching, and put the call on speaker.

"I wanted to let you know that we won re-election," Buck said, "by a landslide majority due in part to our ability to stop Al-Qaeda, bring the two major political parties together to solve more of the real problems with the economy, bring world powers to the bargaining table, reduce the threat of nuclear war and solve the energy problem by making nuclear power affordable."

"Congratulations Mr. President!" Doc said, smiling. Lillie knew these two men were on a first-name basis. It was funny hearing Doc speak to the president that way, even though that's exactly how she would have said it.

"Did you keep Art as your running mate?" Doc asked. Lillie hadn't heard his name come up in reference to the twin world. Art Klemp had died of Smallpox in the old world, but was apparently alive and kicking in the twin world.

"You know better than that, Doc," Buck said. "Luckily, he isn't my vice-president, or even in my cabinet, so I don't have to look at his sour face all the time. Jim Seymour agreed, reluctantly, to be on the ballot with me. When I dropped a few hints about his role in the terrorist cleanup, our approval rating climbed almost ten percentage points."

"Great. He's a good man and will serve the people well," Doc said. "So, where is Art?"

"He's still a senator, from California. I don't know how they put up with him; but they must not know him the way we do. You might be interested to know what's been happening since you left."

"Of course, I am."

"Well, I appointed Dr. Chandra Robertson as Chairperson of the NRC. I had to fire the entire commission, just as you said, and Chandi is doing a fabulous job as chairperson, replacing the old guard with younger, more dynamic engineers. And she's building mini nuclear reactors as fast as she can get the materials."

"A wise decision, Buck. She'll do well," Doc said.

"She's already revolutionizing the power industry. Do you remember asking me if I knew Dr. Terry Stephens?"

"Did I? I don't remember."

"Well, I hadn't heard of him, but because you asked, I looked him up. It seems to me quite a coincidence that he has been nominated for a Nobel Peace Prize in medicine because of his work on non-intrusive medical diagnostics. Do you know anything about that?"

"Not a thing," Doc said. Lillie was grateful they weren't on a smartphone, looking at each other. She was sure there was no way Doc could have kept that secret if Buck was looking him in the eyes.

"I asked," Buck said, "because in his nomination acceptance speech, he said that your work had influenced him. Are you sure you don't know anything about that?"

"I'm sure, Buck." Doc said.

"Do you know what your team of scientists has done?"

"I know what I suggested to them."

"Then, you probably won't be surprised to learn that they've gone into business together and have landed several lucrative government contracts around the world to remediate radioactive hazardous waste sites."

"You're right, Buck. No surprise there."

"You know, Doc, the next election is only four years away. If we start floating your name now, there's better than even odds that you could be the next president."

"No thanks," Doc said emphatically. "You know how I dislike politics. That's the farthest thing from my mind right now. I'm keeping a low profile, working at becoming a decent doctor, and playing at my hobby. I don't want to be bothered."

"How are you enjoying retirement, really?"

"Loving it!" Doc looked over at Lillie and smiled.

"Well," Buck continued, "I'm giving you all the credit for the things that are now working. Everyone is asking where you are. You've got to come back to Washington."

"Sorry Buck. Not interested."

"Doc, there's something you're not telling me. We've been friends for a lifetime and I feel like you're keeping secrets. I know you didn't just happen to know how to cure that mutated Smallpox. Where did you get it? And what's the coincidence that your new girlfriend is named Lillie? Come on, Doc, tell me what's really going on."

☢

Doc debated telling Buck what had happened. The questions were good. The president wasn't an idiot.

Doc wasn't worried about whether Buck would believe him. Buck would believe anything he said, regardless of how crazy his story sounded. It was more that he couldn't stop at telling him just a little bit. Asking him to believe everything seemed like too much to ask. But too many coincidences led to one big secret. He decided the time had come to tell Buck.

He looked at Lillie, trying to convey both his understanding of the importance of the secrets and his need to tell the president.

"Go ahead," she said.

Doc mouthed a 'thank you', then spoke again. "Buck, you're not going to believe this."

28

Two Worlds

Old World—Logan, Utah, 24 December

The military cargo plane landed at the Logan, Utah airport and taxied to the end of the runway, stopping next to the small terminal building. Doc had been concerned about the radiation level in Logan, so he had been sending the Outcasts to treat the air to reduce the contamination. He had sent them to the airport that morning to check the equipment and had reported to Greg that it was safe to land.

The tail ramp lowered and two stretch limousines exited, followed by four SUVs, all driven by military personnel. Two of the SUVs and their occupants, four fully-armed Special Forces soldiers in each, pulled out of the line and left immediately for the Logan Utah Tabernacle to check security before the president arrived. The plane turned around and took off almost immediately.

A few minutes later, Air Force one—the president's personal airplane—landed. President Gregory McCormick exited the plane, surrounded by his six-man security detail. His family, key advisors and Dr. Chandra Robertson followed.

Technically, the Logan airport was only a Class G, uncontrolled airport, but with a nine-thousand-foot runway, it was long enough for the 747 to land, which only required about seventy-five hundred feet. The pilots had no trouble landing once they confirmed that the sky surrounding the airport was free of private aircraft for their approach.

Everyone piled into the limousines and the string of cars drove to the Logan Utah Tabernacle on Main Street. Everyone was ushered quickly into the building and down to the basement. Doc Blund, who the president would think was Amos, was there waiting.

"Greg," Doc said, "Thank you for coming."

"My pleasure, Amos," the president said. "I can't wait to see what you've been hiding from me."

Doc shook hands with the others as they found seats in the small room. Immediately after his conversation with Buck, the president in the twin world, he had called Greg, president in the old world, and invited him and his entourage to the wedding.

"Liz, Jen, Jim, Tom, Cy, Eric, and you must be Chandi," he said to the young, pleasant-looking woman in professional dress.

"It's a pleasure to meet you in person, Amos," Dr. Chandra Robertson said. "Greg said you have a few surprises for us."

"That I do," Doc said. Buck and his crew had been invited to the wedding too, and that crew included Dr. Robertson from the twin world. The surprises waiting for *all* of them were certain to be startling. "I fear that you'll all think I'm crazy when you hear what they are; but seeing is believing, so hopefully, you'll all be satisfied before the end of the day. Please have a seat."

They all sat and Doc stood in front of them, trying to keep from appearing nervous. He was pretending to be another man—Amos—but if anyone could pull it off, it was Doc. He knew that, but he still fought the urge to fidget as he spoke to the small group.

"Ten years ago," Doc said seriously, "I was faced with the most difficult decision of my life; stay with medicine and medical research, or work for the government on a Senate science committee for Senator Gregory 'Buck' McCormick."

"I haven't been called Buck since college," Greg said, interrupting Doc.

"Bear with me, Greg," Doc said. "Apparently, fate knew that my decision would impact the future of the United States. I believe that is why there was a split in the river of time, and parallel worlds were created."

Nobody spoke, but everyone stared at Doc as though he were crazy—as though they couldn't believe that he had just said that.

"You're right," Jim Seymour, the president's secretary of Defense said a few moments later. "I think you're crazy."

"Thanks, Jim," Doc said with a smile at Jim, then continued.

"Believe me or not, there are at least two worlds coinciding on the same plane, with different timelines. In the other world—Buck McCormick's world, what *we* call the twin world—my family died in a terrorist bombing in London on New Year's Eve. Then I helped Buck stop the terrorist threat that caused their deaths."

"*You* did it, Amos?" Greg asked. "How did you do that? If there are two worlds, *you* live in this one."

"Just a moment Greg," Doc said. "I'll get to that. In this world, what we call *the old world*, Greg, I stayed with medicine, invented medical devices, then built a Preserve in Logan Canyon and stocked it with enough supplies and power to survive for thirty to fifty years. With the help of my good partner, Terry Stephens, I built a machine that can diagnose medical problems as well as open a portal in space between the two worlds."

"Uh huh," Greg said, obviously not buying the story. Doc was surprised that nobody else was speaking. Sure, they were looking at him like he was crazy, but at least they were listening.

"Hang in there," Doc said. "Greg, this should explain some of the questions you've had about events in your world."

"Hold on," Greg said, "you did it again. You said *your* world, as though you weren't in it; but you're right here."

"I know. Confusing. But we'll get there. In your world, following the war, there was a battle for our little valley in Logan Canyon, and Amos Blund, my counterpart in your world, was killed."

"Ha, that's it!" Greg said. "You're saying, you're not Amos. So, who are you?"

"For the last nine years, I've gone by the name *Doc Blund*, first as a member of Buck McCormick's Senate committee, then as a special advisor to the president, Buck McCormick. After Amos's death, his son, Mike, and his partner, Terry Stephens, devised a plan to contact me. They used technology developed by Amos Blund called the Gemini Gate. They came to Buck's world—*my* world. We spoke, and exchanged information. And believe me, whatever you're feeling about this story, I felt too. Of course, I had the opportunity to see something that I'm going to show you later. But Buck's world was on a course toward global thermonuclear war which your world had just experienced. Mike and Terry found me and gave me all the information I needed to help Buck avert nuclear war. In exchange. I gave them research on how to cure radiation sickness and how to clean up the environment."

"Mini nuclear reactors?" Greg asked.

"Yes," Doc said, "and water treatment plant design, electric substation design, and other things."

"This is beginning to make some sense," Greg said.

Jim looked at him, his eyebrows raised.

"It does, Jim. It explains a lot of things."

Jim didn't speak. None of them had spoken. It made Doc nervous, particularly since he'd never met any of them. They were the same names as those in his own world—the twin world—but they weren't the same people.

"Thanks for understanding, Greg." Doc said. "And as for the rest of you, I know you're having a hard time believing me. I'm telling you that I'm a person you've never met, from a world you've never known. That's a lot to take in. But in a few minutes, Terry will be here to escort all of you to our Preserve in Aspen Valley, using the Gemini Gate. Terry will give you a tour while you wait for the rest of our guests. And I should probably tell you who they are, so no one has a heart attack."

There were a few snickers, but they came from people who were obviously skeptical of all of this.

"We've invited President Buck McCormick and his advisors from the twin world to join us for this special occasion. His advisors are *you*, from a different world!"

Finally, there was commotion. Many of the people gasped or made other audible sounds. Doc knew he had them now. Whether they wanted to believe him or not, they clearly hadn't denied the story outright. They were now facing the prospect of facing themselves.

Doc let the commotion die down some before continuing, with a wide grin. "When you see someone who looks just like you, keep in mind that the person you're looking at has a totally different memory than you have, of the last ten years, and will not recognize you, other than from your appearance."

Suddenly, a small circle appeared in the air a few feet from Doc, which grew to just over six feet in diameter. In the middle of the circle stood Terry Stephens, holding what looked like a computer keyboard in his hands.

Liz McCormick fell over backward in her chair, while Chandi tried to grab her to hold her up. Jim and Tom stood simultaneously and knocked into each other in their surprise. Cy looked as though he was going to faint. And Doc just stood there, smiling.

"Hello ladies and gentlemen," Terry said. "Doc, if you're finished, I'll show these folks to the Preserve."

"Ready, Terry," Doc said. Then he held his hands out to invite his guests to follow Terry through a hole in the air.

"Great," Terry said, then looked at the guests. "If you will please take turns placing an arm through this opening, I will calibrate the gate to your nervous system, then you can step through into the community center of the Preserve. Who wants to go first?"

Nobody spoke. Greg helped lift his wife off the floor. Jim brushed off his pants, clearly trying to look nonplussed. But nobody moved toward the Gate.

"Come on folks," Doc said. "Nothing to worry about. And maybe now you believe me?" He raised his voice at the end as though he were asking a question.

"What . . . what is this?" Greg asked. "Is this what you called the Gemini Gate?"

"Exactly," Doc said. "It is a gate between your world and Buck's world—a hole in the fabric of space." Doc waited for a response, but still nobody moved.

"Chandi," Doc said, "do you trust me?"

"Absolutely," she said quietly. "Well, I trust Amos—I guess, you—so . . ." Her voice trailed off, but she stepped to the gate, thrusting her arm through in a brave display.

"All set," Terry said after a moment, "step through. It will tingle a bit, but won't hurt you."

Chandi took a step forward and turned to the left, disappearing from view. "It tingled," she said from the other side of the gate.

The others looked at each other, at Terry, at Doc, at Chandi on the other side of an apparent rip in the fabric of space. Doc was amused by their confusion.

"Come on, who's next?" Terry asked. The men didn't appear any less nervous about stepping into the unknown, Doc thought, but they apparently weren't going to be shown up by a young woman.

Jim, Greg, and Tom all hurried to be next, bumping into each other as they approached the hole. Jim and Tom giggled nervously, then stepped aside to allow the president to go next.

Eventually, they had all gone through. Doc followed. When he stepped into the twin world, he grasped Greg's arm and turned him around.

"You know my family," he said, pointing to Lillie, Mike, Emily, and Rachel, standing off to one side. Lillie came right over and gave Greg, then his wife, Liz, a hug.

"Good to see you again, Lillie," Liz said. "You are the *real* Lillie, aren't you?"

Lillie laughed. "Yes, I'm the Lillie you know so well. Welcome to my home," she said. "It's good to see you again, too."

"Have you really been living underground for a year now, in this Preserve?" Liz asked.

"We're used to it now," Lillie said. "It feels quite natural. Let me show you around."

Terry got everyone's attention, then suggested that anyone who wanted to go on Lillie's tour should follow her, and the rest should follow him, then he started walking toward the airlock. Lillie headed for the kitchen and dining area. Doc took the portable gate control and opened the gate to his estate in the twin world, then stepped through into his living room, taking the control with him.

Twin World—Logan, Utah, 24 December

A similar scene took place at the Logan, Utah airport in the twin world, at about midday, the limousines however, took President Buck McCormick and his entourage to Doc's estate on the west side of Logan. The soldiers cleared Doc's home, then Buck's security detail escorted him, his family, his advisors, Doc's former team and supreme court justice Andi Reynolds into the living room, where Doc waited and greeted each one warmly. "Buck, Liz, Jen, Jim, Tom, Chuck, Cy, Eric, Judge Reynolds." He greeted each of his former team leaders with a hug. "Brian, Nick, Sterling."

"Buck," Doc said, finally, "Thank you for coming."

"I wouldn't have missed it, Doc," the president said. "Now I can find out what's so secret."

"Your wait is over," Doc said. "But I fear that you'll all think I'm crazy when you hear what I've been doing. Hopefully, you'll all be satisfied before the end of the day. Please have a seat."

They all sat and Doc stood in front of them. He relayed the story almost as he had with Greg and the others, except from the opposite perspective. He shared details about Amos' death in the old world, and was beginning to tell them of the technology exchange between the worlds when Buck stopped him.

"I remember," Buck said. "I really wondered where you'd disappeared to. It wasn't like you. That's when things started getting strange."

"Right, strange is an understatement. For me, I saw and experienced, for the first time, everything I've been talking about. But for me, at least I got to *see* it. You're just *hearing* about it. But would you like to see the Gate? The old world?"

"Oh man," Buck said. "Would I? I can't stand it anymore. Show us!"

Others nodded and shared similar sentiments.

"Thanks for understanding, Buck." Doc said. "In a few minutes, I'm going to escort all of you to our Preserve in Aspen Valley; not Amos's original Preserve, but a copy that I've had built in the same place in your world."

"Yes!" Chandra Robertson said, standing, obviously excited. "Sorry, I'll sit back down."

Doc laughed. "No need to be sorry. When you see all of this, you will all be excited. It's incredible! But, I need to tell you who else is here so no one has a heart attack."

Buck was the last to go through the gate. Doc placed a hand on his arm to stop him.

"You know that my family died in London," Doc said, lowering his eyes.

Buck grasped him by the shoulder and squeezed. "I do. I'm sorry, again, for your loss."

Doc raised his head, then nodded sideways at Lillie, Mike, Emily, and Rachel. "This is my new family . . . almost." Lillie came right over and gave Buck a hug. She had just greeted Liz, who now stood beside her.

"Good to meet you, Lillie," Buck said, seeming awkward with the greeting.

"Welcome to my home," Lillie said. "Thank you for coming."

"And you really live underground, in this Preserve?" Liz asked.

"Actually, we've been living in the one in the other world: but yes, we do, and we're pretty much used to it after a year. Would you like a tour?"

"I'd love that," Liz said.

Doc clapped his hands to get everyone's attention. "This is the community center of the Preserve," he said. "Those of you who would like a tour of the rest of the house can follow Lillie. She'll bring you back here when you're finished."

Half an hour later, Lillie walked back into the community center, followed by Buck's entourage. Doc took the portable control with him, and, walked everyone out through the secondary door into the valley.

"If you would all take a seat, we're about ready to begin," he said. "Dinner will be served after the ceremony, and there will be plenty of time to mingle and continue your tour if you want to see more. Thank you."

Then Doc stepped back and watched the group. They believed now, just as Greg's group had. Seeing was believing, after all.

☢

Doc watched as people as they studied the Valley. The trees surrounding the clearing were decorated festively in a rainbow of colors. Tables and chairs filled the clearing, with place settings set at each of the tables. The ground was covered with artificial turf to cover the snow on the ground, and portable heaters had been set up next to each table.

The guests began filling the chairs set up at one side of the clearing, and Doc took Judge Reynolds aside to explain the plan to her. Lillie had mentioned that she had met Justice Reynolds at a White House party with Amos, years earlier. Lillie came to love the Judge, in just a short amount of time. When Doc suggested that Justice Reynolds might be able to perform their wedding ceremony, Lillie was thrilled. It turned out that Justice Reynolds was thrilled as well. Now, here in the Valley, Justice Reynolds couldn't stop smiling.

Minutes later, when the gate opened and Terry led Greg and the others from Greg's world into the valley, there was a loud commotion as people recognized themselves and realized what Doc had meant. Doc had asked them to refrain from socializing until after the ceremony and Terry had done the same. So far, everyone seemed content to obey their wishes. But Doc knew it wouldn't last long. They had to keep things moving.

As the talking died down and people took their seats, quiet music began playing from speakers mounted in the trees. A few minutes later, Lillie appeared at the back of the clearing, having just stepped out of her she-shed, dressed in an ankle-length, slender, white dress, carrying a bouquet of flowers. Faces beamed with understanding. It was a wedding! Doc had kept that a secret, but it wasn't a secret any longer.

Lillie took Terry's arm and they walked up the isle between the tables and chairs, amid oohs and aahs. Doc stood at the front of the crowd, standing sideways, waiting, dressed in his black tuxedo. Judge Reynolds smiled as Terry and Lillie began the slow walk toward her.

Doc watched, in awe, as his soon-to-be bride stopped across from him, facing him at an angle while she looked at the Judge. She was beautiful!

"Justice Reynolds, I'd like to say something before you begin," Doc said.

"It's your party," Judge Reynolds said, motioning for Doc to proceed.

"Those of you gathered here today," Doc said, facing the group, "are our dearest friends. We've invited you here to share in both the creation of a new family, and the forming of a new alliance between our two worlds. Lillie Blund, Amos's widow, has agreed to marry me and I'll consider myself to be the luckiest man in the world until I pass away, and even after that.

"You have already experienced travel between the two worlds, using the newest mode of transportation, the Gemini Gate, the door between twin worlds. No one else in either world knows about this new technology. I don't intend to tell anyone and would appreciate each of you promising to not share what you have learned today.

"We want you all to make yourselves at home here. You are welcome to visit anytime and visit any portion of the preserve."

"Like the pool?" Chandi asked, uncharacteristically loud, from the back of the group.

"Absolutely, Chandi. Anytime," Doc said, "You realize, however, that you need to give us advance notice, so we are in the correct world to receive you." There were a few chuckles and Doc turned back to face judge Reynolds.

"We're ready to start, your Honor."

The ceremony was concluded quickly and the bride and groom kissed. Then they walked back down the aisle, hand-in-hand, amid cheers and a shower of wheat, rather than rice, from those of the family who knew the day was going to hold a wedding. The wheat would sprout and become the first of many grain crops in the valley,

Lillie thought about how grateful she was for all these people and how they had made her life better. Later, she threw her bouquet. Her daughter, Rachel caught it, then headed back to her seat next to Chris Stephens, who congratulated her and gave her a kiss.

Becca, with the help of family members and the Outcasts, who had been seated behind the other guests, brought armloads of food to the tables, through the gate, and filled the tables. All of the guests, including the security teams, moved to the tables and helped themselves to a buffet dinner.

Doc leaned over and spoke to Lillie, as they stood next to a table nearest the cliff walls of the Preserve. "It's not surprising where these people have chosen to sit."

Lillie studied the tables and saw that each person had elected to sit next to or across the table from their counterpart from another world. She was certain they would spend the evening comparing life stories, and pinpointing where each life had divided into two.

Later, as Lillie and Doc were finishing their meal, Buck and Greg walked together toward their table.

"This has been wonderful," Greg said.

"My sentiments exactly," Buck added.

"Thank you, gentlemen," Doc replied, smiling. Then he bent over and looked down the table. "Hey Mike, do you have it?"

"Yeah," Mike said, standing. He walked over to Doc and placed something in his hand. Lillie watched as Doc held the object out to Buck.

"What's this?" Buck asked.

"Is that my satphone?" Greg asked at the same time.

"Sure is," Doc replied. "Buck, Greg and Amos used this to speak to each other in the old world. Amos didn't join Greg's team, as you've heard, but he was still instrumental in helping save lives, or so I'm told."

"Indeed, he was," Greg said.

"Well, we haven't been able to modify it to call between the two worlds. But we've done the next best thing. We've set up an automatic relay through the Gate to the phone that Greg has. That way, you two will be able to speak to each other."

"That's amazing," Buck said.

Greg nodded his obvious agreement.

"But if you give the phone to me," Buck complained, "Greg won't be able to contact you."

"If he has you," Doc told Buck, "he won't need me. You two are smart enough to work out your problems and let me go on my honeymoon."

Lillie laughed. Then the others who had been listening in joined her.

After the ceremony, everyone was given the opportunity to tour the Preserve again, swim in the pool or visit with each other in the warmth of the community center. Hours later, when it was dark and cold, Terry shuttled the people from the two worlds back through the Gate to transportation waiting for them. It was time to go home. As the last of the guests departed, Lillie smiled again. She had married a wonderful man. The two worlds had joined. Amos never would have predicted this outcome, but she hoped he was smiling from Heaven.

Epilogue

Lillie stood next to the black stretch limousine. Her children—Michael, Emily and Rachel—were close by, with hundreds of other people surrounding them. They were on the Embarcadero in London, celebrating New Year's Eve. Doc hadn't been able to join them, and it was a bit depressing to be spending the holiday without her husband, but that was the life of a politician's wife.

Suddenly, there was a blinding flash of light and the next moment, she was . . . somewhere else. She stood next to a shining turnstile, a man in a white, starched uniform standing on the other side. He was holding out a slip of paper to her. Michael, Emily and Rachel were right behind her, forming a line, but none of them were paying any attention to her at the moment.

All around her, people came from every direction, out of a haze, which her eyes couldn't penetrate, and stood in line behind them. She recognized two of her security guards and others that she, somehow, knew were from the Embarcadero. She felt no anxiety, fear, or confusion. She was at peace with the situation, even though something incredible, and perhaps terrible, had just occurred.

Lillie stepped through the turnstile and took the paper. It was a ticket. Looking past the uniformed man, she saw a red train that extended as far as she could see in both directions—perhaps miles long. She knew the ticket was for the train. She took a few tentative steps forward to a door, which was locked. There were no markings on or next to the door, but she knew this was her berth. She remembered the ticket and raised it to her face to read it, but it was now a silver key. She slipped the key into the lock on the door. It entered effortlessly and turned easily. She opened the door and looked inside. A lavishly-decorated mini suite, complete with a small dining table, adorned the room. The table was laid out with expensive, white plates, silver cutlery and crystal glasses. There were serving trays piled high with steaming dishes and food. She didn't immediately recognize the dishes, but the smells were overpowering and wonderful. There was a bright blue couch on one side of the berth, against the wall, and a rich leather chair against a window.

Before taking a step to enter the train, Lillie looked down the train and saw that Michael, Emily and Rachel each stood before doors similar to hers, looking into berths that she knew were just like hers. Other people stood at other doors up and down the train.

She knew that she had died, but felt no anxiety or fear. She felt . . . at peace.

She took a step into the room, was tempted to sit and rest. Instead, she walked to a center aisle and looked to her left, the direction she'd last seen her children. She saw that her children had done the same. They came to her and they all hugged. It was reassuring.

A man approached, down the aisle from the right. He looked familiar.

"Amos?" she asked as he got close; she didn't know why she'd asked. He had shoulder-length hair and roguish features, as though he spent a lot of time outdoors, instead of in government meetings, like the 'Doc' she had married and spent most of her life with.

He turned and looked at her. He smiled, making him look just like her husband. "Lillie?" he asked. He moved toward her, holding out his hands to her.

She needed to sit down. Who was this man who looked and smiled just like her Amos? She sat on the beautiful couch in her berth. Her thoughts paused as the man ran a hand through his hair in a manner familiar to her from years of living with Doc. She choked up at the sight.

Lillie patted the seat next to her and Amos sat. There was no threat here, only peace.

"Where's my Amos," she asked casually, wondering if this man would know her husband.

"He's with my Lillie," he said. "They have some time before they'll join us. I noticed that your children came with you. They're good kids, just like mine."

"Yes, they are," she replied.

Preview:

Heritage of Aspen Valley

(Book 6 of the Gemini Gate series)

David Murdock breathed a sigh of relief as the ribbon cutting ceremony ended. He hadn't been asked to make a speech, and his tense body finally relaxed. Technically, the upper Logan Canyon project was his, but Evans, his supervisor, and his superiors in the highway department were taking all of the credit and the bows for its successful completion, on time and under budget. The parking lot and all of the folding chairs that had been set up in First Dam Park at the mouth of Logan Canyon had been filled by state, county and local politicians and reporters, which bothered him only because his team of engineers, who had helped him design the road and manage the project, had had to sit on the grassy, sloping verge of the parking lot.

David loved Logan Canyon; it was his favorite place to hike, camp and fish. He had been lobbying for this project ever since he'd graduated from the University of Utah and gone to work for the highway department, ten years earlier. With the mushrooming population around Bear Lake, the highway from Logan to Garden City had become overstressed, unable to handle the traffic load. That had been the case ten years ago. The population growth in Utah had been high for decades, especially along the

Wasatch Front, and had spread out from there. Highway 89 had been a lower priority than the interstates and other highways; but its time had finally come.

When the request for proposals had gone out from the state, several large design firms and construction contractors had submitted proposals. David's proposal was the only unsolicited one and it was rejected out-of-hand by Evans because, As Evans said, there was a conflict of interest, since David worked for the department that would manage the construction. But David believed Evans felt threatened by his potential for promotion, above Evans, if the opportunity presented itself.

David had a good eye for design and trusted his design team to help him put together the perfect proposal for the new road; but Evans's rejection meant that they would not even be given the chance to prepare their proposal. As it turned out, the newly elected governor was a family friend of Ty Davis, one of David's team members; and before David knew it, Ty had asked the governor whether Evans had the right to reject their proposal.

The governor spoke to the head of the state highway department, two levels above Evans, who passed the word down that David's proposal would be accepted, because they wanted the best design for the road and didn't want to restrict where it came from. Evans had reluctantly notified David of the department's decision, with a warning that none of the proposal preparation could be performed on department computers or during normal work hours. So, the entire proposal was drafted in the basement computer lab of Ty Davis's parents' home, where Ty designed virtual reality computer games in his spare time. Ty, who had a lucrative side business in VR games, had agreed to delay the release of his latest invention while the design team worked on the road proposal in evening and weekend sessions.

The proposals were submitted and judged by an independent team of industry representatives and university professors appointed by the lieutenant governor. David's team design won, which surprised Evan's because of all the roadblocks he'd placed in David's path, and the project moved forward to the solicitation for road construction bids. David's team had no construction resources, so they didn't bid, but they were given responsibility to manage the project. That had suited David just fine; after all, he was a professional project manager and this was his design.

The construction had been completed on time and under budget, which was rare for a highway project, and David credited his team for their close supervision of the contractors and his innovative ideas for cutting costs without compromising quality or integrity. His team members had spent so much time in the canyon that they knew where all the good fishing holes were and where the wildlife roamed.

Now that the speeches were finished and the ribbon across the highway was cut, the dignitaries that wanted to be seen as supporting a successful project piled into their cars and headed up the canyon to the starting point of the project, near Cottonwood Canyon, the upper twenty-one miles of highway 89 ending at the Bear Lake Highway in Garden City.

David had thought that with this project completed, Evans would find someone else to pick on, but it was not to be. Evans had already refocused on another of David's projects and wanted to micro-manage it like he had tried with the Upper Logan Canyon project.

David clicked the remote to unlock his red Camaro convertible, lowered the top and fired up his new ride. The car had been his gift to himself for a successful project, paid for from his bonus, and he loved it. He loved the smooth ride and the horsepower under the hood. He'd only had it a week and he'd already noticed the looks he got from women, and the notes left under the wiper blades with phone numbers and the words, 'Call me'.

David looked around again before following the motorcade, making sure there was nothing impeding his imminent departure. The three team members who had helped manage the project were walking toward him.

"Climb in!" David called out.

Ty opened the passenger side front door, set himself carefully in the seat and closed the door softly, showing the proper respect for David's baby. Tanner and Cody climbed in the back and buckled their seat belts. David revved the engine and within seconds, was cruising just below the speed limit up his favorite canyon. He loved the fresh smell of plants and trees that were still wet from recent rainstorms. As they drove, the sun broke from behind a cloud and the sunlight glistened off the wet, vivid green leaves.

David listened to the rolling of the tires on the wet asphalt and noticed the pools of rain water in the ditches on the sides of the roadway. He smiled. *This is my world. This is where I belong.* He felt like he had entered a new and pristine world meant only for him.

He noticed how the sun, warming the asphalt, caused steam to rise from the roadway, creating a mirage of shimmering light ahead. One of the absurdities of nature, that mirage, giving the impression of something being there that was not, like a lake in the desert.

He chuckled at the thought and shook his head. The absurdity in his life was that he was taking a trunk full of potted plants, jewelry and other presents to propose to a woman he wasn't sure he loved. He wasn't sure he was capable of loving another woman, not since Heather's automobile accident and death twenty months earlier. It was so difficult for him to open up to people anyway. He had lost a big part of himself when Heather had died after the accident. The two weeks that she lay in the hospital in a coma, hooked up to all the machines, had seemed like an eternity. He had spent every spare moment in her hospital room, talking to her and listening for any response, but there had been none; and she had passed on, likely not knowing he had been there.

The guy who had run into her car was convicted of a DUI and spent six months in jail. Through some legal technicality, he hadn't been convicted for any crime involving Heather's death. A week after his release, he was arrested again—another DUI. It had taken David a long time to forgive the guy, but he had eventually managed. Now, he didn't know if he had anything left of himself to give to Stefani. Perhaps he was afraid of losing her, too.

As the motorcade reached Cottonwood Canyon, the starting point for the project, some cars stopped, their occupants getting out to look around; but most of the cars turned around and headed back to Logan without stopping. They had shown their support and the local media had been on hand to take video, so they would be remembered at election time.

David stopped and let his team members out so they could catch a ride back, then he continued up the canyon, admiring their work. From that point on, his travel took him along a divided highway which hugged the contours of the canyon, crossing the river when there was insufficient space on one side or the other.

His Camaro swept around a banked curve, one that David, himself, had designed. *We did this right*, he thought. Then, *Stefani should be pleased with the potted plants.* She was studying botany at Utah State University and was always talking about this or that plant. She thought David wasn't interested and accused him of not paying attention when she talked about her plants. But he had spent weeks looking for just the right ones. When he had asked her, "Why botany? You can't make a living with a botany degree," she had disagreed, becoming almost hysterical, and insisted that there was a demand for botanists.

As the Camaro swept across a bridge over the river, he thought about the care his team had taken to ensure that the new road blended in with the landscape. Even the bridges were partially hidden by the trees and brush, and decorated to look like the forest around them.

Anyway, Stefani figured she'd get married and settle down with children and home-making before too many more years; and she already had the family cabin in Garden City, which she'd inherited from her grandparents upon their deaths in a plane crash; so it wasn't like she had to make a lot of money to live. She had told David on several occasions that thy could live there once they married, but it was always, 'her home' they would live in, which grated on his nerves.

He guessed that it was her self-confidence and sense of direction that attracted him to her. *'Well, that's great for her to know what she wants. But what am I doing with a carload of plants, the names of which I can't even pronounce; about to make a commitment I'm not sure of?'*

David snapped out of his musings suddenly, realizing that the mirage ahead of him was not acting normally. The roadway had just curved to the left and was about to make a long, gentle sweep to the right before climbing to the overlook. The sun was now slightly off to the left, so the mirage should have disappeared, but it didn't. David was about to pass off this phenomenon as a result of the bank of the road surface, but his eyes were playing other tricks on him. He knew a mirage should move forward along the roadway, keeping about the same distance from the car at all times, due to the angle of the sun. But he could swear the mirage was closer than a few moments ago.

He thought about that place south of Rapid City, South Dakota, where the trees didn't behave normally, bending in toward each other due to some strange energy field phenomenon, so they said. It taxed the imagination. This mirage was like that, catching his attention because it wasn't behaving normally. Maybe there was a similar energy field in the canyon, but he'd never encountered anything like this, in all the time he'd spent here.

As his engineer's mind recalled, reviewed, evaluated and rejected data, he wanted to pass this off as an optical illusion, but his mind and attention were totally captured. Even so, he was about to cast aside his mental exercise and accept the fact that nature is full of surprises, when yet another oddity shook him. He was now close enough to notice that the mirage was not lying flat on the roadway, but was standing on edge, intersecting the pavement. It appeared as an oval shaped plate of glass or polished steel might, if erected on the road. He guessed steel, since it reflected blues, greys and browns from the hillside instead of the natural greens.

With his attention totally focused on the odd shape and color of the object, it took a few more moments for his mind to grasp the fact that he was on a collision course at high speed with an object, the consistency of which he had no idea, which by then had grown to completely block the roadway. He suddenly realized that if he that if he didn't stop the car, he was going to hit it and do who-knew-what kind of damage to the car, and to himself. There was now no way around the object.

David's body tensed and he slammed on the brakes, throwing the car into a drunken skid on the slick roadway. He instinctively turned the wheel into the skid to keep the car from leaving the roadway or turning sideways and rolling. His mind raced as his eyes searched for an escape around the grotesque object which now, against all logic, had grown so large as to almost rest against the embankment on the left side of the road and extended beyond the edge of the roadway on the right.

With no time left, and certain death imminent, his heart raced.

Author's Note

This story is a work of fiction. All of the characters in the book are from the author's imagination and any resemblance to known persons is purely coincidental. Location names, government organizations and functions and the effects of man-caused and natural disasters mentioned in the story are accurate to the best of my ability to determine.

About the Story

The Gemini Gate series combines real-world geopolitics, including a detailed, behind-the-scenes look at the White House and the possibility of a global thermonuclear Armageddon, with a fictional technological discovery that just might hold the secret to saving the human race. It takes a component of science fiction—a hypothetical, fictional technology—and embeds it in a realistic, present-day world.

Background: The Three Mile Island Nuclear Generating Station, reactor number 2 (TMI-2) in Pennsylvania, suffered a radiation leak and partial meltdown on March 28, 1979. It was said to be 'the most significant accident in U.S. commercial nuclear power plant history'.

At that time, I worked as a project engineer at a nuclear power plant construction site in Washington State. Eventually, four of the five power plants that were under construction in Washington, were cancelled due to spiraling construction costs, that resulted from safety concerns and a labor dispute, at the same time that energy consumption declined in the northwest. The Washington Public Power Supply System (WPPSS, or Whoops, as it became known in the media and on TV in the eighties) was forced to default on $2.25 billion worth of municipal bonds—a humiliation for the financial industry. You can read about it on my website, *www.stevenewilde.com.*

The failure of the nuclear industry to provide reliably safe, low-cost energy to the public made me wonder what would happen if an accidental or—heaven forbid—intentional nuclear accident occurred in the western United States, and my story about the Gemini Gate was born; but it took a few years for it to mature into a series. It led me to speculate on the ability—or inability—of government leaders to work together to prevent thermonuclear war, and what it would take to survive the resulting chaos.

The great question behind the Gemini Gate series is that, when faced with the prospect of nuclear weapons in the hands of terrorists and corrupt political leaders, how would the United States defend itself and its people? News headlines lead us to believe that there are people throughout the world with radical ideologies who would welcome another world war. Would the United States government be able to protect its citizens if those terrorists were successful in obtaining the technology, materials and logistics to perpetuate a terrorist plot of such significance? Who would suffer from the resulting chaos? Certainly, governmental leaders would ride out the storm in bunkers, and people like the fictional Blund and Stephens families, who anticipate war in advance, would likely survive. But the end result for the vast majority of regular, normal people would certainly be terrible.

When the idea for the story came to me, Aspen Valley existed, but only in my mind. Having travelled extensively throughout Utah over the years, visiting the beautiful and unique natural treasures of Utah's State and National Parks and forests, I tried for years to match up what was in my head with a specific location.

Driving up Logan Canyon to a family vacation at Bear Lake a few years ago, I realized that we were in the right canyon. I just needed to find Aspen Valley. It's there, a little different than I've described it in the story, but close enough to recognize it. If you're ever in Logan Canyon and spot it, send me an email to let me know.

One of my goals in writing this story was to give each character a unique and believable personality. So, many of the characters in the series are patterned after people that I know or have known. Just to be sure that I don't offend anyone, let's just say that if you identify with one of the characters, he or she was meant to resemble you—except for Jason, who is a composite of all the bad character traits I could think of.

Acknowledgements

I need to thank the people who've helped me develop, edit and publish the books in the Gemini Gate series. Steve Brown, Kevin Cook, Dan Duvall, David Noble, Felicia Osborn, Chris Palmer and Dan Wilde reviewed one or more of the volumes and provided valuable feedback on content and grammar. The people at IndieBookLauncher.com: Nas Hedron for editing the first two books and educating me on writing styles; and Saul Bottcher, for painting the book covers, setting up the books for publication, and putting up with all my questions. I couldn't have gotten this far without all of you pitching in to make me look good.

Most of all, I need to thank Marilyn for putting up with my obsession to tell this story. She's been my best critic and greatest supporter through the long hours at the computer.

For your patience at all the interruptions, to run my latest ideas past you, and each time I jump out of bed to finish a scene that has suddenly come to me, I love you.

About the Author

I grew up in Salt Lake City and graduated from the University of Utah with a bachelor's degree in engineering. My wife, Marilyn, and I have five children and fifteen grandchildren. Together we enjoy camping, hiking, travel, and family get-togethers. I love to read, and enjoy most genres, particularly murder mysteries and science fiction. In my quiet time, I enjoy reading, writing, gardening, genealogy, and emergency preparedness.

My career as a project manager took me to several countries around the world, and multiple industries and specialties, including electric utilities, nuclear power plant construction, water management, global mining, and aerospace, with each of those experiences contributing to my interest in, and the broad perspective needed to write this story.

This story is meant to entertain. I hope you enjoyed it. The sixth and final book in the Gemini Gate series is called *Heritage of Aspen Valley*. It's the story of Mike's programming artificial intelligence into the observer, as Doc challenged him to do, and the problems introduced to the families as a result of the Observer using AI to play matchmaker. Don't miss it.

Thank you.

Steven E. Wilde

Facebook: StevenEWilde_GG
Email: StevenEWilde@gmail.com
Website: www.StevenEWilde.com